IN THE
SHADOW
OF THE
CYPRESS

THOMAS STEINBECK

G

GALLERY BOOKS

NEW YORK   LONDON   TORONTO   SYDNEY

IN THE
SHADOW
OF THE
CYPRESS

G

Gallery Books
A Division of Simon & Schuster, Inc.
1230 Avenue of the Americas
New York, NY 10020

First Gallery Books hardcover edition April 2010

GALLERY and colophon are registered trademarks of Simon & Schuster, Inc.

For information about special discounts for bulk purchases, please contact Simon & Schuster Special Sales at 1-866-506-1949 or business@simonandschuster.com.

The Simon & Schuster Speakers Bureau can bring authors to your live event. For more information or to book an event contact the Simon & Schuster Speakers Bureau at 1-866-248-3049 or visit our website at www.simonspeakers.com.

Designed by Joy O'Meara

Manufactured in the United States of America

1   3   5   7   9   10   8   6   4   2

Library of Congress Cataloging-in-Publication Data

Steinbeck, Thomas.
In the shadow of the cypress / Thomas Steinbeck.—1st Gallery Books
hardcover ed.
p. cm.
1. Chinese—California—Fiction. 2. Immigrants—California—Fiction.
3. California—History—1850–1950—Fiction. I. Title.
PS3619.T47615I52 2010
813'.6—dc22
2009033355
ISBN 978-1-4391-6825-7
ISBN 978-1-4391-6988-9 (ebook)

This modest volume is dedicated to
Rubilee Knight,
Heaven's testimony that angels live among us

ACKNOWLEDGMENTS

Bringing any book into print is as much a team effort as staging a play, or producing a film, and in that regard there are a number of very able people who are owed not only credit for this book, but also my full store of gratitude and appreciation.

First I wish to thank my very talented wife, Gail Knight Steinbeck, for her tireless efforts as my agent. Her mastery of complex contract negotiations has saved my bacon on numerous occasions, and her support and skills as a first-draft editor have proved invaluable over the years. In that same vein I wish to thank Dan Smetanka, a truly professional and thoughtful editor, for helping me with this book long before it found a home with Simon & Schuster. In fact, I'm convinced that it was due to his insight and expertise that it found a home at all.

I would also like to express my deep appreciation to Anthony Ziccardi at Simon & Schuster for giving me the opportunity to come in out of the rain for a while. My gratitude stimulates a natural desire to always be worthy of his confidence and generosity. I would also like to express my gratitude to my new editor at Simon & Schuster, Kathy Sagan. Her compassion and patience in the wake of many difficulties have been truly inspirational. I look forward to luxuriating in the warmth of her support, her consummate literary sensitivity, and her vast experience for the many tales as yet unborn.

Family support and encouragement has always been the abiding grace for those artists who are fortunate enough to lay claim to it in any form. And to those of my family who have helped to keep the ship on an even keel all these years, I must first thank the indomitable queen of our clan, Rubilee Knight, a paladin of the "greatest generation," and in its older and more romantic connotation, a true flower of southern womanhood. "She is a creature of many intricate parts, and all the parts are true and well fashioned."

In that same vein, I wish to express my sincere gratitude to Mike and Patti Hilton for all their loving support. This also stands true for my dear friends Myrica Taylor and Mary Jean Vignone. Their sympathetic concerns and timely assistance in turbulent seas is much appreciated.

For love, inspiration, courage, and music I'm blessed to have Johnny Irion and Sarah Lee Guthrie as a part of my family. But I especially owe their two beautiful and talented daughters, Olivia and Sophie, a mark of personal gratitude for remaining constant reminders that I have readers yet to come, and that's a weighty responsibility for someone of my tender years. I would also like to thank my friend Gerry Low-Sabado for her valuable insights concerning the coastal Chinese communities of Monterey, and my old mate Kent Seavey for his concise historical perspectives and timely assistance in all things arcane and mysterious.

And I wish to express my sincere thanks to Harry Lewis, who has every right to lay claim to being a true patron of this work. His patience and kindness has engendered great affection and loyalty. I also wish to acknowledge my dear friends, the O'Connell family. They have generously looked after the balance of my sanity for the better part of five years, with marginally interesting results. I am looking forward to a complete recovery one of these days when I have nothing better to do.

And last, I would like to personally communicate my sincere gratitude to the nation and people of China for having gifted me a lifelong focus of study that has never once disappointed my historical interest or dampened my enthusiasm to know more.

PROLOGUE

WHEN I WAS A CHILD in Monterey my two best friends were gifted Chinese boys named Billy Chen Su and B. D. Chu Mui (better known as "Bee-Dee" Mui to his friends). It was from their respectful relationship with their own parents that I ultimately learned the obligations and abiding value of familial respect, and the cultural pride that comes from being able to name one's ancestors back through the ages. Despite their pressed financial circumstances, my childhood friends lived with the confidence that they were inheritors of an ancient culture grounded in well-documented history, literature, medicine, and art, while I was the product of a race that, until the eleventh century, most likely painted themselves blue, lived in vermin-infested hovels, slaughtered their neighbors for sport, and stole cattle by profession. My envy of my Chinese friends was truly palpable. Thus, it is to those intrepid Chinese fishermen and farmers of Monterey that I owe the inspiration for this historical flight of possibilities. The past may indeed be prologue, but it is the future that invariably answers the questions of history.

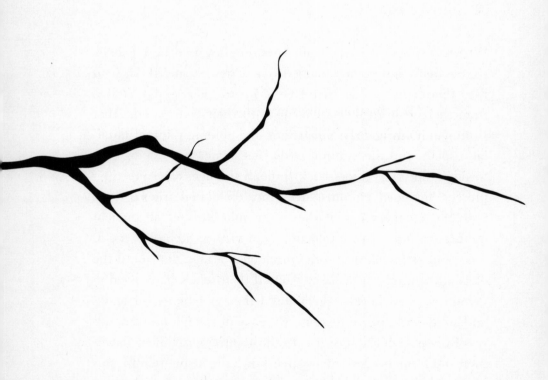

JOURNAL EXTRACTS OF
DR. CHARLES H. GILBERT

Stanford Professor of Marine Biology

"True wisdom comes at great cost.
Only ignorance is free."

— TAOIST PROVERB

IN 1906, AT THE TIME these entries were written, Dr. Gilbert was a highly respected instructor and researcher at Stanford University's Hopkins Marine Station in Pacific Grove, California.

Dr. Charles Lucas
Stanford University
Department of Marine Studies
2008

Partial diary entry: June 1, 1906

The raging China Point fire was an experience that must be forever etched in the memories of everyone who witnessed the tragedy, though I presently suspect there were those who perceived only profit in the flames. On the night of May 16, 1906, aided by predictably seasonal winds from the southwest, the fifty-year-old Chinese fishing village on China Point was completely burned to the ground in less than one hour. It was the most horrifying conflagration I have ever witnessed. My heart was wrenched with concern for the poor occupants of the village, and I feared the worst for the plight of those trapped in their shanties. The dwellings seemed to burst into flame like boxes of kitchen matches, but there was nothing anyone could do without suffering death for their efforts. By dawn the whole village was nothing more than a black, smoldering skeleton. It was only through the grace of a merciful God that no Chinese were killed in the racing inferno. But it is a certainty to all witnesses that they had lost most of what they once possessed, including some of their nets, sheds, and beached fishing boats.

The fire's ignition point was most certainly a Chinese-owned hay barn at the south end of the village, and I'm persuaded the deed was initiated with the strong seasonal winds in mind. Though it disturbs me to say so, I am thoroughly convinced that the consequential inferno was the result of a determined and planned act of arson.

If armed with the perspective of hindsight, one can easily deduce that the following narrative has roots that stretch back more than sixty years, and perhaps more than several hundred years if the truth was known. The one person who might be said to have set the engine of destruction in motion is a strange fellow who I came to know in early June of 1898. The man's name, appropriately enough, was William "Red Billy" O'Flynn.

By any definition, Mr. O'Flynn is a unique-looking individual. Roughly in his midforties, weathered and apparently used to hard labor, the man comes across as keen and observant, and considering his lack of formal education, he shows good sense in most all things. His novel appearance, despite his being born in Ireland and saddled with a brogue broad enough to occasionally make his speech almost incomprehensible, bespeaks a colorful parentage. He once volunteered that his mother's people were of Moorish blood. "All thoroughgoing Gypsies to the bone," he said, and "all armed to the teeth with endless batteries of the most chilling curses imaginable." He had thus inherited his mother's soft, dark complexion and black eyes, as well as a moderate knowledge of European Spanish, which our local Mexican population disdains for historical reasons.

Mr. O'Flynn's father, according to his son's recollection, was "a large and dangerous fellow with a ruddy, moon-pocked face, and hair as red-crested as God makes a peckerwood." As a result, the young man also inherited a prodigious mane of copper-bright curls. And though he possesses marginally pleasant features, and a muscular physique tempered by hard labor, the abiding contrast between his dark Mediterranean complexion and his vivid red crown of hair is truly a most striking sight to behold. One never quite gets used to his appearance. Every time I came across him at his duties, it was like a novelty surprise all over again.

Only once did Mr. O'Flynn reveal a portion of his history to me, and to this day, knowing his verbal habits as I do, I can't imagine what inspired him to do so. It was on the day that he first applied to me for part-time work at Hopkins Laboratory. I suppose that, as I was the prospective employer, he felt somehow compelled to reveal that he "first drew breath overlooking the tar-blackened docks of Cork." His father was a brawling shipyard-pipe fitter, "built like a Birmingham brickbat, but lacking all the wit and modesty God gave a cobblestone."

Mr. O'Flynn gave me to understand that when he was fourteen years old he escaped Ireland altogether. His father, he said, had long since matriculated well beyond his amateur standing as a tavern tippler, and had gone on to become a renowned professional whiskey drinker. This all-too-common situation, with its predisposition toward physical cruelty, evidently distressed the family sorely. At last Mr. O'Flynn's long-suffering mother felt she had endured more than enough. Circumstances obliged her to call forth her mortal quiver of Gypsy curses. Two days later, the senior O'Flynn was discovered facedown in a rain-filled gutter. The coroner formally declared that the notorious and unrepentant boozer had drowned in three inches of rainwater.

I record this here only in passing, because this tragic incident seems to have deeply influenced Mr. O'Flynn, for as far as I can deduce, he has always expressed a total aversion to alcohol. He impresses me as the driest Irishman I have ever encountered. He has for some years been confirmed to the Methodist faith and vehemently speaks against the use of spirits, as well as "all those misbegotten fools what do indulge."

On the whole, I have always found Mr. O'Flynn a man of simple, if somewhat cautious, honesty. As far as I can discern, he has always spoken the truth, but only as much truth as warranted by the question. On most occasions his natural reticence induces him to say as little as possible, and with the greatest circumspection. Unlike most of his race, Mr. O'Flynn never indulges in idle conversation or even bemused observation. In fact, for an Irishman, he exhibits not the least vestige of Celtic humor. However, he is at all times a stable, capable, and dependable worker, whose efforts rarely if ever draw the slightest criticism from myself, or the laboratory staff.

When Mr. O'Flynn first applied to me for a job, he stated that he had worked for the Southern Pacific Railroad for twelve years. He said he had started as a gandy dancer and worked his way up to roadbed foreman with a crew of twenty men to supervise. Then one day a slowly passing engine accidentally ruptured a steam release valve on a piston feed line and badly scalded Mr. O'Flynn and four of his crew. Two of his Chinese workers later succumbed to their burns by way of infection, and O'Flynn almost died himself. Happily, he was pulled back from the brink through the careful ministrations of his hard-nosed

Portuguese wife. She bartered housecleaning chores for burn creams and pain medications; these were compounded for her by Charles K. Tuttle's Pharmacy and given to her at cost. When he later asked the Southern Pacific regional manager for compensation to cover the expense of his injuries, Mr. O'Flynn was given seventy-five dollars and told that he need not come back to work, as his position had been filled in his absence.

The Chinese victims of the accident received forty-five dollars each, and the families of the dead were given thirty-five dollars to help defray burial costs. These latter particulars concerning Mr. O'Flynn I eventually learned from Mr. Tuttle, but only after I'd already engaged Mr. O'Flynn on a part-time basis. Indeed, once I understood the man's predicament, I found myself quite pleased to be of some small assistance in his financial restitution.

I soon discovered that Mr. O'Flynn kept himself adequately solvent by working six part-time jobs every week. On Mondays and Tuesdays he worked for the county on a road maintenance crew. On Wednesdays he came to us. He was taught how to properly clean fish tanks and assisted with all the equipment maintenance at the laboratory. Thursdays O'Flynn worked making deliveries for Tuttle's Pharmacy, or carefully dusting the hundreds of large glass-stopped medicine bottles that lined all the walls. On Fridays he ran a steam-saw for Thomas Work's wood yard. But Saturdays were O'Flynn's special delight, for he alternated between carting and stocking at Steiner's grocery store and working at Mr. Hay's ice cream parlor. He cleaned the large copper kettles in the candy kitchen and redressed and oiled the stone taffy tables. A bemused Mr. Tuttle helped him find these additional jobs when he realized that Mr. O'Flynn was in possession of a sweet tooth the size of Seal Rock. The proprietors of both establishments proved very generous with free samples and token prices. His Sundays were just as regular. The mornings were spent worshipping at the First Methodist Church on Lighthouse Road. And, weather permitting, his Sunday afternoons were dedicated to fishing for the Sabbath table with his Portuguese father-in-law. In general, one would appraise all of Mr. O'Flynn's habits as quite regular, sober, and disciplined. I must here record that these factors, like the man's sobriety, are indisputable facts that should be taken into account for later consideration.

There was one additional curious facet to Mr. O'Flynn's social intercourse within the local community. Though he seemed to possess few friends besides relatives acquired through marriage, he spent much of his free time in the company of his Chinese acquaintances. In particular, he was often seen associating with the well-to-do proprietor of a successful Chinese laundry in Pacific Grove. This rather popular fellow goes by the name of Master Ah Chung. O'Flynn has also been known to keep company with Ah Chung's younger brother Jim Len. I have since been informed that despite all modest appearances to the contrary, both these gentlemen are alleged to be heavily involved in diverse business interests up and down the California coast. It is widely believed that they receive lucrative stipends from the Three Corporations of San Francisco. This mysterious organization represents the most powerful Chinese clans in California. It is under the auspices of these secretive and financially powerful families that ninety percent of all Chinese imports and exports are bought and sold.

The improbability of our Mr. O'Flynn enjoying social congress with the Chinese stood out as an oddity, until I recalled that he had worked for years supervising Chinese road gangs for the Southern Pacific. And it appears that during his time in that capacity he learned to speak a fair smattering of Cantonese, which I understand is the predominant dialect spoken among our local Chinese.

I discovered these obtuse facts quite incidentally one summer day about thirteen months after Mr. O'Flynn came to work for us at Hopkins. One afternoon a Chinese fisherman and his wife came to visit the laboratory from China Point. They accompanied a rude donkey cart that had been tailored to carry a shallow wooden tub four feet in diameter. The tub had a two-sided hinged lid to keep its contents from splashing out. As they walked along, the fisherman's wife worked a clever double-channeled hand-bellows. This device, I later learned, pumped a steady flow of air into the tub through a hose end wrapped in a sponge. They had come to our laboratory with a very rare specimen indeed. It was a small, black-skinned, deepwater shark. They had caught the ruby-eyed creature on a deep trotline over the Monterey marine canyon.

I should note that there are a good number of Chinese fishermen on the bay who specialize in hunting unusual species of marine life specifically for their use in an assortment of esoteric Chinese pharmacopoeias. I'm given to understand that the export market for these perplexing products is thriving. Commodities like preserved sea cucumbers, sea urchins, needle fish roe, basking shark eggs, and various species of small kelp crabs and azure-colored sea snails are in great demand. All these and many more are highly prized, and can easily pull their weight in gold or silver on the export tallies.

The visiting fisherman and his wife bowed and introduced themselves in thick pidgin English. The man said that Master Ah Chung had sent them along with something special.

As my negotiations for the exotic shark continued, our Mr. O'Flynn suddenly appeared. Smiling broadly, and in a torrent of pidgin Chinese, Mr. O'Flynn suddenly greeted the fisherman as an old acquaintance. They spoke together rapidly for a moment, and then O'Flynn turned to me and asked what price the fisherman asked for the shark. I told him we had settled on a price of two dollars. Mr. O'Flynn quickly confirmed this with the fisherman, and then turned back to me and said, "For two dollars he's making you a present of the fish, and he's delivered it more or less alive, no mean feat if you ask me, but he's done it only at Master Ah Chung's insistence. You can safely wager there's some binding obligation involved. To be sure, you're barely paying for this fellow's time. He tells me the shark's liver alone is worth five dollars, and the tanned skin another twelve. I'll be begging your pardon for the impertinence, Professor, but if I were you I'd up and give this good fellow eight dollars. That way he can honorably fulfill Mr. Ah Chung's instructions and perchance realize a pittance of profit so as to save face with his family."

O'Flynn grinned, winked, and went on. "Mark what I say, Professor, the good word will soon race about that you're an honest man of business, and before you can recite the saints' names, you'll be up to your braces in all manner of fishy God-knows-what."

I managed the transaction just as Mr. O'Flynn had so earnestly recommended, but I did so in a confused fog of amazement at his hitherto unknown, and totally unsuspected, ability to make himself perfectly well understood in brogue-laced pidgin Chinese. I was dumbfounded to say the least, but I paid out the eight dollars all the same, and was later happy to have done so, for we managed, with constant diligence, to keep this rare specimen alive and healthy for almost fifteen weeks.

The fisherman and his wife were quite pleased with the arrangement, and a minor festival of bowing, smiling, and amicable chatter ensued. It was then I noticed that the fisherman and his wife treated Mr. O'Flynn with particular deference that entailed bowing even lower with hands clasped together as if in prayer. I found this more amusing than interesting, and didn't reflect on its significance at the time.

After I had instructed some of my more stalwart students to transfer the exhausted shark to one of the large, bay-fed tanks, the proud fisherman and his wife happily took their leave. I recall that they departed in the company of our Mr. O'Flynn, all the while chirping a seemingly endless exchange of Cantonese salutations and polite laughter.

The discovery of O'Flynn's hidden linguistic talents opened new and vigorous channels for acquiring specific species for our research and preservation. Mr. O'Flynn even suggested that a reasonable bounty be paid for specimens delivered alive and in reasonable health. This we did to great effect. The demand for our scientifically preserved laboratory specimens had grown fivefold in five years. We at Hopkins soon found we were servicing six other universities, as well as smaller research institutions. We even managed to set aside a complete catalog of preserved specimens to satisfy the needs of the state biologists for whom the Hopkins Marine Station is almost a second home.

Mr. O'Flynn, though he was only employed every Wednesday, made his presence felt by the ongoing delivery of marine specimens from the various Chinese fishing villages. Due to his admonitions and the bounties offered, all but the most delicate or vulnerable creatures were delivered alive. We even occasionally received (free of charge) orphaned sea otter kits, sea lion pups, and the odd storm-stressed, fledgling pelican.

In all respects, Mr. O'Flynn had quickly proved so successful acting as our purchasing agent that we soon were at liberty to offer him a decent commission on all accepted purchases, and a five percent wage increase. He expressed himself completely satisfied with this arrangement, though he insisted on an understanding that should we "find ourselves in want of anything particularly big and dangerous," he wanted the right to renegotiate terms to compensate for the obvious increased risk all around. Personally amused by imagining what exact picture Mr. O'Flynn envisioned for such unspoken dangers, I so stipulated, and it was all agreed.

Since then, I'm pleased to recall the intervening years at Hopkins have passed most agreeably and very constructively, with Hopkins functioning well, albeit at a metered academic gait. And over time Mr. O'Flynn and I have become better acquainted, but only marginally better than I am with most of my own students. As I have previously stated, he is not a fellow who reveals much if he can help it. But after working for the laboratory for a few years, O'Flynn had come to witness a great many marine oddities; most of these specimens he never would have even suspected of existing. This novel if mostly untutored interest seems to have led him to indulge in a sincere if arcane Methodist interpretation of the Creation. In that vein Mr. O'Flynn's interest became remarkably focused, if not fixated upon the more bizarre and seemingly pointless examples of "the Almighty's Grand Design." Creatures "kin" to the common flea, or the "blood-hungry" mosquito, were most assuredly of Satan's dark creation. "And I ask you honestly, Professor, just what purpose would a caring Christian God have for a man-killing jellyfish no bigger than a nickel? It just doesn't make sense in the great scheme of heaven's design."

Perhaps it was my position as a tenured old pedagogue at Hopkins that encouraged Mr. O'Flynn, on a number of occasions, to call upon me at the laboratory, or at my home. Hat in hand and head slightly bowed, he would beg my indulgence for a few minutes. He appeared interested in a remarkably wide range of seemingly disjointed subjects, as though he'd chosen them from a fishbowl, like a lottery ticket. He diligently and innocently inquired about pole stars, blackamoors, slack tides, narwhals, whip snakes, monsters, and misanthropes, and all with equal interest, intensity, and enthusiasm. And then he might ask some spiritually obtuse question on the subject of biology. To be honest, I was somewhat taken aback by his interests. The very fact that a man of his limited education could actually frame such questions, I regarded as something of a novelty. The man piqued my interest in numerous ways, and his interests were always remarkably unpredictable.

With each visit Mr. O'Flynn would bring by some living aberration or semifossilized oddity. Then he would ask me to explain what I saw in light of the Almighty's faultless reputation for perfection. Following this vein, he showed me numerous examples of two-headed snakes and turtles, frogs and toads with six legs or two, a wingless chicken, and other creatures with all manner of strange malformations.

I attempted to explain to Mr. O'Flynn that there were obvious differences between those creatures that in the majority exist within their own zoological perfection, and those that are accidentally conceived with genetic imperfections that usually result in such malformations. I told him such imperfections could occasionally be found in every species of creature, including humans.

It had long seemed to me that our Mr. O'Flynn had been

undergoing some small crisis of faith, perhaps aggravated by his peripheral acquaintance with our marine studies at Hopkins. On several occasions I tried reminding him, in a good-natured manner, that it was generally deemed unadvisable, if not impossible, to attempt to reconcile religious faith and pure science in absolute terms of correlation, faith being highly subjective in nature, and pure science (whenever possible) primarily objective.

I'm persuaded that I made no appreciable impression on O'Flynn whatsoever. It appeared that some complex amalgam of "bog-bound Irish superstition," a rank amateur's appreciation for the laws of nature, and certain orthodox dictums of faith had all collided at once. It appeared he couldn't, or wouldn't, acknowledge the proposal that measuring scientific validity using religious calibrations was a fool's errand. Just how this impasse affected Mr. O'Flynn, I really can't say, but it certainly did not appear to dampen his enthusiasm for our occasional interviews.

He once appeared at my door with a very small human skull that had obviously been buried for centuries. I saw at once that it was not a child's skull, but rather a fully formed adult whose defined features, though less than half scale by contemporary measurements, were all quite proportional and well formed.

On another occasion he brought me an unusual bronze-shanked iron arrowhead. It appeared to be of considerable age and was obviously not of indigenous design. The shank was approximately six inches long, and the point remained embedded in the neck vertebra of what later proved to be a very large and extinct species of bear. The arrowhead itself was of a fluted, three-edged design and had much in common with medieval bodkins I had seen illustrated in museum catalogs years ago. I asked Mr. O'Flynn how he'd come by such an unusual item.

He was reticent at first, as is his way, but when pressed he explained that clearing and grating the county's roads brought up all manner of strange and wonderful things. I didn't quite take to this explanation, and he seemed mildly amused by my incredulous response. He took pains to point out that most of the present roads in California, like roads everywhere in the world, were laid out to follow long-existing paths and trails, which had probably been traveled upon for centuries. He went on to speculate that a good number of those thousands of travelers were always losing things along the way while moving from here to there, and to his way of thinking, it only stood to reason that at least some of those lost articles would come to light again one day. He confided that every now and then he came across various items that put a few odd dollars his way, but mostly it was discarded junk, with a few curiosities thrown in every so often. I was obliged to admit that O'Flynn's serendipitous methods of discovery were impeccably suited to the needs of an incidental seeker of errant roadside treasures.

It was about this same time that I became aware (through the normal channels of idle gossip) that Mr. O'Flynn was spending more and more of his time with his Chinese friends and acquaintances, and less with his fellow parishioners at the First Methodist assembly hall. A later interview with one of the church elders suggests that Mr. O'Flynn's attendance at services fell off considerably over the years since 1900, until at last he ceased going to church altogether.

Further reports of Mr. O'Flynn's close social affiliations were verified by his presence as an honored guest at an elaborate Chinese wedding held in Pacific Grove. On December 18 of 1900, the locally popular, and deftly inscrutable, Ah Chung hosted his own elaborate wedding and reception in front of his prosperous laundry establishment on Grand Avenue. I'm told the bride was a well-connected Chinese maiden from Santa Cruz. However, I was mildly surprised to later discover that a handsomely attired Mr. O'Flynn was one of the appointed groomsmen sent to welcome the prospective bride's train at the depot. The groom even arranged to have a twenty-piece brass band in attendance. Nuptials of this scale and expense are all but unheard-of in Pacific Grove. It was said that only a Chinese New Year celebration could have rivaled Mr. Ah Chung's wedding in color, ceremony, or festive largesse. An abundance of food and drink was made available to one and all. I was amused to learn that a good number of our local citizens attended, some out of simple curiosity, but most to enjoy the festive nature of the celebration, the copious fireworks, and the colorful Chinese lantern processions. I'm sorry to say I was in Santa Cruz on laboratory business at the time, or I too would have been easily lured to attend the spectacle.

A number of our students did witness the festivities, which is how I discovered that Mr. O'Flynn had a noticeable participation in the ceremonies. This particular fact I did find very interesting, as the Chinese are well-known for being every bit as racially and socially prejudiced as we are, and thus rarely if ever admit "barbarians" to the inner circles of family ceremonial life or clan business. And what proved even more curious, though not totally unexpected, was the fact that Mr. O'Flynn never hinted at his participation in the wedding ceremony. As he was only a part-time worker, I felt any pointed inquiries would be deemed impertinent, and most likely go unanswered for all my curiosity. I chose to err on the side of civility and let the matter pass. If I were to hear anything on the subject, Mr. O'Flynn would have to volunteer the information, and my odds were not favorable in that respect.

Life and work went on in like fashion for a good while. I was privileged, at least for the present, to be unburdened by the requirements of any prospective marital constraints on my time and concentration. This freedom allowed me to indulge in all manner of agreeable research until the spring of 1905, when the warmer southern currents flowed north, and with them came a remarkable change in the local fish populations. The salmon and herring stocks were driven farther north to colder water. They were subsequently replaced by southern species like Mexican mackerel, Humboldt squid, and basking sharks, to speak of just a few. As one can well imagine, we became extremely busy collecting, preserving, and cataloging the encroaching species throughout the year. Even the state biologists were up to their waders in triplicate reports on the fluctuating fish stock appraisals, and the depleted projection of fishery revenues. But even with the increased workload, our two agencies managed to be of enormous service to each other.

At this point I must record that without the enigmatic relationship of our Mr. O'Flynn with the local Chinese fishermen, our ability to assemble a current and relevant collection, and to then preserve and catalog to such a professional standard, would have been very much impaired, if not altogether impossible.

But our success and gratification aside, all normal activities on the bay changed for the worse during the last four months of 1905. The warmth of the southern currents had a detrimental effect upon the weather. The unseasonable storms that raged out of the southwest caused widespread damage, of which the coastal Chinese seemed to suffer the worst material losses. Many of their seaside shanties and storage sheds were blown down, and a fair number of their fishing boats were badly damaged, if not destroyed altogether.

The endless days of sharp, contrary winds and torrential rains brought on inland flooding in the Salinas Valley and beyond. Needless to say, the local fishing industry and tourist trade all but withered on the vine, and we locals could do little better than hunker down to ride out the storms as best we could. In retrospect, one wonders if the dangerously inclement elements only presaged the disasters yet to come. The storms claimed a fair number of big trees all over the county, and in several cases these old-growth monsters had crushed a few barns, outbuildings, and parts of houses. Others had blocked all movement over important streets and roads.

One blustering, black day an oilskin-clad Mr. O'Flynn appeared at the laboratory to say that for the next two weeks he would be obliged to work for the county helping clear the roads. The situation had been voted an emergency by the county board, and they needed qualified men at once.

Due to travel difficulties by land, rail, and sea, the laboratory had temporarily suspended operations; therefore I had no objection to Mr. O'Flynn taking as long as he liked. Remembering the inherent danger in that line of work, I wished the fellow all the best of luck. I didn't see O'Flynn again for more than a month.

Then one cold, fog-bound Sunday afternoon, while I worked on student papers in my fire-snug study at home, the bellpull at my front door clanged twice. I answered the summons and was mildly surprised to find Mr. O'Flynn, hat in hand, standing under the portico. He bowed his head modestly and apologized for not seeking a proper appointment. Nevertheless, he asked if I might be so generous as to oblige him with a few minutes of my valuable time. I could tell from the look in his eyes that this was a serious application. He declared there was something very important that he wished to consult with me about.

Fully prepared to be shown almost any variety of exotic object or malformed wildlife, I invited Mr. O'Flynn to come warm himself by the fire. He thanked me and sat toasting his hands while I poured out hot sweet tea. He began by saying that his work with the city and county was almost at an end. He was proud to say that he and his crew cut up and hauled away 137 "widow-makers" in less than four weeks. The city of Monterey had even awarded the road crews a modest bounty for speed, which was paid over in addition to their county wages.

O'Flynn paused, scrutinizing me closely, as if deciding whether or not to tell me the purpose of his visit. I must have passed inspection, as he cautiously commenced his story again. He informed me that part of his job was to survey those trees that had been blown down, and determine in advance what kinds of tools and how many men and wagonloads would be required to clear them away. He confided that the city and county were recouping a reasonable portion of their costs by selling the timber to Mr. Work's wood yard and the railroad.

Mr. O'Flynn had been instructed to ride out to the cypress groves overlooking Moss Beach. One of the older trees near the road had blown down and was effectively blocking most of the route south. He rode out to the location in a very leisurely fashion, free to enjoy the quiet and make his own hours, as there was no county supervisor about to hurry him along.

When O'Flynn came upon the scene of the fallen tree, he was surprised to see how large a root ball the cypress had pulled up with it. He said the collapse left a deep, eight-by-eight-foot hole in the ground. While he was examining the scale of it all, something entwined at the bottom of the torn root ball reflected a strange pink light, so he jumped into the hole to get a closer look. As he patiently brushed away the dirt with his fingers, he realized that he was looking at a very large piece of finely polished pink stone. Using his sheath knife, he carefully cut away the remaining tangle of small roots that enmeshed the stone. He declared it took him almost an hour to free the figure. Once it was liberated, he gently withdrew the oddly shaped object from its ancient cradle in the roots. But it was only after wiping away the dirt that O'Flynn realized the object was a carved stone figure of some kind of animal, and sculpted from very beautiful stone. Evidently, it was while he was climbing out of the hole with his prize that his foot accidentally dislodged a decorated stone plaque. Again it took some time to carefully cut the object free of its root-bound nest, and by then it was getting too dark to examine his finds in any detail. He then packed up the stone in a burlap sack and stowed it in his mule cart. The animal figure he wrapped in his poncho. O'Flynn made his way home as quickly as possible, unloaded and stashed away his discoveries, and then returned the work cart to the county stable.

O'Flynn made a point of saying that his wife had been away for a few nights looking after her ailing father, so when he returned home from the stable later that evening he found ample opportunity to clean and examine his discoveries unmolested by witnesses.

I asked O'Flynn to describe the objects in complete aspect while I took careful notes. My curiosity was palpable and my instincts sharpened.

O'Flynn described the stone plaque as a rectangular, headstone-like slab, approximately thirty-five by twenty-five inches in area, and a little more than two inches thick. The stone itself was finely cut, detailed, and highly polished. It was carved and engraved on one side only. He said it was also remarkably dense and heavy for its small size. The animal figure, on the other hand, was beautifully carved from a large piece of opaque pink stone with slight streaks of white marbled throughout. It too had engraved script on its base. O'Flynn said the stone animal looked almost brand-new, highly polished, and not a chip anywhere.

To say that Mr. O'Flynn had by now thoroughly piqued my interest would be a bald understatement. I'm sure he could read the look of inquisitive anticipation that must have colored my expression. I asked him if he had brought me anything to see, and without another word he withdrew a soft leather parcel from his coat, untied the laces, and carefully unrolled the contents onto his lap. From a protective hide of rabbit fur he removed the magnificent figure and set it on the table between us.

The first sight of this treasure took my breath away. From the presence of knobbed horns, I presumed the long-necked creature to be a stylized Asian representation of a giraffe. The figure was approximately nine inches tall, and was posed resting on its knees in the fashion of a camel or llama. But what proved the most enthralling feature of the treasure was the fact that this noble object was obviously carved from one perfectly flaw-less piece of milky-pink jade. I gently turned the object around on the table several times to examine it from every quarter with my big magnifying glass. I found myself openly praising its intricate engravings, and the simple but aristocratic proportions chosen by the craftsman who created this magnificent work of art. The very posture of the animal, with head facing left and slightly down, seemed to have been chosen specifically for the purpose of allowing the darker pink jade to form a continuous bright crest for the creature from head to tail.

I was so completely preoccupied that it took me a moment to acknowledge that Mr. O'Flynn had spoken for the first time.

"Now, sir, I ask you fair as a university man, a doctor and all, just what kind of animal is that supposed to be?"

It amused me to ask, "What does it look like to you, Mr. O'Flynn?"

"To be sure, Professor, to my untutored eye it looks blood-kin to a hump-shy camel what's been hung for the untoward loss of it. And I ask you, sir, just what are those odd stumps on its head? What kind of animal is it?"

"Well, Mr. O'Flynn, for centuries, books about mythical beasts called it a Quilin, but one day people were forced to acknowledge that the animal wasn't a myth after all; in fact, it was modestly abundant in Africa, so people began to call it by a version of its African name, giraffe. The animal is most assuredly a giraffe, Mr. O'Flynn, and those stumps on its head are short horns."

"So you are saying this 'gee-raff' creature is an animal that lives in dark Africa?"

"Yes, Mr. O'Flynn, except for the few that reside in some of the world's better zoos, giraffes are native to the savannahs of central Africa. I'd be happy to show you a picture if you like."

Mr. O'Flynn looked confused, but he nodded his head, and I reached for my zoological atlas. I showed him a photograph of a small herd of giraffes pictured in their native African veld. O'Flynn looked at the picture, and then looked at the figure, and then back again to the photograph. He silently repeated this back-and-forth comparison several times, and then closed the atlas with a bang. He sat back with a frustrated sigh and took up his tea. He appeared to be pondering some troubling question that forced him to knit his brows, occasionally suck his teeth, and stare off into space. After a minute O'Flynn spoke up again. "Africa, you say, Professor? And how long have these animals been common knowledge in the old countries?"

"Mr. O'Flynn, the giraffe is unquestionably an African animal.

And I'd say it's very likely the early Egyptians, Persians, and Greeks, and subsequently the Romans, would have come across such animals in their extensive trade networks."

"And what about the old-country Chinese, Professor, would they be in the know about such things?"

"I really can't say without further information. Africa is a long way from China, but I've learned with the years that nothing is impossible. I see no reason why a culture as advanced and curious as the Chinese could not sail, or even travel overland, to Africa. Why do you ask?"

"Well, Professor, I don't claim to be any kind of expert, mind you, but I have seen a fair number of downed trees in my time, and you can tell a lot about them from the root ball, you can even come close to the real age of a tree if you know what to look for. I'm told the old cypress groves hereabouts are spot-on rare, even for California. And they don't thrive well at all in other climates. Well, sir, that's what the county surveyor told me when he came out with the cutting crew the next day; the county man wanted to inspect this particular tree, mind you, and when he'd had an eyeful he politely asked that we cut him two sample disks from the trunk for the county forestry office. We were right pleased to oblige, but before he left I asked what they would use the samples for. He said they could date the tree to within a couple of years, and even read the weather for those years."

"That's a very common forestry practice."

"So I was told, sir. I then asked the surveyor if he could take a look at the cuttings and give me an unofficial count of the tree's age, if only to satisfy the curiosity of the men who would have to spend many hours taking the poor tree down to cordwood. Well, the fellow said he wasn't really a forestry technician, but he showed me how to count the growth rings for myself. He told me that to make it easier, a man counts off by tens, and then pencil checks each ten. When you've reached the core, you go back and count the checks and multiply by ten. And I did just that."

Mr. O'Flynn gently picked up the jade figure with callused hands, drew it close, and looked deep into its opaque luster. He spoke in an odd fashion, as if the power of ancient superstition now came into play. "Now, there's something to truly ponder, Professor. This valuable object was purposely buried along with that stone plaque at the bottom of a hole over which a cypress sapling was planted. Do you follow me so far, Professor?"

"I believe I'm keeping abreast for the moment, thank you."

"Well, sir, if all is as I say it is, then you'll appreciate that this jewel of a beast and the stone plaque were actually buried in that very spot at least four hundred years ago. And that's the best evidence accorded by the rings on the tree. You see, I cut a trunk sample of my own and ciphered the rings twice more to be sure. What do you think now, Professor?"

"If what you say is true, Mr. O'Flynn, I'm far more than just interested. Your find begs any number of historical questions, and certainly merits further study and research."

"Well, then this will give you something more to think about, I'll wager." Mr. O'Flynn carefully handed me the figure. "If you'd be so kind, sir, look what's carved into the bottom."

I turned the figure over and was surprised to discover that the base was a large, fully inscribed seal. There were ten vertical lines of beautiful Chinese script, each character inset with remnants of gold foil. The same foiling was used on an elaborate oblong cartouche at the bottom right of the inscription. The engraved characters still showed slight traces of the red cinnabar used to print the seal on documents.

I was thunderstruck to say the least, but my curiosity leaped even farther ahead. I asked Mr. O'Flynn if the stone tablet had any writing on it, and he said it had. Three different types of script were displayed, and one of them seemed to be Chinese, but he had no idea what the other two were. He'd never seen the like before. Then I asked whether the lettering on the stone plaque showed any signs of having been inlaid or painted with gold. He answered in the affirmative. He said the stone had been highly polished on one side, and the characters cut into its hard surface. He also mentioned that the whole inscription was bordered within a carved design of flying serpents, flowering vines, and bats. With a perplexed look, he said that the stone had an odd property. When dry, it looked mostly coal black, but when he flushed away the dirt using clear water, the stone appeared to shimmer a beautiful dark green.

Reexamining the superbly engraved characters on the bottom of the jade figure, I told Mr. O'Flynn that while I was certainly no expert in the field of Chinese artifacts, it was my considered opinion that no further useful progress could be made on this mystery until the Chinese characters on both objects had been translated. I asked him what his Chinese acquaintances had thought of the inscriptions. His answer surprised me.

"To be honest, Professor, you and I are the only two people who have seen this carving in centuries. But begging your pardon, sir, the last people I'd wish to know about this are the Chinese. Mind you, they're a remarkable race, and I have a great deal of respect for their strength of character and ingenuity, but they're a right proprietary and dangerous tribe when they construe that a Chinese grave has been despoiled, especially by a Christian. And to be sure, Professor, just because I personally saw no bones doesn't mean they weren't there hundreds of years ago. Until we can make out what all this means, I'd far prefer to keep our local Chinese friends ignorant of the discovery, if such is even possible."

O'Flynn leaned forward and lowered his voice in a slightly conspiratorial manner. "Just between you, me, and the gatepost, Professor, when those cheeky fellows care to put their crafty minds to it, they can also become the finest thieves and bandits in the world. And it's a fact that I wouldn't have this treasure very long if certain Chinese elders knew about it and felt they held a binding interest. I wouldn't stand a tinker's chance in Hades if those gentlemen truly wanted them back. As of now I can trust only you to help me."

I was gratified by the man's confidence, and said as much. I admitted that I was honored that he consulted me, but reminded him that anthropology was not quite my field. Nonetheless, I was deeply fascinated by the prospects of sinking my teeth into such a rare discovery. I suppose no thinking person in my position would be averse to daydreams of scholarly glory, but I already knew the pitfalls inherent in such ambitious endeavors, and believed I could keep a tight rein on my perspective.

In careful consideration, I informed Mr. O'Flynn that translating the inscriptions was still of paramount importance. And if he wished no one to see the objects as yet, then reliable copies of the originals had to be made. He inquired whether I knew of a method for accomplishing such a thing, and I said I believed I did, and using only materials readily at hand.

O'Flynn thought for a moment, and then politely asked me if I might demonstrate. From a large roll of sturdy white Japan paper, which I keep for mounting botanical specimens, I cut a piece that would overlap the base of the jade seal. Using a wet cloth, I moistened one side of the paper and pressed it firmly against the engraved text, using my fingers to pressure the paper firmly into every detail. Then, using a clean, dry handkerchief, I continued to pat and press the paper into the stone while holding it near the Franklin stove to help it dry. When it was done, I took a soft charcoal pencil and, working gently, began to make a rubbing across the surface. The process worked quite well, as I expected, and the text was handily duplicated as white on black. Mr. O'Flynn paid close attention to every step of the process, but when I told him he would have to come by with the plaque so that I could make a rubbing of that text as well, he seemed very hesitant to comply.

After pressing him to explain his reticence, I learned that O'Flynn was very fearful of removing the plaque from its hiding place for such an errand. On the other hand, if I gave him the proper materials, he thought he could copy what I had done. I agreed, but insisted that he first make another impression and rubbing of the jade figure's base, so I could be sure he'd done the work correctly. O'Flynn happily agreed, and his third attempt was every bit as good as mine.

As I packed up the materials he would need, Mr. O'Flynn asked what I planned to do with the rubbings once I had them. I said that, with his permission, I would consult with suitable colleagues at Stanford University, but do so without telling them the origin or present location of the originals. If they agreed to help me, then we might well be on our way to solving the mystery of the burial. O'Flynn asked how long I thought it would take to get the answers, and I told him that I honestly couldn't say. It all depended upon how difficult it was to find someone qualified to translate the texts. If they were as old as O'Flynn believed, based on the tree-ring count, then a true Chinese scholar might be required to do a proper translation. Understanding the difference in language usage over the centuries might be as complex as translating ancient Gaelic runes or Mayan hieroglyphs. I told Mr. O'Flynn that the process could not be rushed, and the outcome was by no means predictable, or necessarily profitable. However, I made it known to him that whatever happened, the value of the jade seal alone made it a formidable treasure in its own right, considering the quality and size of the jade, worth perhaps many thousands of dollars.

I admonished him to keep the figure hidden and safe until I should receive some response from the university. I also asked him if I might see the tree-ring sample at his earliest convenience. If I was expected to continue with the necessary research on his behalf, I felt scientifically obliged to make the ring count for myself, and this time using published botanical scales for reference. Mr. O'Flynn happily agreed to every particular. Then he carefully rewrapped the jade seal, took up the materials I had given him, and, with brogue-laced phrases of gratitude and confidence, quietly departed just as the setting sun peeked between the thick gray clouds and the ocean's horizon. Suddenly, golden shafts of azure-flecked fire lanced through the trees, and the belly of the clouds all turned flame red. The whole experience took O'Flynn and myself quite by surprise, and we stood speechless in my little front garden watching the dramatic play of light as it changed color and intensity. Out of the corner of my eye I noticed that my guest made several furtive gestures with his hands that appeared ritualistic in nature, as if to protect his soul from the darker powers. Perhaps it was just an errant quiver of his Gypsy blood, but it led me to wonder how O'Flynn's superstitious temperament was managing this unusual series of events.

I must admit that at this juncture I was feeling childish pangs of excitement. Like a little boy with a secret to share,

I longed to have somebody to tell about these matters. I was saved from such indiscretions by circumstance alone. I had no wife to wheedle me into making premature confessions. My housekeeper, old Mrs. Bailey, already believed I was but a few steps from being committed to a mental institution, and thus never listened to anything I said, and I knew better than to share my special knowledge with any glory-hungry academics, who just might feel free to poach in their neighbor's woods. I cast no immediate aspersions, of course, but I have personal knowledge of several such examples of academic chicanery, and I flatter myself that I wisely chose not to test my luck in that dangerous arena.

The following Wednesday O'Flynn appeared at Hopkins for his regular day of work, and he brought with him a package containing two rather well-executed rubbings of the stone plaque, as well as a pie-cut slice of the disk of wood taken from the cypress trunk. From heart to bark it was thirty inches long, which would have made the whole trunk a hefty sixty inches in diameter. Even a cursory glance at the wedge convinced me that there were at least three centuries recorded there. But I waited to examine it and the rubbings until I got home and could be guaranteed uninterrupted privacy.

I thanked Mr. O'Flynn for his fine work on the rubbings and invited him to call upon me at home on Friday evening after supper. I felt sure that by then I would be able to tell him more. I also requested that he bring back the jade figure so that I might make a camera image to verify the origin of the inscription. I pointed out that it would be helpful to have an image of the plaque as well, but I understood his natural reticence to move it about.

I had decided against using the specimen camera at the

laboratory because it was too large, too heavy, and too cumbersome to transport with ease. Besides, my use of the equipment would attract unwanted attention, and awkward questions were sure to be posed by the curious.

After considering my alternatives, I went to visit my friend Charles K. Tuttle at his pharmacy. Besides being a good friend and Hopkins's principal supplier of bulk chemicals, Mr. Tuttle is the county's most reputable and successful druggist, a man trusted by all who know him.

But the real reason I approached him was because Mr. Tuttle is a keen and ardent photographer, and the owner of several very fine cameras. He also keeps a well-stocked darkroom to process his own plates and print his own photographs. Locally, he's quite famous for the quality of his work, and I am the proud owner of six of his prints.

I asked Charles if he could set up one of his cameras in my house, with all the distances, focus, and lighting predetermined, so that I could photograph a certain object at a later time without making any adjustments beyond changing the negative plates and triggering the shutter.

Mr. Tuttle was kind enough to visit me that same evening to better understand my needs. I felt obliged to tell my friend that the project in hand had a somewhat clandestine aspect about it. And I went so far as to divulge that the proposed photographs involved something that might or might not have historical significance. The problem lay in the fact that the person in possession of the artifact wished to keep its existence confidential until more was known of its origin. In this way all parties might avoid undue embarrassment if existing presumptions and appraisals should prove to be in error. I explained that many important archives abound in undiscovered forgeries of every description.

Charles Tuttle was in total sympathy with my constraints and subsequent requirements. I might even say that he warmed to the mystery of it all and promised to be of any assistance he could. He helped determine where the table and the object should be placed for best effect with the camera angle, and since the photograph would most likely be taken in very poor light, he recommended that I gather together six to eight bright reflector lamps, and a number of small standing mirrors to help increase the light value focused upon the object to be photographed. After that, success depended upon the right lens for the distance, a properly placed and undisturbed subject, and, of course, the correct length of exposure. To help with this variable, Mr. Tuttle promised to write down all the settings and timed exposures in detail.

By Friday afternoon everything was in place. Charles had generously set up one of his better cameras, along with oil lamps and mirrors all preset to his professional satisfaction, using a porcelain platter as a stand-in for the unnamed artifact. When he departed, Mr. Tuttle left me with a case containing a dozen negative plates, and he added that he would be happy to help me develop them in his darkroom if I wished. I thanked him for his kindness and said I would take the utmost care with his equipment. Not wishing to slight his open generosity, I decided not to tell him that I planned to do that job at Hopkins, as we possessed all the necessary equipment. I felt bad about misleading a friend, but it was the strict need for confidentiality that precluded his kind offer. I knew Charles Tuttle to be a gentleman of consummate discretion, an essential qualification for one whose profession entails a long catalog of personal and medical confidences. If it were my secret to share, I'd go to Charles Tuttle first. However, this was O'Flynn's discovery, and

I was determined to prove myself worthy of his trust and confidence, such as it was.

Mr. O'Flynn failed to put in an appearance at the appointed hour, which I found most exasperating after all the arrangements had been made. Evening came and went, and after a light supper of grilled abalone, I decided to forgo any further waste of my time by going to a warm bed with a folio of scientific journals that I had put aside for study.

I had just banked the coals in the fireplace for the night and doused most of the lamps when there came a knocking at my front door. I answered the summons and my lamplight fell upon a bedraggled and sour Mr. O'Flynn. The heavy night mists had thoroughly dampened his clothes and his demeanor, for he answered my surprised greeting with a frustrated grunt and a burdened shrug. It was then that I noticed my guest was shouldering a heavy, damp gunnysack. By its shape and apparent weight, I knew at once that he must have brought along the stone plaque.

I ushered my moist and disgruntled visitor into the parlor and sparked up the hearth with fresh kindling and split pine. Mr. O'Flynn set his burden down near the fire, removed his coat to the rack in the hall, and sat down to warm his hands by the fire. He said nothing at all at first, so I went to the kitchen and returned with a hot mug of sweet cider and a tin of shortbread biscuits. He looked up and smiled at last when I presented him with these refreshments.

After taking a few moments to enjoy his cider, Mr. O'Flynn volunteered an explanation without the least prompting from me. He said that he was aware that he had arrived at an untimely hour and apologized for doing so without sending some kind of notice. He was forced by circumstance to change his plans at the last moment. He went on to lament the necessity, but he had felt obliged to move his discoveries to a new hiding place away from his home. He suspected that word had seeped around the Chinese community. He'd heard that people were talking about the ancient fallen cypress, and the fact that he had been the man who had supervised its final destruction.

"Now, you may not know this, Professor, but our Chinese friends hold the local cypress groves as sacred. Some say those trees were planted for a purpose generations ago. They believe that tampering with such things can only bring down a cruel fortune on a man's head." O'Flynn shook his head in frustration. "But why pitch the stink at my door? It surely wasn't my bloody idea to blow down the damn tree. It had nothing to do with ir-reverence or anything like it. And if I hadn't discovered those stones, someone else was sure to. And it seems some of the vil-lage elders have taken on a different view of the situation. Those old men should be harping at the county supervisors, not at me. I've heard they're complaining that a vile desecration has taken place." O'Flynn shrugged with an air of resignation. "To be sure, I suspect my usefulness among those people is fast coming to an end." He mustered a slight grin. "My sterling reputation is under something of a cloud at present, and I wouldn't be at all surprised to learn that they have someone watching me."

I asked O'Flynn if any of the Chinese suspected that he had discovered something important buried under the tree. He shook his head and said that not even his wife knew about it. Then again, he affirmed that no one could ever fathom what the Chinese really knew about anything one way or another. But in that vein, O'Flynn did acknowledge that if, in fact, it had once been a local tradition to bury important people in such a man-ner, then yes, the elders might have every reason to suspect that something other than a root ball was removed from that hole by the road.

I thought for a few moments and then pointed out that the situation could be easily amended to his benefit, his profit, and even his standing among the Chinese. All he had to do was make their community a gift of what he'd accidentally discovered as a result of an act of God.

O'Flynn shot me a look of surprise. "That won't do at all, Professor. No, no. You can't just hand some Chinese elder a couple of ancient treasures and expect him to share with the others." O'Flynn smiled indulgently, as though addressing a rank freshman. "God bless you, sir, but it won't work that way; any old burgher you choose will just keep the stones to enhance his own clan's prestige. And you can't pass them over to just any old tong or the fraternal corporation, because they'll do just the same. No. If I might make so bold, Professor, until we know what all this means, I intend to stand on the side of prudence and caution. Once you've recorded the objects with your camera, I intend to hide these petards where discovery will be all but impossible."

Mr. O'Flynn obviously intended to leave the whole question of propriety and ownership till some later date, but I got the settled impression that he intended to profit from the circumstances one way or another, if only to compensate himself for everything he'd been through so far.

Now, it must be said that Mr. O'Flynn never struck me as a man easily given to fits of philanthropy, nor was he, on the other hand, perceptibly materialistic or acquisitive. To his credit, he has a fine head for balancing funds owing against labor spent and the going price of such services. Thus he appears to modestly balance his accounts in the black, more or less. And I never heard him mutter an envious sentiment toward those who possessed more wealth or property than he did, or ever voice an ambition based on serendipitous wealth. For all intents, O'Flynn seems to have accepted his station in life, and appears to have all he needs, if not all he desires. And though there are no scales to judge unspoken aspirations, I'm persuaded that his decidedly circumspect and suspicious nature would not allow him the luxury of indulging daydreams of instant wealth based on what little we had in hand.

Perhaps this instinct was buttressed when I informed him that the only true value of the plaque, and what I perceived to be an official seal, was the importance and context of the inscriptions carved upon them. It seemed to be a case of the message outweighing the value of the gilt-edged parchment upon which it's written. Once these elements had been properly cataloged and recorded, the objects themselves, regardless of all commercial considerations, would ultimately take their place in some well-endowed state institution where they would most likely be displayed as the historical curiosities they are. I reminded Mr. O'Flynn that he was not the only one who had something to gain or lose. My time spent on research could easily still prove little more than a study in academic frustration. With that, I encouraged the man to forgo his suspicions for a few hours and assist in the evening's labors.

With Mr. O'Flynn's help I lit all the reflector lamps, adjusted the mirrors, and prepared to photograph the jade giraffe seal. In consultation we agreed to take six plates of the jade figure, and six of the stone plaque. As this was the first time I had laid eyes on the latter, I spent quite a while studying the stone, examining the engraving, and matching the charcoal rubbing with the plaque for accuracy. I can testify that the stone was a beautifully executed piece of work. The inscriptions were set out in three distinct languages and scripts, with slight hints of gold foil inlaid here and there to highlight certain characters. It appeared, from remaining traces, that similar foil had also been used to highlight details of the border decorations.

The uppermost text was comprised of thirty-six vertical lines inscribed in what I assumed was Chinese. The second segment, though I couldn't be sure, looked to be of equal length in text, and marginally akin to a medieval form of Persian. But the lowest and most cryptic segment was set out in an alphabet I was totally unfamiliar with, and subsequently unable to identify with any reference available from my meager library at home.

With Mr. O'Flynn's assistance, I readjusted the lamps and mirrors to accommodate the photographs of the plaque. But even with our best efforts, and all the light available, viewing the inscriptions through the lens was difficult. Mr. O'Flynn solved the difficulty by suggesting that we brush wheat flour over the stone and then wipe off the surface so that the engraved characters would appear white in contrast to the dark surface, and this we did with some success.

By half past midnight, Mr. O'Flynn and I had finished our task. Without further ceremony, he carefully gathered up his treasures and went off into the night to hide them somewhere new. I never asked where he intended to deposit the artifacts, which I believe added further confidence to our informal association. I had all I needed for the present. The photographs, if they proved legible and credible, stood as solid testimony to the existence of the originals. I'm not sure O'Flynn quite understood that the patent value of his discovery rested primarily in the translation and publication of the texts. He was oblivious to all such details. His abiding concern remained focused upon securing the originals against future loss.

Since I presumed it would take some months to track down the proper academic assistance to initiate the work of translation, I agreed with Mr. O'Flynn's decision to place the artifacts out of harm's way. However, I encouraged him to consider writing down the location of the hiding place, and placing the envelope in the custody of a trusted third party like a bank or a law office. If something untoward should suddenly happen, the document would be the only way to recover the artifacts. O'Flynn listened politely to the suggestion, as he always did, but I got the definite impression that he had no intention whatsoever of following my advice. This realization led me to harbor a nagging suspicion that I would probably never see those artifacts again.

The following weeks were marked by more unseasonable weather that, though not as severe as the last storms, kept the harbor closed and business generally buttoned down all over Monterey. Only those people bent on serious errands bothered to leave the shelter of their homes, and so I was mildly surprised late one drenching afternoon when there came a knocking at my front door. I answered to discover the oilskinned figure of Mr. O'Flynn standing in the downpour. I invited him to enter, which he did, but he also apologized that he could only stay for a few moments.

As usual O'Flynn came right to the point, but now he seemed slightly uneasy and embarrassed. He talked rather quickly and refrained from eye contact lasting more than two seconds. He announced right off that he'd come out to give personal notice of his departure to all his fine employers. He said he was leaving town to take on more serious and lucrative work now that he was completely recovered from his injury.

I noticed that O'Flynn fidgeted with his hands as he informed me that he would soon be back to work for the railroad up north. In an attempt at affable informality, he justified his choice by bragging that being a road foreman, working the long rails out in the countryside, was a "right-soft berth." He seemed happy to recall with some degree of sarcasm that "way out on the line" a "family man" might enjoy domestic tranquillity, unfettered conversation with friends, relative safety, and "right-fine" victuals served without complaints. In spite of all this nonsense, I knew the crux of O'Flynn's reckoning. Like any man in his position, a fat pay packet every two weeks beckoned like an irresistible muse. I imagined this fortunate circumstance would go a long way toward making his wife happy, whether he was at home or not.

As surprised as I was, I hadn't for a moment forgotten his discovery, or our mutual involvement in its fate. I tried to interject a question concerning its future, but O'Flynn shook his head and insisted we could attend to that matter later. At the moment he pleaded more urgent matters elsewhere. Despite my serious concerns, I saw no reason not to wish him the very best of good fortune in his future endeavors. O'Flynn smiled and thanked me heartily, but upon departing he reminded me that Wednesday would be his last day at Hopkins, and if possible he wished to settle up his wages at that time. I happily agreed and he thanked me again with a handshake. Before I could discover anything further, O'Flynn quickly departed into failing light and pelting rain.

The last time I ever saw Mr. O'Flynn was that following Wednesday at the laboratory. I had especially brought along some of the photographs to show him in the privacy of my office, but he seemed only partially interested. In fact, I noticed that he appeared slightly agitated and distracted. When I asked what was disturbing him, he threw up his hands and shook his copper mane with an irritated exclamation. "Ach! But it's the same as before." Then he leaned closer and confided to me that he was positive the Chinese were still dogging his heels. He had twice caught sight of his shadows where they had no business being. He swore he didn't know how, but he alleged the Chinese elders knew, or at least suspected something. O'Flynn even said that he was fairly sure someone had very carefully searched his cottage when he and his wife were away. He warned me that their obstinate suspicions might soon spread out to include me, especially since they would know of our past associations.

In that vein I asked about the artifacts and his plans for them. Mr. O'Flynn flatly declared they were well hidden and beyond all discovery by the Chinese, or anyone else for that matter. The question must have acted like salt in a wound, for O'Flynn became agitated and stated that as far as he was concerned, "those bloody stones can stay hidden until Satan comes up for trial, or until some cunning fellow shows me how to profit from their retrieval." Then he softened his words and once again showed himself concerned with my particular situation. "But if I were a clever gentleman like you, Professor, I'd see to the safety of those papers of yours. Those rubbings and photographs are the only proof you have that such articles rightly exist at all. And mark me when I tell you that those courteous Chinese elders across the way are the canniest lot of old badgers on God's earth; you can take my word for that. And, if you can help it, never but never get between them and something they want. No matter what's thought of them hereabouts, I can tell you those people can skin you alive with such agility that you won't even know your hide is missing till you shuck off your pants for a bath."

I smiled and thanked Mr. O'Flynn for his timely advice. I then asked where he might be found if I should discover something important about the artifacts. O'Flynn thought for a moment and said I should place a notice in the *Railroad News*. It would eventually catch up to him anywhere he was.

In conclusion I thanked Mr. O'Flynn for his years of hard work and dedication on Hopkins's behalf. O'Flynn somehow managed a modest blush, and with many thanks in return he signed the receipt for his wages. Then we shook hands and he departed.

As an aside, I ultimately acted upon Mr. O'Flynn's admonition about the existing evidence and decided to secure my notes, the rubbings, and the photographs in a proper fashion. I sorted the material down into three complete packages, each carefully pressed and secured between folds of unbleached linen and boxed in a cedar packing case that would stand up to the rigors of transport and storage. The first I posted to a colleague at Stanford to hold in trust for me. The second I prepared for eventual shipment east to Harvard University, where I was reliably given to understand the esteemed Professor J. L. Andeborg still held tenure in early Asian languages and texts. Once I had written to him to get his approval, I would ship the materials back east for his opinion. The last package was for myself, and therefore the most complete. Nonetheless, I chose to side with caution. I took the other parcels and temporarily deposited them in the property vault at the Bank of Salinas, where I knew they would be safe until I could turn my attention to their future.

———

BETWEEN THE END OF MARCH and early April of '06 the increasingly angry spates of stormy weather were sometimes interspersed with curious and unexplainable periods of dead calm, clear skies, and motionless, millpond conditions upon the bay. In fact, it was very early in the morning, perhaps five o'clock, on just such a motionless day that two of my graduate students drew my attention to the stillness of the water. Classes for some students had been called at that difficult hour to facilitate collecting specimens in the rock pools and traps with the outgoing tide. However, the tide seemed to be going out at an unusually accelerated pace.

I had gone outside to stand with my students and noticed at once that even the birds and animals seemed to be holding their tongues. All the seagulls had departed, and the sea lions were mute for once. But even with all that, I was still quite amazed to witness every boat from the various Chinese fishing villages loaded to the gunwales with men, women, and children. They were simply floating about the glassy bay without apparent destination or purpose.

From the sounds that traveled to us from across the still water, it appeared they had also taken along their dogs, geese, piglets, and God knows what else. I took note that the bay had become so still, in fact, that there ceased to be even the smallest ripple breaking along the surf line. I must confess that I found the unnatural quiet and apparent motionlessness palpably disturbing, almost to the point of vertigo; it was as though the whole planet had stopped moving, and now waited in hushed anticipation for some great and climactic event.

And then it happened. Just as my students and I turned

to go back up to the laboratory, the three of us were violently tripped off balance and thrown to the earth by a tremendous shaking of the ground. I'd experienced several small earthquakes before, but nothing of that intensity or tenacity. The brutal tremors continued unabated for at least twenty of the longest seconds I have ever experienced. The disorienting momentum was sharply accompanied by the familiar signature of shattering glass. Instantly my mind's eye foresaw crashing laboratory cradles cluttered with beakers and test tubes, overturned aquariums, and hazardous shards of laboratory glass liberally distributed everywhere. Hardest of all to dismiss were the distressed and frightened pleas for assistance, and the screams of the students still trapped within the laboratory. And then abruptly, in a nerve-wrenching instant, the quake ceased. And again it was still, motionless, and even more frightening.

Upon regaining our feet, we three immediately went about searching for those people who had cried out for help. Thankfully, there were few injuries requiring serious attention, and the cries for help were coming from people who were trapped by jammed doors or upended equipment. The physical damage to the laboratory itself was not quite as bad as my fears and ears had led me to expect. Most of the broken glass had come from the many windows and dry aquariums stacked for storage, though we did part with a fair inventory of expensive and necessary laboratory glassware. I gauged that replacing all the broken windows would require more labor than all the other repairs.

On one of my trips escorting dazed students out of the building, I happened to look back toward the bay momentarily, and there I spied a curious sight. The water, which had been glass-smooth but moments before, now rippled out in all directions without the benefit of wind or swell. The moving water appeared similar to the effects of a large pebble tossed into a still pool. And out of the silence emerged a sound I shall never forget. It was the broad release of laughter, both joyful and nervous, coming from the villagers on board the fishing junks. I found this fascinating, and ten minutes later I took the opportunity to look out over the bay once more. I was pleased, if somewhat confused, to find the sea conditions had returned to normal and that all the boats had safely returned to the beach with their precious cargo of children and livestock. I have since been plagued with the nagging suspicion that the Chinese knew what was about to happen long before it occurred, and trusted their safety afloat better than they did ashore.

As we went about our search and recovery, my students and I were relieved to discover that aside from a few cases of shock and disorientation, the injuries suffered were indeed minor. I only wish I could say the Almighty had been as kind to the rest of northern California.

With the telegraph wires down, and rail travel at a standstill, it took days for us to discover the terrible scope of the tragedies inflicted upon San Francisco, San Jose, and numerous smaller towns. Even Salinas, which is far closer to home, had its whole main street reduced to smoldering piles of broken masonry in just moments. I was later informed that the parcels I had placed in the bank there were destroyed in the subsequent decimation.

Perhaps it was because Pacific Grove rests upon an extensive granite shelf, or because the town is mostly of newer timber-frame construction and therefore more flexible, but in general the community suffered only modest structural damage. In many cases little was really noticeable beyond drifting porch pillars, toppled garden walls and arbors, or doorjambs and window frames skewed out of all true alignment.

At every church in town, the bewildered population expressed prayerful gratitude for its survival. And afterward many people noted that, aside from the shared demolition of window glass, storage jars, household crockery, and mantel-ensconced family treasures, the overall destruction in Pacific Grove and Monterey was mercifully kept at a minimum. Indeed, coastal communities like Santa Cruz fared far worse.

Barring the loss of a score of roof tiles, a half-collapsed rose arbor over the walk, and a few shattered potted plants, my own little cottage was where I had left it, more or less. However, I soon discovered that the homey interior of my quaint residence had been transformed into a chaotic mound of collapsed bookshelves, scattered books and papers, broken crockery, dinner dishes, and shattered lamps; in short, an unqualified disaster that took many weeks to sort out. Nonetheless, my first obligation was to help get Hopkins Laboratory back in working order, and for a while that hobbled all other priorities.

In the long, distressing weeks following the earthquake, Monterey County experienced a noteworthy increase in population. The influx consisted of shocked and jaded refugees from the more heavily damaged areas to the north. They came to seek shelter with parents, siblings, cousins, distant relatives, or just friends. Some arrived in tatters, friendless and alone, and just camped out where they could.

My friend Mr. Henry Kent owns the Mammoth Livery Stables. When I mentioned all the sad-boned strangers in town, Henry shrugged with Christian resignation and told me he was presently supporting seven heartbroken relatives, late of Hollister and San Jose, at his own house. He said they had all lost their homes and intended to move to someplace safer like Pacific Grove or Monterey.

In that same vein Mr. Tuttle informed me that since the disaster, a general indulgence in mercenary practices had taken hold, and property values had climbed rather considerably. I now believe it was this situation, coupled with traditional racial bias, that caused further hard feelings in the community. It also brought to the fore a renewal of serious interest on the part of the Southern Pacific Railroad and the Pacific Improvement Company (owners of the El Carmelo Hotel and other lucrative commercial properties) to increase the value of their estate holdings by manipulating which land leases, whether commercial or domestic, they would continue to service, and which they would terminate to facilitate their own future development.

Serious land speculation thrives now that Pacific Grove and Monterey have achieved a notable status as popular visitor's destinations. With the peninsula presently serviced by two scheduled railroads, the number of visitors to places like the splendid Hotel del Monte or the El Carmelo Hotel or Chautauqua-by-the-Sea, increases every year. Even Pacific Grove, as small as it is, can boast a fine little depot of its own. In fact, profits and prosperity are increasing in most all areas of endeavor, and for all classes of our population, except one, the Chinese. I have noted that they seem to function on an arcane monetary philosophy that is incomprehensible to westerners. The Chinese receive less compensation for their labors than anybody else, but they also prudently subsist on far less than most people could imagine. Therefore, they realize profit and, to a greater or lesser degree, even property and prosperity.

———

THE CHINESE FISHING VILLAGE AT China Point had been in existence for over fifty years, and its profitability had been such that, in all those years, not once had the village ever been in default or arrears on its lease payments to the Pacific Improvement Company, which owns the land. For that matter, the Chinese are acknowledged for their prompt attention to debts of any kind. They are just as insistent that others do the same.

The village corporation is managed by what the Chinese refer to as a tong. I don't know about other Chinese enclaves, but in Pacific Grove the village tong is more like a mayoral arrangement: the tong supervises all the village's business and maintains social order within the community. In effect, it is judge and jury in all matters of local importance. I'm well aware that in places like San Francisco, Seattle, and other large ports, some tongs are little more than organs of criminal extortion backed by threats of violence, but that wasn't really the case at China Point. There, the local tong was, for the most part, a righteous set of old gentlemen who genuinely cared for the well-being of their constituents and conducted village business on their behalf.

I am convinced that the underlying conflict was basically aesthetic in nature, though racial considerations certainly buttressed the fundamental discord on both sides. And no one in their right mind would ever claim that the coastal Chinese fishing villages were pleasant to the eye. Their fragile shanties were slapdab affairs made from anything at hand, and looked as though they had been washed ashore by some terrific storm. And this is not far from the truth, since driftwood supplied a good portion of the construction material used. Many of the buildings are precariously perched on the coastal boulders, with the odd piling driven here and there to hold things in place during a heavy blow. The wobbly, rope-lashed appearance of China Point, for instance, may have been quaint to the visitor's eye from a distance. But for the local white population, it was an eyesore and, in some important instances, far worse.

In all fairness it must be said that when the Chinese dried their abundant catches of squid, which they laid out on every conceivable flat surface in the village, the odorous stench could become quite overpowering. If the wind was hauling from the right direction, the reeking odor could bring up the gall of an individual living at the top of Forest Avenue. For some reason the smell never seemed to bother the Chinese, leading some locals to speculate that the Chinese had no olfactory sensibilities whatsoever.

In short, I believe this conflict between the land agents and the Chinese came about as a result of the confluence of all these elements in an environment of rising property values and much increased revenue brought in by visitors who came to enjoy the pristine beauty of the Monterey Peninsula. As far as the Pacific Improvement Company was concerned, lease or no lease, China Point, with its accompanying perfume, was anything but a jewel in the crown of civic pride, and naturally the company sought any legal means to reclaim the land.

The Chinese, however, would not be bullied. They held a well-drafted, ironclad ninety-nine-year lease, and were not about to relinquish it without very substantial compensations, which the PIC could ill afford after the added damage expenses brought on by the earthquake. Even with the tacit backing of the railroad, which held a strong vested interest in the increased tourist trade, little or no legal progress could be made on the matter.

It was soon after the earthquake that the commandant of

the Presidio sent a company of the First Squadron of the Ninth Cavalry down to their old tent camp and parade ground adjacent to China Point. They were sent at the request of Sheriff Robert Nesbitt to help keep order and prevent looting after the quake. These hearty buffalo soldiers had recently served with distinction in the Philippines, and they presented a formidable and reassuring presence. This move also served the Army commandant's purposes, as his troopers' new barracks at the Presidio had also sustained damage. Thus he needed to bivouac some of his men until proper repairs could be completed.

A short while later I made the acquaintance of the dashing young cavalry officer in charge of these soldiers. His name was Captain Charles Young, and a more intelligent and perspicacious officer would be hard to find. To tell the truth, I was somewhat surprised by the extent of this officer's education until I discovered that he had graduated fifth in his class at West Point. Indeed, he was only the third black cadet to matriculate with honors from the Army academy, and had shown special aptitude in engineering and the sciences. Since his men were encamped close by, Captain Young often came by the laboratory to pay his respects. He displayed knowledgeable interest in our work, and was in the habit of asking the most intelligent and interesting questions. As fate would have it, Captain Young and I would become involved on the periphery of a local tragedy.

ON THE EVENING OF MAY 16 I enjoyed a very pleasant dinner with Dr. Trimmer and his wife. It was during after-dinner coffee that Rhoda Trimmer drew our attention to a strange glow to the west. Soon afterward the sound of fire bells was heard.

Concerned with the safety of the laboratory, I took my leave and went off with Dr. Trimmer to see what was happening, and to lend our services to any who might be in need. When we drew close, we discovered that the Chinese fishing village at China Point was fully engulfed in flames and smoke. Due to the steady winds and the poor building materials employed by the Chinese, the furious conflagration traveled unimpeded across the length of the village in less than fifteen minutes. The presence of our intrepid volunteer fire company meant little to the sad outcome of the disaster, as there was no adequate water source to feed the pump wagon aside from the bay. However, there wasn't enough fire hose to reach that far, and even if there had been, the pump wagon didn't possess the power to lift the water that high. As a result, there was little chance of extinguishing the flames, and so everybody just stopped and watched the village burn to the ground.

Captain Young sent his men to help the fire company, but it was obvious to everyone that the fire had grown out of all proportion to the abilities of even the bravest bucket brigade. The sole grace to the whole tragedy was the fact that, though they were now homeless, no Chinese had lost their lives or been injured. Realizing that the survivors must be sheltered from the elements, Captain Young ordered his sergeant major to gather up as many campaign tents as he could find from the Presidio's storehouse, and to erect them on the parade field adjacent to his own encampment. He also made sure that food and drinking water were brought in for the dispossessed.

The next day, on the way to work, I returned to the scene of the fire to survey the damage. I was disgusted to find a good number of local ne'er-do-wells scavenging through the smoldering wreckage for anything of value. They brazenly looted charred scrap right under the tearful eyes of the traumatized survivors. Sadly, the Chinese were helpless to stop them until Captain Young told his men to run off the looters and guard the Chinese while they searched for whatever possessions they could still salvage from the fire.

Eventually, small collections were taken up by various church groups to help feed and clothe the survivors, but little else could be done to assist in their relief, as more than a few citizens were quite satisfied to see the village gone. These whispered sentiments saddened me more than anything else.

Two days later, while teaching a class at Hopkins, I was surprised by a visit from Sheriff Nesbitt and Captain Young. They were accompanied by a demure young corporal who seemed rather downcast and distracted. Once I had dismissed my students, I invited my visitors to retire to my office for what looked to be a very serious conference indeed. I only assumed this because Sheriff Nesbitt, normally a smiling, good-natured peace officer, bore the appearance of a fellow now deeply haunted by serious concerns.

Sheriff Nesbitt informed me that he was now quite sure the fire that destroyed the fishing village had been an act of arson. The blaze had begun in a communal hay storage barn on the south end of the village. The prevailing winds blowing south to north, as they usually do at that time of year, had rapidly driven the conflagration through the tightly packed village.

When I asked Sheriff Nesbitt why he suspected arson, Captain Young quickly interjected that six of his men had seen a man run from the barn just before the flames broke out. His men were squadron buglers and concert musicians who had gathered about a small campfire to practice pieces for a company concert. The troopers had evidently seen the arsonist quite well when he ran away.

I told Nesbitt and Young that I couldn't imagine what the crime had to do with Hopkins, as I couldn't imagine we harbored any blatant arsonists. Sheriff Nesbitt didn't find my response the least bit amusing, and I will never forget the exchange that followed. Sheriff Nesbitt looked at me with knitted brows. "Dr. Gilbert, just when exactly was the last time you spoke with a man in your employ called Billy O'Flynn, known in some quarters as Red Billy?"

I was of course stunned by the question, but I told him all that I knew of Mr. O'Flynn, his rather sudden departure from our employ due to some kind of reconciliation with the Southern Pacific, and how he and his family had left Pacific Grove some weeks past as far as I knew. I asked Sheriff Nesbitt if he had made inquiries with O'Flynn's other employers, and he answered that everyone interviewed had stated the very same facts and presumptions.

"But why would you be asking after Mr. O'Flynn?" I asked.

Captain Young then spoke up. "My men are the best skirmishers and pickets in the Army. General Abernathy called us his Night Owls. My boys can spot a vole at fifty yards on a moonless night. That's how we stayed alive all those months in the Philippines." Captain Young looked to his corporal for confirmation and received it with a nod. "And to that end, they swear that they witnessed a man run from the barn just before the flames appeared at the doors. The culprit was remarked by my men as a figure of unusual appearance, primarily because he seemed to have a dark complexion crowned by a mane of bright, copper-colored hair."

Sheriff Nesbitt stepped in to save time. "The only man that fits that description is Mr. Bill O'Flynn . . . The question is, to what purpose would a man, who has supposedly migrated north to work for the Southern Pacific Railroad, secretly return to burn down an innocent Chinese fishing village where, according to what you've told me in the past, he was so well received and respected for his fair dealings?"

I admitted to them both that I had no idea why these presumed crimes might have transpired, all the time secretly suspecting that some dangerous impasse had taken place between O'Flynn and the Chinese. Perhaps the conflict had something to do with O'Flynn's secret discovery. I'm ashamed to say that this scenario suddenly fit and reinforced all my irksome suspicions. But at the time I saw no reason to express them publicly.

Sheriff Nesbitt went on to say that he had set an investigation in motion, but that without more substantial evidence, he knew not where to turn. He could petition for a general warrant of arrest against Mr. O'Flynn, of course, but not knowing where he had gone, or even if he was indeed the true perpetrator, left the sheriff with little to take before Judge Kimmerlin as proof of culpability.

Further inquiries made with the Southern Pacific Railroad revealed that Mr. O'Flynn had most assuredly not been reemployed in any capacity whatsoever. The company claims to have had no dealings with their erstwhile employee since he'd been paid off and invalided out years before.

In the following weeks nothing could be discovered of O'Flynn's whereabouts or place of present employment. The Southern Pacific adamantly denied any knowledge of him and offered to open their employment rosters for official inspection.

In any case, I was never again officially consulted on the matter. Nonetheless, for warrantable reasons, my interest was understandably affixed, and I continued an informal investigation of my own, which I'm sad to report has revealed little to illuminate the situation aside from my affirmation that the facts presented here are true and unadulterated.

For the life of me, I cannot fathom the purpose or motive for what O'Flynn has been accused of doing. He might well have had some troubling disagreement with the Chinese, but could it have been so dire as to drive the Irishman to arson and possible murder? But on second thought, it cannot be denied that over the centuries the Irish have been known as masters of the incendiary art. Cromwell's General Monck was once quoted as saying that an Irishman would happily burn down his own house just to enjoy the pleasant afterglow, but he would much prefer to burn down his landlord's manor first. Be that as it may, Sheriff Nesbitt is of the opinion that perhaps O'Flynn committed arson on behalf of a third party, but without hard evidence he doesn't propose to cast a wide net to find the culprits. Suspicion and implied accusations would only cause bad feelings all around. And though it saddens me to say so, I find myself in total agreement. Justice, I fear, will have to wait upon future events to sort matters out.

THE PLOT HAS NOW TURNED as we expected. The Pacific Improvement Company is more than happy to honor the Chinese lease to China Point, but they adamantly refuse to allow them to rebuild, and they have had a city ordinance passed to put teeth in this repudiation of reconstruction. The Chinese, in response, and under the stewardship of their tong, have enlisted the legal services of one Albert Bennett Fox, Esq. I am reliably informed that he is a rabid antitrust advocate with an abiding passion for going after the railroads on any pretext whatsoever. I can only offer the fishermen my best wishes. Though, in truth, I'm sadly persuaded it will be a very long trek in search of recourse, compensation, or even justice.

As it now stands, aside from those few diehards who are taking shelter under canvas so as to continue to fish at the height of the season, most of the Chinese have already moved on from China Point. Some joined relatives in other rickety, rock-bound coastal villages like Point Alones, Cypress Point, Pescadero Point, and Point Lobos. However, other, more intrepid souls simply moved on and leased more land on McAbee Beach in Monterey. The Chinese refugees were back in full operation within two weeks. By way of comparison, it will most likely take the city of Salinas two years to accomplish full recovery.

All the while, the fishing has never stopped, and another Chinese village just seemed to appear overnight like a fairy ring of mushrooms on a fresh-mowed pasture. I have an abiding respect for the ingenuity these people display in every aspect of their lives. I truly believe they could build a viable community from almost anything at hand. They let nothing go to waste and find purpose for discarded materials that others would overlook. They are tenaciously loyal to family and clan first, but usually come together in solidarity where their mutual interests are concerned. I'm convinced the Chinese will always garner profit in whatever field they employ their considerable talents.

November 23, 1906

A FEW MONTHS HAVE PASSED since my last entry concerning this matter. Recently I received word from Dr. Fiche, only now returned from his field trip. He said he had stored my material in the antique documents vault at the university before he left, but would return them forthwith. He added that he had not been able to discover as much as he would have liked about the artifacts, but the objects were most certainly very old. Dr. Fiche stated further that he thinks the three scripts carved into the stone might be fifteenth-century Mandarin Chinese, Medieval Persian, and possibly an Indian script that he could not pin down without further research. He assumed it was a form of Tamil Cyrillic, or some other closely linked language. He believes the large jade seal was an artifact of some importance, and he put forward that it must have been the property of a notable Chinese official. A valuable piece of pink jade of that size and perfection, carved and engraved as it was with such precision, could only have been the property of someone of great importance. But until accurate translations could be made of the archaic inscriptions, nothing more could be determined.

I wrote back to Professor Fiche and thanked him for all his help, promising to communicate what details, if any, I could discover about the inscriptions. I asked him to use his best efforts to locate a Chinese-language scholar, which I assumed would be no easy matter under the circumstances.

The arrival of my package from Dr. Fiche has occasioned many hours of cold and painful introspection. No scholar trained in the sciences can ever relish the idea that an important discovery, no matter how culturally obtuse it may seem, can be arbitrarily withheld or hidden based on the whims of those who are too ignorant to comprehend the importance of such knowledge. For those educated to understand these matters, and who thus appreciate the significance of such information, all attempts at suppression would seem like rank cultural hubris or worse. My own profound disappointment was almost too painful to acknowledge. How much more so would it be for those dedicated scholars who had spent their professional careers in search of examples of the very objects I had seen, touched, and, in my poor way, cataloged. I didn't know offhand who those scholars might be, but I was sure they were out there in the world somewhere. My frustration concerning the now hidden artifacts was only matched by my anger at being hood-winked by that rascal and rogue, Red Billy O'Flynn, may he ultimately suffer the agonies he so blithely intended for others.

Sheriff Nesbitt has done his best to track down the ac-cused arsonist, and his office has sent telegraph alerts to every county in the state, but Nesbitt is still at a loss for a clue in any direction. It is as though O'Flynn and his people have simply dropped off the earth. This mystery can only lead me to believe that there has been a criminal conspiracy afoot all along, and that O'Flynn, on behalf of the propertied interests, played a key role. The obvious motive aimed at driving the Chinese from China Point so that property values adjacent to that location would find parity with the rest of Pacific Grove.

Still waters may run deep, but any competent douser can find them, and though the truth of the matter may not have been spoken of openly, it was known to most thinking citizens. Unfortunately, few people chose to speak out with anything akin to a moral opinion that might muddy their own wells. Too many people had too much at stake to indulge a controversy that would only come back to haunt other aspects of their com-mercial and political interests. So in the end I believe nothing viable will be done to compensate the Chinese for their losses.

I personally, and on my own account, went so far as to fol-low O'Flynn's parting suggestion. I therefore advertised for two months on the message page of *Railroad News*. Without men-tioning O'Flynn's name, in case it had been changed recently, I requested only that "a recently departed employee of Hopkins

Laboratory in Pacific Grove contact me on a matter of mutual interest and dire importance." As I should have suspected from the first, no response has been forthcoming, nor do I really expect that I will hear any word from that quarter again.

December 18, 1906

THOSE IN POLITICAL CIRCLES HEREABOUTS have informed me that the case for the people at China Point will not be resolved any time soon. Some interests are predicting a year or two, but the odds in favor of the plaintiffs are slim indeed. Unfortunately, this eventuality only fuels my sense of injustice and the absolute need for fair dealings all around.

Embracing a circling flock of guilt-tinged sentiments, I determined at least to restore what little remained of the treasure Red Billy O'Flynn had discovered and sequestered away for his own profit. I began to believe that perhaps the return of my historically pertinent documents (in lieu of the artifacts themselves) might at least mitigate some small portion of the loss the Chinese community had recently experienced. Either way, my evidence could be of little use to anyone beyond a truly dedicated scholar of fifteenth-century Chinese inscriptions, or to the local Chinese themselves.

I berated myself again and again for not insisting that O'Flynn tell me where he had hidden the stones before he departed. But then I have to acknowledge that I'm not really a person who finds overt confrontation a viable approach. Such a coarse contention between us might have inspired O'Flynn to make off with the rubbings and photographs as well.

Since I could do little at present to alleviate my sense of culpability, I determined to unburden myself of the problem as best I could. With this in mind I sent word to Master Ah Chung, who I was given to understand was now the majordomo of the local tong at Point Alones. He soon returned a polite reply by messenger requesting I pay him a visit at the tong's meeting hall on the following day at noon, which I did.

Master Ah Chung met me promptly at noon and invited me to share tea. The small meeting hall was deserted except for three tong elders who sat to one side and said nothing during the whole proceedings. Ah Shu Chung, to use his formal name, spoke an educated English that was flawed only by the chronic Chinese difficulty with the consonants *l* and *r*, which one might easily get past with patience and a close attention to context.

It was affirmed that he was acquainted with my erstwhile employee, Mr. Bill O'Flynn. He said that many people in the village had done business with Mr. O'Flynn, and that he was always held in high regard for his fair and honorable dealings. I then took the opportunity to inform him that, after what I had to impart, such an opinion might be significantly degraded. He invited me to speak at liberty, and so I went on to tell him everything I knew of O'Flynn's activities and his subsequent discoveries at Cypress Point. I told Master Ah Chung all I knew of the Chinese artifacts that O'Flynn had unearthed under the fallen cypress and then brought to me for a scholarly examination and appraisal. I then presented Master Ah Chung with the portfolio containing the stone rubbings and photographs. I invited him to inspect the material in detail.

What followed surprised me more than I can say. Master Ah Chung opened the folio and examined the contents in what appeared to be a very cursory fashion. Though he examined the rubbings and seemed to be reading a small part of the text, he showed no outward emotion whatsoever. Indeed, after a short perusal, he closed the folio and passed it back across the table to me without comment.

This gesture so surprised me that I found myself at a loss for words. I was stunned that there should be so little interest or recognition of the obvious. My frustration instantly inspired me to stir the pot in the opposite direction. I changed the subject by asking my host if he was aware that there was an official contention that the fire that destroyed the fishing village had in fact been a matter of arson, and the suspected perpetrator was none other than their friend Mr. Billy O'Flynn. I further stated that there were several reliable witnesses who would attest to the fact that O'Flynn had been seen leaving the China Point barn after the flames broke out. Again I was surprised by the lack of appreciable reaction on the part of my interlocutor.

After a few moments of silence, my host turned to the three elders discreetly seated at the side of the hall and spoke to them in Chinese. These gentlemen spoke among themselves for a few moments, and then turned back and nodded to Master Ah Chung. He in turn pleaded for my patience and requested that I not speak of this matter with anyone else until our next interview, which he proposed should take place the following Monday at the same location.

I agreed, of course, but in a state of some confusion, which led to several sleepless nights as I speculated and wondered just what the Chinese had perceived from my statements. I was also puzzled by the fact that Master Ah Chung had so easily, and without the least hesitation, returned my evidence as though it was only a matter of passing interest at best.

I arrived back at the tong hall on the appointed day and time, and was again kindly received by my host, Master Ah Chung. However, this time he was accompanied not by the silent elders, but by a Chinese gentleman of unusual aspect. This gentleman was introduced to me as Dr. Lao-Hong, and a more prepossessing figure would be hard to imagine. Unlike Master Ah Chung and many others who still wore Chinese dress and kept their hair in the traditional queue, Dr. Lao-Hong was Western in every possible detail. His hair was fashionably dressed, he wore an expensive gray suit, and he sported a blue silk waistcoat and highly polished boots. The doctor peered through gold-rimmed spectacles, and across his waistcoat hung a heavy gold watch chain from which was suspended a unique-looking fob of translucent amber mounted in gold. But what astounded me most was the fact that Dr. Lao-Hong spoke perfect English without the least trace of an accent, though his pronunciation hinted that he might have studied somewhere in the east, perhaps Boston or New York.

Again tea was served, and it was then that I was introduced to the purpose of Dr. Lao-Hong's visit. The gentleman explained that he functioned as a trade representative for the Three Corporations of San Francisco. In that capacity he handled the export of dried squid for the local fishing villages. He also dealt in exports of salt-cured eels, smoked abalone, and quality abalone shells, which were used in China to manufacture mother-of-pearl buttons and other decorations.

After a polite pause to enjoy our tea, Dr. Lao-Hong asked after my own background. I gave him a modest biographical sketch, as well as my academic credentials and present position. Dr. Lao-Hong seemed somewhat impressed, and said that he had attended Harvard University for three years before being summoned west at the request of his uncles who were officers of the Three Corporations. Unlike them, Dr. Lao-Hong had been born and educated in America. His knowledge of Western traditions and business practices were thought to be of considerable value to his uncles' extensive commercial interests.

When all the polite amenities had been dispensed with, Dr. Lao-Hong asked me to repeat what I had said to Master Ah Chung on my previous visit. Again I passed over the folio of rubbings and photographs and reiterated all I had to say about O'Flynn, his discoveries, and the subsequent charges of arson that had been laid against him.

Dr. Lao-Hong's examination of the material seemed just as cursory and disinterested as Master Ah Chung's had been, and he soon passed the folio back to me. Something about their lack of real interest aroused my suspicion, which in turn, I confess, inspired a twinge of tension if not outright anxiety.

Dr. Lao-Hong turned to Master Ah Chung and spoke in simple Cantonese. After a contemplative pause, Master Ah Chung nodded thoughtfully and rose from his seat, gesturing for me to follow. Dr. Lao-Hong smiled at me and stood to follow as well. I was escorted to the back of the hall, where a curtained alcove stood. On my first visit, I had noticed the embroidered silk curtain and had assumed that it formed a partition to a back room.

As the three of us stood before the curtain, Dr. Lao-Hong spoke to me in a lowered voice that denoted either reverence or a fear of being overheard. "I believe, Professor Gilbert, that you may have misjudged Mr. O'Flynn. But then, there would be no way for you to know the truth of the situation. We Chinese may have our failings, like all the rest of humanity, but one of the things we are brilliant at is keeping secrets. It has proven our salvation throughout history." The doctor smiled knowingly. "If we had not, then gunpowder, the compass, printing, and paper money would have found their way to the West three hundred years before they did. Can you imagine the bloody chaos that would have ensued if Charlemagne, for instance, had been able to bring cannons to bear upon his enemies? On the other hand, some secrets, my dear Professor Gilbert, are so powerful that they inspire disbelief no matter how loudly you proclaim them to the world. And we are faced here with just such a secret. So you see, it was Mr. O'Flynn who helped our efforts to preserve it. For we are sure that knowledge of the information you recorded could only hurt our position here in California and elsewhere. Some things are better left unspoken if one is to survive the slings and arrows of ignorant incredulity as well as racial and cultural prejudice."

Dr. Lao-Hong turned to Master Ah Chung and nodded. That gentleman drew back the curtain to reveal not a doorway, but an alcove housing what I took to be a shrine. I had seen others like it before. Every village had a shrine dedicated to prosperity, peace, and domestic felicity. Almost every house had smaller but similar shrines dedicated to household deities and ancestors. But this shrine was slightly different insofar as, at its center, there was a shallow, two-door wooden cabinet covered in ornate Chinese calligraphy. I noticed that the cabinet was secured with a small brass lock. Dr. Lao-Hong must have noticed my bewilderment, for he nodded again to Master Ah Chung, who in turn lit tapers on either side of the altar, clapped twice ceremonially, and unlocked the cabinet. Then he opened both doors and stood aside so I could get a better view of its contents. The astonishment on my face must have been palpable, for there in the muted light of the tapers I saw the stone tablet and the jade seal. The artifacts had obviously been meticulously cleaned and polished so that they shimmered like jewels in the candlelight. I well remember being at a loss, for I attempted a response that came out as a stutter.

"But . . . but . . . but how did you come by these artifacts, Doctor? Mr. O'Flynn expressly told me that he was going to hide the stone and the seal where no one could find them until he was ready to disclose the location."

Dr. Lao-Hong smiled once more and nodded. "And so he did, Professor Gilbert. He brought them to Master Ah Chung for safekeeping, and I assure you he was handsomely rewarded for his fidelity. You see, Mr. O'Flynn is respected by our community, and accepted into our homes as a faithful friend."

I was stunned. "But he was the one who was seen setting the fire that destroyed the whole village. How can you count such a villain as a friend? Besides, what's so significant about these artifacts that they should inspire such clandestine dealings? Surely they can do no harm in and of themselves."

Dr. Lao-Hong took on a contemplative expression, as though weighing his alternatives. "I hope you will forgive the impertinence, Professor, but you are quite wrong. But to satisfy your justifiable curiosity, I shall answer your second question first, if that's agreeable."

"Any explanation would be most appreciated, Doctor. I fell into these present circumstances quite by accident, and would be most grateful for any information that would set my mind at rest."

The doctor nodded. "Well, sir, under the reign of the third Ming emperor, Zhu Di, a great fleet of massive ships was commissioned to explore the known world and bring back ambassadors from those far lands to serve the emperor's court. Now, you must understand that many of these great ships were over four hundred and eighty feet long, the largest sailing ships in the world at the time, and were powered by as many as twelve sail-crowded masts, and crewed by thousands of sailors, soldiers, and diplomats. The grand admiral of this tremendous expedition, which consisted of over two hundred and fifty vessels of every variety, was the renowned Zheng He, a man of remarkable talents and industry. Zheng He accepted the commission and set about accomplishing his master's designs. At some point during that extended journey, Admiral Zheng He divided his fleet into separate squadrons and sent one of his vice admirals, Zhou Man, to explore the lands in the far eastern Pacific. To that end, and as far as we can tell, he sailed south to north along the coasts of the Americas and possibly set up small exploratory enclaves along the way.

"At some time during that journey, approximately June 1422 by your Western calendar, Admiral Zhou Man's squadron anchored in Monterey Bay. We now believe, evidenced by the inscriptions on the stone tablet, that he must have landed and set up camp at a place that is presently known to you as Cypress Point. Indeed, you might like to know in passing that the Monterey cypress trees that the locals are so proud of are in fact not indigenous to this place, but instead come from the coasts of southern China. It has long been the custom of Chinese sailors to plant trees native only to China in places where they could be seen as recognizable landmarks for those who followed. The stone tablet records just such an endeavor. The plaque was then buried, along with the seal, under the cypress saplings to mark the importance of the place as one that owed its allegiance to the benevolence of Emperor Zhu Di."

To say the least, I was enthralled and astounded by all I was hearing. "But, Doctor," I said, "how can you be so sure of these facts? As far as I know, there isn't the least mention of such an occurrence in local Indian traditions."

"I'm well aware of that, Professor. The jade seal belongs to Admiral Zhou Man. It affirms his rank and authority and carries his personal chop. And who is to say whether some Chinese sailors left on these shores did not intermarry with the local inhabitants? You must admit that the indigenous Indian populations along the coast of California look a great deal more Chinese than they do Spanish. Wouldn't you agree?"

That interesting fact had never really occurred to me, and in lieu of a pointed response I just nodded. Then a question popped into my head. "But if that were indeed the case, Doctor, why keep such an important piece of historical information secret? These revelations could change our whole view of history. As a teacher and scholar, I could no more suppress such information than I could suppress a newly proved truth about science."

Dr. Lao-Hong barely held a laugh in check and then apologized for any offense. "You must forgive me, Professor, but would you truthfully say that we Chinese in California are accepted as anything more than cheap labor? Would you say that, like other European minorities, any serious efforts have been expended to help us assimilate as equals, or that our contributions to society are respected in any way beyond that already accorded us as peasant laborers who dig for your railroads, work your mines, do your laundry, and demean ourselves as household servants? In truth, wouldn't you go so far as to say that we Chinese are viewed as little more than an inconvenient necessity, and that most white people might wish us to depart if it weren't for the fact that very few occidentals could carry on with business as usual without our labors?"

I nodded modestly, and he continued. "And what of your Spanish and Mexican compatriots, the people who settled this coast before a greedy and shameful war tore their possessions from them? Are they treated as honored equals? Don't bother to answer, Professor, for we both know the answer. And in that vein, let us suppose that a modern-day Hernando de Alarcón did sail into Monterey Bay and marched ashore with banners flying and made territorial claims based on prior discovery and occupation. Just what kind of a reception do you imagine he would receive? You need not respond to that either."

I was having difficulty following the relevance of the doctor's contentions and said as much as politely as I could.

"Well, Professor, perhaps we should look at the question from another perspective. Just imagine what people would do if they even suspected that we poor Chinese held a prior claim, albeit distant in time, to the West Coast of America and beyond; how do you imagine we would be treated then? We already live under a cloak of cultural and racial suspicion. What would our taskmasters do if they thought for one moment that we might one day register a prior claim to their land? Of course, these are but rhetorical questions, since it is our intention to send these voices from the past back to China as soon as proper arrangements can be made. In that way our brilliant maritime exploits shall be maintained, albeit in silence, without giving offense, or causing undue suspicion and cultural paranoia. We believe this to be the best feasible solution for all concerned."

I must confess to the fact that, all things being taken at face value, at this stage of our conversation I felt myself the target of a thinly veiled manipulation that bordered on threat. I confess that it made me slightly angry, but I kept it to myself as much as possible.

"But, Doctor," I said, "unless you propose to take them from me by force, I still have the rubbings and photographs as proof of the existence of these artifacts."

"My dear professor, no one here would think of depriving you of your property. But on the other hand, you must admit, as a scientist, that without the original artifacts your evidence would hardly influence matters one way or another, as such things are easily forged. Indeed, forgeries are hardly a rarity in any culture. They are usually created to dupe the faithful, fleece the gullible, and influence the wealthy. After all, if one assembled all the bones of all the known saints that now reside in treasured reliquaries in Catholic churches all over Christendom, you'd certainly have more bones than saints." Then he said, "You are welcome to publish your findings once you've made your own translations, but just who do you imagine would put their reputations on the block to defend your flimsy paper evidence? How many Western scholars of Chinese culture are there who might defend your premise, and how many of those scholars can translate antiquated Persian or Tamil? For I tell you, Professor, that this plaque, like the Rosetta stone, makes the same claims in all three languages, which means that all three cultural groups were involved in these voyages. So who of those chosen scholars, Western in the main, would believe that these diverse cultures were all in nominal service of Imperial Emperor Zhu Di and sailed as trusted colleagues in his treasure fleets? Not that I mean to belittle your position, Professor, but you are a teacher of marine biology at a small Western university. Thus it is my qualified opinion that your information will never see the light of serious academic inquiry."

I found myself racked between the wheels of frustration and anger. Frustration at the knowledge that Dr. Lao-Hong was correct in his assumption, and anger at Mr. O'Flynn for not taking me into his confidence about his relationship with the Chinese. There remained only a profound sense of disappointment.

Whether or not the treasure came within my field of study made little difference to me. I had come across an extraordinary piece of history. I had touched the evidence, duplicated the text with rubbings, and even photographed the stones from all angles, and yet it seemed I was to have no part in sharing the information with the world without putting my reputation as a teacher in some jeopardy. And if the very Chinese concerned in the case insist on denying the veracity of my evidence, I'm left standing in quicksand. The sensation made me very angry, and in a fit of pique I mentioned O'Flynn's involvement in the arson.

Master Ah Chung interjected by saying that Mr. O'Flynn had only done what he had been asked to do. My look of surprise must have been more than obvious.

Dr. Lao-Hong explained that Mr. O'Flynn had early on informed the elders at China Point that there was a plot in hand to drive the Chinese from the village in spite of their ironclad lease with the Pacific development company. This plot was covertly seconded by the Southern Pacific Railroad, which intended to construct an extended railroad line down the shore, and then engage excursion trains so that tourists might enjoy the beautiful sights. And by all means, the Chinese fishing village at China Point, with its cloying, fetid odors, was judged neither a salubrious nor desirable experience for their paying passengers.

Dr. Lao-Hong went on to elucidate. "These powerful interests conceived a diabolical plot to drive the Chinese fishing families from their holdings with an allegedly accidental conflagration. When the local tong elders learned of their plans from Mr. O'Flynn, they decided on their own response. Knowing they would most likely lose everything without apt and timely preparation, they sent a Caucasian emissary to San Jose to purchase fire insurance to cover any losses at China Point. And just whom would you think we got to insure the property? I'll save you the speculation by saying that it was the Southern Pacific Railroad. They very conveniently maintain their own public insurance company, and since the right hand had little notion of what the left was doing, an insurance policy for ten thousand dollars was drawn up in the name of the tong at China Point against any community losses from fire. Then the tong very secretly arranged to have all the inhabitants of the village pack up their most precious possessions to be removed to a place of safety at Point Alones, leaving behind only those items, like stoves or ovens, that could not be removed without drawing suspicion. Most all the boats, nets, and fishing gear were moved to the south end of the beach below the village, where the flames of the fire could not possibly reach them. Only the older boats and nets were left to burn. When Mr. O'Flynn came to us and said that he had heard reliable rumors that something untoward would soon take place, we set our plans in motion. On the appointed evening our brave friend Mr. O'Flynn secretly returned to town and set the barn aflame as was arranged. The tong elders, of course, notified the villagers what to expect and when, which is why there were no injuries or fatalities as a result of the fire."

To say the least, this information rocked me back on my heels. I asked Dr. Lao-Hong where Mr. O'Flynn was now, but he said that information could not be divulged. O'Flynn had protected them at the risk of his freedom, and they would do no less for him. He was in a place of safety and future prosperity. "Besides, Professor Gilbert, if they can't find the alleged perpetrator and coax a confession, then nothing can be proved either way, and the onus of responsibility remains an open question."

"But Mr. O'Flynn is already under suspicion. He was witnessed setting the fire by a group of soldiers. Even Sheriff Nesbitt thinks he is the arsonist, which goes a long way toward putting a cap on the matter."

Dr. Lao-Hong smiled in the most inscrutable manner. "I have no doubt of what you say, Professor, but Mr. O'Flynn was first and foremost a railroad man. He had worked for the Southern Pacific for years before his injuries, and the infidelity of his masters forced him out with a tawdry pittance. Knowing that, where do you think the most suspicion would be aimed? Perhaps one might argue that the Pacific Improvement Company and the railroad made him an offer that impending penury obliged him to accept. Who can say? We believe the question should be left to the courts. Don't you agree? But either way, Mr. O'Flynn will not be present to stand in the dock to take the blame or point fingers. So the question of responsibility will remain a mystery for quite some time, and indeed may never be resolved to anyone's satisfaction, which is perhaps as it should be."

"But what about the villagers and their homes?"

"That was also seen to. In preparation for the impending destruction, the tong arranged to take an extended lease on some property over on McAbee Beach in Monterey. The fishermen were back on the bay three days after the fire, and the villagers will soon replace everything they lost, thanks to the prompt attention of the Southern Pacific Insurance Company, which under the circumstances could find no reason to disavow the claim. They were mired in their own machinations with nowhere to turn. They will drag their feet, no doubt, but they'll pay up in the end unless they wish to see their Chinese labor force go on strike. It was all very well thought out, I assure you."

Here I found a chink in the doctor's reasoning. "But, if

secrecy was so paramount, why have you told me all this? What prevents me from taking what information I have to the authorities?"

"Because, Professor, you are an honest and empathetic man, and were once a friend of our Mr. O'Flynn. You also know about the seal and the stone. But you are also a highly intelligent man and aware, I'm sure, that without absolute proof, your hearsay testimony would be scorned as improbable, if not altogether ridiculous. And I'm quite sure you'll agree that neither the Pacific Improvement Company nor the Southern Pacific Railroad will acknowledge that any such plot to burn us out ever existed. But if, however, you did choose to take such an action, the tong would vehemently deny all knowledge of Mr. O'Flynn, of you, and this meeting, to say nothing of the artifacts you claim to have examined and copied. For I assure you, Professor, no American will ever lay eyes on those treasures again."

I left the village at Point Alones feeling quite giddy. It was almost as though the whole situation had been conjured in a murky dream and, as such, perched beyond explanation. Even to those of my contemporaries who might be willing to give me the benefit of the doubt, the lack of all corroboration would mark me as a crank or, worse still, the victim of an elaborate hoax perpetrated by a disgruntled employee.

I slowly realized that Dr. Lao-Hong was right. Anything I might publicly say on the matter would most likely be ridiculed as pure invention or, at the very least, idle speculation. For it's certain that the white population hereabouts would never acknowledge or believe that these supposedly ignorant and lowly Chinese could have so deftly arranged matters for their own benefit, or so thoroughly hoodwinked those who had planned their destruction.

Though I'm now sure that the chain of events will live on only in my journal, and probably go no further, I'm left with a very intriguing source of speculation. What would history have been like if that famous Chinese admiral and his great fleet, armed as they were with highly developed technology and political expertise, had stayed behind in California to protect their claims of discovery? After all, Columbus managed to make a sizable impact on history with far fewer resources and much less intelligence. But of one thing I'm now quite sure. If those medieval Spanish conquistadors, lacking as they did all enlightened self-interest, should have come upon a thoroughly entrenched Chinese presence in California, they wouldn't have stood the remotest chance at conquest, much less trade. It's my studied opinion that men of violence rarely indulge in honest commerce.

—*Dr. Charles Gilbert*

THE THORNS OF WISDOM

"No man needs more than one blade to cut
his own throat."

—CHINESE PROVERB

THE IDES OF JUNE FOUND Dr. Lao-Hong in his San Francisco study writing a long letter to an old college friend in Boston. Indeed, the doctor had received a number of concerned letters from old colleagues and friends asking after his well-being since the disastrous earthquake two months earlier, but he was only now finding the time to respond. But in doing so he discovered that the very act of setting down recent events from his own perspective led him to sort out and scrutinize all his thoughts and reflections for the first time in months. He made no attempt to write down everything, of course, but he pondered everything in as dispassionate a manner as he could muster. His one discomforting obstacle rested in the knowledge that he was, to some degree, little more than a yarn ball in the cat's paw of fortune. For in truth there were really two diametrically opposed experiences inextricably knotted together in his thoughts; one was but the shadow manifestation of the other. But he could only share one part of the story, the rest he would have to take to his grave, and at age thirty-seven he believed that was a long time to keep a secret, but he would do it. Betrayal was out of the question.

The doctor's letters were gracious. He was sincerely gratified by the solicitude of his friends, but he only felt comfortable writing about the basic facts as he viewed them, and for the most part he recomposed general news and personal observations. The outline remained principally the same for each letter.

Dr. Lao-Hong wrote that 1906 had been a most distressing and disagreeable year for a great number of people in northern California. The range of deadly earthquakes and their aftermath meant that most everyone except undertakers suffered serious financial loss in one form or another. A destroyed business, of whatever size and importance, meant no employment. But it was all the same, as there were no customers, and there were no patrons because there were no accessible funds for them to spend. Credit was all but impossible to get because many banks, along with their records, had been severely damaged in the earthquakes, or subsequently destroyed by fire. Hard cash money had dried up almost overnight because the price of every conceivable commodity, from goat's milk to buggy whips, became shockingly exorbitant. Prices for the simplest staples rose astronomically, and good whiskey and other spirits became so rare and costly that even a number of gambling dens, dance halls, and back-alley saloons went belly-up. But by far, the worst scandals were perpetrated by the blackguards who manipulated the trade in essential medications and medical supplies. Their dealings were nothing if not blatant and merciless criminal extortion. And though it was probably only a slight exaggeration, it was wildly rumored that in some parts of San Francisco, a badly injured person needed gold to enjoy the privilege of staying alive.

The consequences of this series of events rippled out in all directions, substantially affecting all strata of society. Leaving himself till last, Dr. Lao-Hong was pleased to report to his friends that his family was safe and well, and presently staying with relatives in Oakland. He was grateful that his own dwelling suffered only moderate structural damage, though its contents had been liberally thrown about. Anything that could be broken had been.

On a more sanguine note, the doctor went on to observe, perhaps with some pride, that there was one group of people who seemed to have endured the recent calamity with the least amount of devastation, disruption, or corruption, and that was the local Chinese community.

It was said by some people that the Chinese lost the least because they had the least to lose, but this was only evidence of their blind ignorance. The truth is that they lost the least because they took better precautions to preserve what they had. The doctor wrote that a long history of similar disasters in China had long since encouraged the development of methods to secure both personal and financial survival. Centuries of experience had made the Chinese familiar with such implacable catastrophes. But somehow, in spite of long wars, bloody revolutions, and devastating natural disasters, the pulse of banking, commerce, and trade never really ceases. Their fiscal system operates under a purely pragmatic tenet of extended accountability. If a man carries debt, his whole family must shoulder the burden until the obligation is resolved. It's simple and it works. And to that end every commercial transaction floats on a "tranquil pond" of extended credit. Unless otherwise stipulated, official repayment of debt is ceremoniously transacted twice a year, sometimes only on New Year's Day.

Dr. Lao-Hong was pleased to make note that, unlike most people in the city, the local Chinese were essentially self-sustaining in respect to food, clothing, shelter, and especially medical care.

Suddenly the doctor stopped writing in midsentence and put up his pen. With a deep sigh born of frustration, he set aside his letters on the desk. Upon reflection it disturbed him to realize that in spite of the serious subject matter, everything he'd written sounded awkward, superficial, and distracted.

And there was no doubt about it. The doctor was seriously distracted, almost painfully preoccupied with the discomforting realization that the other story, the one he could never document in any form, kept encroaching on his thoughts at all hours of the day and night. He was often reflectively engaged to such a degree that all else, including the present turmoil, became little more than a monochromatic background. But whether he wished to or not, it was very likely that Dr. Lao-Hong would once again surrender his thoughts to the recent past, and again try to envisage and qualify the inscrutable machinations of destiny, a fate that had goaded him onto the course he was now committed to follow with eternal fidelity.

Dr. Lao-Hong had known from the very first that the discovery of Admiral Zhou Man's stone testament, and the accompanying imperial seal, would cause widespread controversy within the higher echelons of the Chinese tongs in northern California. But that aside, he hoped to resolve the issue in an equitable manner. Nonetheless, the young doctor, having been born, raised, and educated in America, and espousing as he did a semi-Western sensibility, knew quite well that he was now embroiled in a thorny situation that could easily erupt into perilous tong rivalries.

Dr. Lao-Hong's predicament was hardly new. In truth, he had been dealing with variations of the same dilemma all his adult life. Simply stated, it centered on the fact that immigrant Chinese, despite the fact that Dr. Lao-Hong spoke flawless Mandarin and Cantonese, perceived him as being too American, while white Americans, of course, treated him like they did all Chinese, no matter how well he spoke English, or how advanced his education.

This fish-nor-fowl quandary had required Dr. Lao-Hong to walk a very narrow path in both worlds, and though his loyalties had always sided with his Chinese brethren, his intellectual sensibilities were Western in the main, and herein lay another ungainly dilemma. Though the Chinese had considered themselves fully literate for many centuries, the truth was at odds with that presumption, at least for those Chinese who had come into the shadow of the Gold Mountain as poor laborers, with little or no formal education of any kind. Sadly, most were illiterate in all but the simplest Chinese characters. In many cases these people arrived in San Francisco from different parts of China and could hardly communicate with one another, much less their white employers. Even Lao-Hong found he sometimes experienced great difficulty comprehending the least bit of the various local dialects. In some instances he found his poorer interlocutors spoke a local patois of Chinese that was totally incomprehensible even to their neighbors in the next province. It was like the difference between French and Norwegian.

The doctor had long been aware that blistering ignorance invariably walked hand in hand with blind superstition, but that was true of all mankind and hardly unique to his own race. However, this tradition did cause some conflict within the Chinese communities themselves. Those who were raised in conservative and better-educated Mandarin societies brought their ancient prejudices east, and so looked down on those fellow countrymen who spoke Cantonese, or any other dialect for that matter. On the other hand, those Chinese who spoke various forms of Cantonese traditionally suspected the high-handed motives and cultural vanities of those who spoke Mandarin, and herein lay one of the problems he was about to confront.

The various tongs represented the cultural tastes and inclinations of their elders and constituents, and in the past their competing interests had sometimes led to outright warfare between them. This was by no means a local novelty. Such conflicts had been going on in China for centuries. Dr. Lao-Hong was reminded of something his esteemed father had told him: "The Chinese Empire had only one all-powerful enemy in the world, and it was the Chinese themselves."

Through his university studies, the doctor had since learned that the same could be said of the Americans, the English, the French, the Germans, and virtually every other nation on earth. The only possible exception was the Duchy of Lichtenstein, whose minuscule population and limited acreage precluded the luxury of having enemies, either domestic or foreign.

For reasons that Lao-Hong could only imagine, Dr. Gilbert had ultimately refrained from publicly divulging what he knew but could not prove, and the local population of Monterey remained ignorant of Mr. O'Flynn's discoveries. The same, however, could not be said of the Chinese community. The Chinese were quite capable of maintaining an ironclad secrecy as far as foreigners were concerned, but within their own ranks, secrecy was next to impossible. Word of the stone tablet and Zhou Man's Imperial seal traveled like a thatch fire throughout the tongs all the way to San Francisco.

Within weeks, a close and heated debate arose among the various factions. Some bearded elders insisted the treasures should be held and guarded by the parent tongs in San Francisco, while others believed they should be sent back to China. But the cold facts were sad, as most just wanted the treasures only for themselves.

As might be expected, possession of these artifacts brought great prestige and honor to the tong that sheltered them, and the Chinese in Monterey felt they held a proprietary interest in the matter. For them possession was better than nine-tenths of the law; it was everything. Regrettably, it was within this context that Dr. Lao-Hong found himself precariously wedged between several tigers at once. He was easily persuaded that if he didn't employ great political dexterity, he might just be crushed by the impetus of conflicting interests, and that would mean defeat and a public loss of face for his family and clan.

Dr. Lao-Hong was the proud scion of a very influential and respected family. Sadly, he was away at school in the east when his mother and father died in the typhoid epidemic of 1887. He was then taken under the collective wings of two aging but extremely powerful uncles. Between them, these venerable gentlemen managed eighty percent of the Chinese export market leaving San Francisco. They also controlled nine seats on the august council of the Three Corporations, which gave them the majority vote on almost every issue. There wasn't a tong in California that dared close its doors to them on any pretext. And though they showed all the outward signs of great modesty and frugality, they were in fact men of phenomenal wealth, influence, and responsibility.

It was to these gentlemen that Dr. Lao-Hong owed the most profound marks of respect and gratitude. They had financed his expensive education and seen to it that he lacked for nothing in his pursuit of academic excellence. Having no siblings to care for, Dr. Lao-Hong was free to indulge his studies for as long as he liked. And though his uncles were of a traditionally conservative strain, they had always treated him with the greatest affection and indulgence, in some cases even more so than their own children. They were very proud of their nephew's scholarship and academic achievements, and came to depend upon his help and advice in matters that related to business dealings with Yankee officials or government placemen. His uncles' indulgence and generosity even extended to breaking with convention and ceding their rights to secure all matrimonial arrangements, and he was allowed to marry the girl of his choice. Happily, she was the jewel of an ancient and prestigious family, and it was a love match from the first. After ten years and three children, his wife, Mui Choi, was still considered a great beauty. The doctor loved her above all else and revered her compassionate and insightful sensibilities.

After his extended interview with Master Ah Chung, the tong elders, and Dr. Gilbert, Dr. Lao-Hong returned to San Francisco by ship and immediately went to his uncles to report in detail all that had transpired in Monterey.

Almost at once, strong opinions concerning the matter were lofted everywhere. At first he too had been in favor of secretly returning the treasures to China. But his wife, with whom he shared everything of importance, had reasonably pointed out that the markers had been buried on purpose. If the grave of the great admiral had been discovered instead, there would be few who would dare play fast and loose with his revered bones, or use them to garner prestige. The desecration would only serve to strip that man and his entire family of all honor and respect. When the doctor asked his wife what she recommended be done, she cast one of her soft, beautiful smiles and said she believed the treasure should be secretly put back where it was found, only much deeper in the ground. They should shelter beneath those ancient cypress trees, where Zhou Man intended them to rest.

A few days later, Dr. Lao-Hong was pondering Mui Choi's suggestion when he received a polite but urgent summons to attend a meeting at his uncles' offices. When he arrived he was not surprised to discover the presence of two austere, bearded elders from the Three Corporations sitting in attendance. For arcane reasons of security as well as tradition, the men who sat on the council of the Three Corporations were always referred to by number, and never by name. Thus, Dr. Lao-Hong politely bowed to Uncle Eight and Uncle Eleven. In the scheme of things, his own uncles were known as Uncle Four and Uncle Six. The numbers reflected a strict code of seniority, with all votes being proportional. Only Uncle One and Uncle Two possessed veto power, which was rarely if ever employed against the wishes of the majority.

After all the social amenities had been dispensed with and tea had been served, Dr. Lao-Hong was informed of the purpose of his presence. He was told by his uncles that after considerable candid and productive deliberation, the council of the Three Corporations had come to what they believed was an equitable solution for the future of Zhou Man's stone testament and Imperial seal.

First of all, they agreed that the artifacts were to stay under the Gold Mountain, and thus in California, but they viewed it as their duty to forestall what they believed might easily become an acrimonious and bloody rivalry between the various parent tongs for possession of the treasures.

By their estimation the stones were now sheltered in a diminutive tong hall on the storm-wracked coast of Monterey Bay, and secured with nothing more than a curtained altar and

---

some vigilant but powerless elders. It was their opinion that a few illiterate fishermen could not possibly know the true meaning or cultural significance of the artifacts in their possession. The council had thus determined that the Three Corporations should offer the security of their wealth and organization to protect and care for the artifacts in the name of the presiding tong of record in Monterey. The uncles would undertake to reveal the artifacts only to the scrutiny of enlightened Chinese scholars, and they were additionally prepared to swear and sign binding oaths promising that the heathen Yankees would never know of or possess the treasure, on pain of a financial penalty if they violated this agreement.

To place the matter in its proper rank of significance, the Three Corporations were generously prepared to secure the interests of the fishermen's tong with a cash bounty of twenty-five thousand dollars in gold, plus a substantial insurance bond to indemnify the loss if any harm were to come to the treasures while in transport and under the protection of the Three Corporations.

As Dr. Lao-Hong well understood, this thinly veiled scheme was, in reality, little more than a gilt-edged act of extortion, albeit plumed with a handsome bribe to assuage dignity all around. It thus represented the price that face, status, and respect demanded in exchange for the inestimable honor of protecting these priceless cultural treasures on behalf of all concerned interests.

On the other hand, though it didn't help him feel any better about the situation, the doctor knew that the uncles were right in principle. For these priceless symbols of a great and proud history to reside within a flyblown tong hall in a peasant fishing village was not deemed appropriate in light of their importance. After all, stealing valuables from the Chinese was not unheard of, and there was a well-worn axiom that declared that one should gather only those valuables that can be most easily secured. The fishermen had little to boast of in that regard. And, as the uncles were well aware, there was still a very good chance that word might leak out through Professor Gilbert, which would only promote another disquieting series of complications.

The conclusion of the interview focused on a detailed set of instructions. Dr. Lao-Hong was to return to Monterey as an official representative of the Three Corporations, and in the most amenable and respectful manner possible make all the necessary arrangements.

Had he been invited to do so, Dr. Lao-Hong could have listed any number of foreseeable obstacles to an equitable and happy outcome. But he was not. Nor did he feel it was his place to taint his uncles' sanguine expectations with pessimistic speculations. Negative sentiments only opened the doors to ill fortune, and joss played a large part in everything Chinese.

Privately, the doctor had drifted around to his wife's way of thinking. He had come to believe that Zhou Man's treasure, whether the uncles suspected it or not, was going to dispense far more than honor or face. It saddened him, but the doctor would not be in the least surprised to hear that blood had been shed in the serpentine wake of the orphaned treasures. And in that regard, he also believed his first responsibility was to make sure that it wasn't his blood.

Dr. Lao-Hong smiled to recall that Mui Choi had been right about something else as well. The only really intelligent course open to him was to assume a benign posture of enlightened disinterest. It was one of those annoying mystical conundrums that always seemed to surface at the wrong time. It was an ancient philosophical puzzle. One defends and protects either everyone or no one. What is the path of an honorable man who finds no principled alternatives at his disposal? The irresolvable questions of justice and loyalty flowed in and out like the tides, and the doctor was quite sure that failure on his part might find his professional "corpse" floating out to sea on one of those tides.

In the broadest sense, Dr. Lao-Hong's family allegiances were as solid as stone. Despite his relative youth, at thirty-seven the doctor occupied important positions within the clan that related to Western business interests. As a result of these lucrative arrangements, and because he had always bowed to his father's call to observe financially modest habits, the doctor was, in all contemporary respects, a very wealthy man. He held deeds covering a profitable range of commercial real estate in San Francisco, and cash assets in a score of gainful business interests. And for all his financial success and familial bliss, nurtured, to be sure, by an exceptional education, the doctor honored a mortal debt to his ancestors, his parents, his uncles, his own family, and, lastly, his clan.

It was that last debt that encompassed the greatest risk. Every family, clan, state, or nation, unless under the thumb of a very powerful patriarch, is perennially riddled with conflicting interests of one stripe or another. It obliged the doctor to recall that, as much as the Chinese universally profess their undying veneration of peace, social harmony, piety, and order, they can rarely get those elements to march in step in their own extended families.

Factions pecked at one another like young cockerels in a never-ending and foolish roundabout of posturing for place and recognition. He was reminded of the cautionary joke about a

half-crazed dog that incessantly chases its own tail, until one
day he manages to catch up with his quarry and, reveling in
his unexpected victory, bites it off. Dr. Lao-Hong knew from
experience that a quarrelsome state of affairs could grow ex-
ponentially with the size of the clan. Inevitably, the resulting
disharmony must somehow be restored to a proper balance, and
only those with great power and prestige can apply real force of
will to make it so.

Dr. Lao-Hong took all this in stride when it came to his own
culture. By his own estimation the Chinese had survived and
prospered under the Gold Mountain by creating for themselves
those institutions of administration and law denied them by the
civil government. It was only reasonable to suppose that, as in
China, the management and supervision of those institutions
followed traditional clan lines of ascending seniority and power.
It was an ancient and proven system with which every Chinese,
regardless of birthplace or dialect, had been familiar since birth.
It was with good cause that they trusted nothing else. And possessed with this historical experience, they had every reason to
be highly suspicious of all Western political novelties. Nonetheless, the doctor knew his people to be substantially pragmatic,
sometimes to a fault. If perhaps some Western innovations
were judged necessary, practical, profitable, and inexpensive to
reproduce, like the telegraph, then the Sons of Heaven could be
depended upon to adopt it at once, and then turn around and
reengineer the device to serve their particular needs.

Dr. Lao-Hong pondered his precarious situation as he took
the coaches south to Monterey. The train rattled and groaned
over the points as it slowly steamed away from the depot, leaving the rusting rail yards and the acrid air behind. With the
passing of the last outlying factory buildings, the gravitational

pull of the city was lessened. Once released, the engine sped up and pressed on past surrounding farms and fields, and then out along undulating hills of ocher-colored grasslands, punctuated here and there with resilient outcroppings of oak and orchards dispensing partial shade to small gatherings of cattle and antelope. Two hours farther south, the upper mantles of the mountains on either side of the valley were showing off small green patches of new grass. Dr. Lao-Hong knew that in a few days, with the continued blessings of rain, the whole vista would transform into a lush, emerald green landscape rolling like sea swells down the valley. The rich hillsides would be dotted all about with thick carpets of brightly colored lupines and pastures rich with bluebells and white cow lilies. The doctor wistfully hoped it might all appear in its verdant glory for his return journey. He believed the natural splendor might reflect a propitious omen, for at that moment he felt in dire need of celestial endorsement to help balance his leaden feelings of inadequacy.

Though he was anxious to please his uncles in all things, Dr. Lao-Hong was not happy to be parted from his wife and children, not to mention his other business interests. As he considered his situation and the many possible outcomes, the doctor found himself being rocked about by a small storm brewing in the Western-educated portion of his brain.

That part of the doctor's American education that had inspired him to revere the imperative lessons discovered reading Xenophon, Euripides, Plutarch, and Livy had also inspired him to mine most of Edmund Burke and all of Thomas Paine. The doctor drifted off as he recalled that once, while attending a Harvard Christmas gathering, he had tapped a fifty-dollar wager by memorizing, word for word, all of Paine's *Common Sense* between the dinner gong and the same chime at breakfast the next day. Just to show off, young master Lao-Hong also threw in Paine's *American Crisis*. He didn't make any friends doing it, but he did pay off his commissary bill with enough money left over to convince Mr. Finch at the bookstore that he wasn't a complete deadbeat.

Suddenly Dr. Lao-Hong came out of his daydream as Thomas Paine, the China Point fire, and Zhou Man's treasure all came crashing together in his mind. There was no question that the fishing families had been doomed from the start, even if they did make accommodations for the inevitable. Nonetheless, recent newspaper accounts concerning the lawsuit instituted by the Chinese against the Pacific Improvement Company indicated that, despite Judge Kimmerlin's predilections to lean toward the interests of the Chinese tenants, the Pacific Improvement Company had harnessed a sleek team of high-priced railroad lawyers to argue their case, and it looked as though an expensive legal struggle might drag on for years without an adequate resolution.

It was here, just as Paine's philosophical specter appeared out of the fog, that Dr. Lao-Hong's cultural struggle came back to the fore. The doctor's personal loyalties could never be called into question, but he was conflicted by the role he was being asked to play in the name of familial obligation. There was definitely no question in his mind that what the Three Corporations were attempting to accomplish was little more than a blend of cultural extortion laced with face-saving bribes plumed with implied threats. But this had always been the way of things, even in China. The greater tongs kowtowed to the Three Corporations, or some such body, and the lesser tongs always bowed to the greater, and so on in a descending scale until one found the poor fisherman or laundryman, who must in turn kowtow to his guild master for the privilege of laboring night and day to feed his family a few bowls of fish, seaweed, and steamed rice each day.

It was painful to admit, especially in his present situation, but Dr. Lao-Hong's sympathies were not totally invested with his uncles, the Three Corporations, or the purpose of his errand. He was scourged not just by history and Burke's First Principles, but also by what he personally felt was basically honorable and just. For the less privileged elements of society to automatically succumb to the arbitrary ambitions of those more powerful might be a primal law of nature, but it made for damn poor politics and did little to cultivate minority cohesion.

The doctor had to admit that in the last decade, disturbing instances of tong conflict had become more frequent and more often bloody. Though many powerful elders preferred to disavow the obvious, the doctor had witnessed a tenacious series of small internal rebellions, each adopting noble guises and espousing selfless motives. But to the doctor's way of thinking, it was as rampant within the tongs as it was within the Californian society at large. Or perhaps the tong elders had deluded themselves into believing that the rise in factional insurgence was just another of those despised Western novelties that some of the younger Chinese had taken a fancy to, and then refashioned to their own covetous ends.

As much as Dr. Lao-Hong wished it were otherwise, he knew full well that if the Three Corporations didn't take charge of Zhou Man's treasures, some other cadet-level tong would pounce on the opportunity to gain the artifacts, even if outright theft had to be employed to gain possession. It had happened before in an unfortunate, murderous incident involving several ancient Taoist texts belonging to a small tong in Seattle. Such crimes would more than likely happen again if the rewards were judged worthwhile and the penalties negligible, as is usually the case when the powerful intimidate and extort from their weaker brethren. Dr. Lao-Hong's father had been right after all. Whether in China or California, the only real enemy the Chinese faced was their own countrymen.

At last Dr. Lao-Hong's thoughts flew back to his family. There, as always, he found great peace and moral resolution in remembering his wife's honest, empathetic insights and her mature and gentle wisdom. As he watched the countryside and the distant ocean fly by his window, he became more determined to follow her prudent counsel, particularly since at present he was bereft of any workable plans of his own.

As it neared Monterey, the train entered a heavy fog bank that seemed to shroud the doctor's mood with increasing misgivings. The train slowed for lack of visibility, and when it finally arrived at the station in Monterey, the fog was so thick the doctor could hardly make out details more than fifteen feet away.

It had been seven weeks since his last visit, and though the Three Corporations had written ahead to say they were sending Dr. Lao-Hong on an important matter of business, no specific date or time had been mentioned. He was therefore surprised to find Master Ah Chung waiting at the station for him with a horse and buggy. He assured Dr. Lao-Hong that his presence was hardly a matter of clairvoyance, since he or one of his associates had met the train for the last ten days. He said he was most pleased to be of service and would take his honored guest wherever he wished to go.

When Dr. Lao-Hong said he had made arrangements to stay at the El Carmelo Hotel, Master Ah Chung simply shook his head. He humbly begged pardon of his guest and said he believed the doctor would not be comfortable there for several reasons, the first and foremost being that the Carmelo Hotel was owned and operated by the Pacific Improvement Company, who were not well disposed to Chinese of any stripe. "Besides," he whispered, "the beds are infested with bugs, and the food they serve is inedible. These round-eyes eat their meat bloody or burnt, and their vegetables are boiled beyond recognition." And this, he said, would hardly be suitable for a man of Dr. Lao-Hong's cultivated tastes. Master Ah Chung said the elders had arranged more appropriate accommodations.

Twenty minutes later Master Ah Chung pulled up to the stone portico of a handsome two-story stone house on a wooded hillside overlooking Monterey and the bay beyond. The broad, walled gardens surrounding the house were impeccably maintained, and the walkways newly swept. Master Ah Chung said that the house belonged to Madame Hammond Yee, the cultured Chinese widow of a wealthy American ship captain who had come to Monterey to retire. Captain Hammond had purchased the house from the estate of Mr. O'Sheen and furnished it to his wife's tastes with treasures he had acquired in China.

Ah Chung quickly communicated most everything he knew about Madame Yee, or Lady Yee, as she was commonly referred to. Lady Yee was of Mandarin descent, and very well educated. Her grandmother had been a lady in waiting to the Imperial Dowager Empress, and her father a very wealthy and influential trader and grain factor. When one day another internal rebellion broke out, Master Yee had found himself on the wrong side of history. Suddenly the Yee family was ostracized from power and position and told to remove themselves to Canton, where, no doubt, they were expected to go extinct with encroaching poverty and shame. However, Master Yee turned the tables on his feather-headed enemies and became even more successful and wealthy in Canton.

It was in Canton that Captain Hammond first cast eyes on his future bride. By any standard, Lady Yee was considered an exotic beauty, and the captain fell in love almost at once. Master Yee was loath to part with his third and most talented daughter, but the captain's persistence and Master Yee's honor were eventually rewarded for the dower sum of eight thousand gold dollars and free passage for a cargo of red wheat bound for the Philippines.

Captain Hammond had passed away ten years ago, and Lady Yee now lived alone except for her four servants and a cook. Those who could appreciate such subtle arts considered her cook, Ah Chu, the finest chef in California, Chinese or otherwise. Because she liked to know interesting and important people, the wealthy widow kept two expensively decorated suites of rooms specifically to entertain important visitors who came to town.

Lady Yee graciously welcomed her honored guests with a soft smile and noble nod of the head. The doctor was surprised to find that despite her supposed years, Lady Yee remained a very handsome creature indeed. She was taller than most Chinese women, but her figure was still slim and youthful in proportion. Her glistening, jet-black hair reflected light like obsidian and was handsomely dressed with magnificently pierced gold and jade combs that indicated her status and wealth. She was attired in a rose-patterned brocaded coat over fine black silk pantaloons decorated with silver cranes and piped in gold. Her features were most attractive and seductive for someone her age. The doctor noted that her general expression was modest, her manner warm and generous, and her ready smile seemed to indicate a person who appreciated the benefits of laughter.

Lady Yee led her honored guest into her beautifully decorated parlor, and after a delicious service of oolong tea and sweet sesame buns, the doctor was shown to his rooms, which were superbly appointed with traditional Chinese furnishings. He was also pleased to discover that Lady Yee's house had been fitted with interior plumbing and elaborately decorated French water closets, a great and warming convenience on cold evenings and foggy mornings.

When they had all finished their second pot of tea, Master Ah Chung, acknowledging that the doctor deserved a good supper and a restful night after his long day on the cars, politely took his leave with promises to call again the next morning at ten, a more congenial hour, to discuss whatever business had brought the doctor so far.

That night Dr. Lao-Hong was served one of the finest meals he had ever enjoyed, and after an edifying and pleasant conversation with Lady Yee, he retired to his suite. And despite his conflicted emotions, that night Dr. Lao-Hong slept the sleep of the innocent.

The next day the doctor was escorted to the tong hall at Point Alones, where he took another official meeting with Master Ah Chung and the council of elders. After another ceremonial service of tea and much polite but necessary banter, the doctor very subtly and courteously presented the offer set forth by the Three Corporations. He also took the time to explain in detail why the proposal had been put forward, and the possible consequences if the proposition was refused.

Master Ah Chung and the tong elders maintained a respectful but inscrutable silence during the doctor's presentation. When he had finished, the elders asked permission to retire to their deliberations, and humbly requested that the doctor return the next day to hear their answer. Dr. Lao-Hong happily agreed. He then rose, bowed to the venerable elders, and retired with Master Ah Chung to attend a celebratory luncheon hosted by his brother. Of course, etiquette and protocol demanded that no business be discussed, but this was not a hindrance to the occasion, as various entertainments had been arranged for the pleasure of their important guest. The gathering went on for quite some time, and a respectable quantity of rice wine was served to lubricate the numerous toasts made in the name of mutual prosperity and perpetual contentment under the mandate of heaven.

Dr. Lao-Hong was unused to drinking wine except on ceremonial occasions, and then only in modest amounts. And, as might be expected, he eventually found himself feeling somewhat light-headed and giddy. He confessed as much to Master Ah Chung, who suggested an invigorating walk along the beach to clear their heads. It was a beautiful afternoon, with no sign of the fog that usually flushed across the bay at this time of year. They talked of many things as they ambled north toward McAbee Beach, where new dwellings were being constructed for the survivors of the fire.

At one point they stopped and watched the fishermen prepare their boats and gear for a night of hunting on the bay. Master Ah Chung explained that tonight there would be a full moon, perfect conditions for taking squid during the height of the mating season. To amplify their chances, each boat was rigged with several fire baskets that hung out over the water. Like the glow of the full moon, the light attracted the shoals of amorous squid, which were then gigged on hooked lures and hauled in by the thousands. The hunt would end with the waning of the moon and only begin again when the full moon returned the following month, weather permitting of course.

Dr. Lao-Hong found that he was impressed with Master Ah Chung's native intelligence, friendly disposition, and good sense. Despite his lack of a scholar's education, Master Ah Chung prided himself on a broad range of reading and self-improvement. The doctor discovered that his host was conversant on a great many subjects, but his quiet, modest demeanor never allowed him to put himself forward as a scholar or expert on any subject. His courteous and applied diffidence spoke well for his upbringing. And the master's honest, pleasant disposition was most congenial. Dr. Lao-Hong could well understand why Master Ah Chung had been chosen to administer business for his tong.

The afternoon shadows lengthened into an orange and azure dusk. The two men sat down on a large driftwood log, and with the comprehension of persons raised to appreciate the natural beauties of the world, they looked out over the bay in quiet reflection. Neither man spoke for thirty long and gratifying minutes. And as such things happen to those who cast a respectful eye upon the wonders of creation, their reverie was soon rewarded by the rising appearance of the full moon in all the goddess's finery and brilliance. Even in the early dusk, the immortal Chang'e cast her immutable splendor out over the bay in penetrating shafts of silver light, each broadening into a highway of dancing reflections leading back to the feet of the goddess herself. As the moon rose still higher, the silver highways glinting on the water became a broad gossamer web of shimmering moonbeams. Then as the enchanted alteration spread across the bay, a score of sampans from Point Alones quietly sculled out onto the iridescent web like a spreading brood of baby spiders just freed from their mother's egg. When the sampans at last arrived at their fishing grounds, the arched fire baskets were set ablaze. Suddenly the whole scene magically transformed into a floating lantern parade, complete with sounding gongs and shouting men.

It was Master Ah Chung who spoke first. Smiling, he asked his guest if he would like to go out and watch the fishermen work. He said it was a remarkable sight to see so many squid pulled aboard. He proudly declared that the bay was a veritable paradise of abundance. The passing seasons brought in all kinds of fish. The doctor looked down at his pressed suit and politely demurred by saying he didn't believe he was dressed for the rigors of a fishing expedition. Master Ah Chung laughed and said that he didn't mean they should go tonight, for he knew that Lady Yee had planned a special meal in honor of the doctor's visit. However, the moon would be up on the following night as well, and an appropriate wardrobe would be happily supplied.

Perhaps it was the beauty of the vision before him, but suddenly, and quite uncharacteristically, Dr. Lao-Hong laughed and found himself saying that he would very much like to go, that is, if his presence was still acceptable after the tong's decision on the matter before them. Master Ah Chung smiled and said the tong elders would not rush to judgment. They never did. Deliberation was their pleasure and a preferred pastime, and now that they had something truly important to decide, they would jealously guard their prerogatives. He laughed and said the venerable elders would savor every morsel until only the bones remained as mute testimony to their meticulous considerations.

Ah Chung cautioned Dr. Lao-Hong that their ultimate decision might take days. There would be plenty of time to enjoy the simple pleasures his surroundings afforded. He went on to mention that two of the most prominent elders of the tong were invited guests that evening at Lady Yee's celebratory dinner. Ah Chung smiled and confided that, like the legendary Indian fakirs, the good doctor would have plenty of time to charm their somewhat reticent instincts out of the basket, but only as long as he did not attempt to influence any detail of their verdict. He went on to suggest that no mention of his mission be made in front of Lady Yee, as the venerable elders might feel they were being held hostage by rigid rules of hospitality in the presence of someone of Lady Yee's eminence and stature. The doctor concurred and promised not to touch on the subject in any manner. He had no desire to compromise the tong's position by divulging their secret possession of Zhou Man's relics. Besides, he was quite confident she already knew everything about the situation, and probably with greater comprehension of the details.

Lady Yee's celebratory feast was a great success all around. The meal was a magnificent fusion of seven courses that featured the bounty of the bay and the Carmel River. The service included a delicate shark-fin soup, baby squid cooked in their own ink, pickled anchovies, grilled mackerel in a sauce of rice wine and Spanish capers, fresh trout from the Carmel River, boned and cleaned from the spine and cunningly posed with their tails protruding from their mouths, and served on a bed of crisp cabbage flavored with toasted sesame seeds. The main course consisted of two young salmon stuffed with mussels and crabmeat, then steamed whole and served on a decorative bed of rice noodles and wild chanterelle mushrooms arranged to look like stones slightly submerged in a shallow river. The whole charming presentation was set to resemble salmon struggling upstream against the current. There were any number of other gastronomic delights, but after a while the company lost count.

Dr. Lao-Hong was good to his word, and though he was un-used to such performances, he regaled the company with amus-ing stories about peoples and cities in the far eastern states. He charmed them with tales of his education at Harvard. He talked about the customs and foods in the east, and how at school he'd formed an unnatural attachment to something called an English breakfast, which he itemized and described in such a way as to elicit laughter, which it did. Dr. Lao-Hong noticed that Lady Yee was always the first to appreciate the humor, but she modestly muted her laughter with a napkin-draped hand. And all the while the doctor never once hinted at the purpose of his visit, and whenever his eyes met Master Ah Chung's, he received an appreciative smile and nod. The master was pleased the ven-erable elders were so thoroughly entertained, and was much amused to see them laugh so freely at every humorous tale the doctor shared.

The feast lasted until almost half past eleven, after which Master Ah Chung drove the elders home, and the doctor, after many heartfelt thanks and compliments, retired to his rooms and slept so soundly that when he awoke the following morn-ing, it took him a few moments to remember where he was. His own household could ill afford the opulent antique furnishings with which his present quarters were so lavishly adorned, so of course his first sensation was one of surprise. It was to augur a whole series of surprises.

His second surprise came at breakfast, when Lady Yee had her cook prepare a special and unexpected meal. After her pleasant greetings and polite inquiries about the comfort of his sleep, Dr. Lao-Hong was invited to seat himself at the table. Then he was presented with a covered silver platter. Lifting the lid, the maid revealed three large fried eggs, a generous rasher of lean bacon done to a turn, a stack of thick buttered toast, strawberry jam, and a large pot of coffee with cream and sugar. The astonishment on the doctor's face compelled Lady Yee to cover her mouth and chuckle with delight. The doctor could find no words to make an inquiry without sounding foolish or rude.

Lady Yee's eyes twinkled with an amused expression as she reminded her guest that he had mentioned how much he enjoyed an English breakfast. She said that the doctor had spoken of it with such fondness that she had her cook prepare the meal just as he'd described.

It proved to be one of the best breakfasts he had ever tasted. And the coffee, of which he consumed three cups, was delicious, sweet and strong, just the way they used to make it back at the Harvard canteen. Toward the end of his meal, while Lady Yee's attention was diverted elsewhere with a caller, the doctor pulled a blank page from his pocket notebook and folded it into a small square envelope. On the front he wrote the characters for "respectful appreciation." Then he pulled a five-dollar gold piece from his coin purse and placed it within the little envelope. When the maid came to take away his service, he gave her the envelope and asked her to present it to the cook with his sincere compliments. The maid smiled politely, put the paper in her sleeve pocket, and took the dishes into the kitchen.

Lady Yee's caller turned out to be none other than Master Ah Chung. He apologized for not sending word first, but had decided to come himself to save time. He lowered his voice and informed the doctor that the elders, as a body, had requested a further interview on the subject at hand. Master Ah Chung said that he knew the request was a little offhand, but elders were elders, and their wishes, no matter how untimely, were best addressed promptly. He gently smiled and said that after the noonday meal, and possibly a pipe of opium to assuage their aches and pains, the venerable elders of the tong had a tendency to drift off the mark, so to speak. Master Ah Chung noted that to do business properly, one had to get their attention early in the day. These old men possessed great powers of recall to be sure, but they generally lost interest in everything but their pipes, dominos, and idle conversation as the day wore on.

Dr. Lao-Hong listened with a bemused expression, then he took one last sip of his coffee, dabbed his napkin to his lips, and declared he was prepared to wait upon the elders at once. After dispensing sincere compliments and thanks to Lady Yee for his breakfast, the doctor retrieved his hat from the hall stand and followed Master Ah Chung out to his buggy.

The second interview, though delivered to a larger audience of aging sages, went very much like the first, with many questions presented that had already been answered the day before. Nonetheless, Dr. Lao-Hong patiently responded to everything he could, and went on to elucidate concerning matters that the elders had neglected to inquire about. He even went so far as to point out one or two weak points in the arrangement and told them how they might adjust the agreement to their advantage. For a while the doctor felt as though he was representing the tong elders rather than the Three Corporations, but he knew that at the very least he was following the tenets of honor, honesty, and fairness that his father had demanded of him. Whether his uncles and the Three Corporations would agree was another matter, and one to avoid if at all possible.

Suddenly, and just as abruptly as the meeting was called, the elders rose and pronounced the meeting adjourned. They then filed out of the hall without the slightest indication of approval or disapproval. Dr. Lao-Hong looked to Master Ah Chung with a perplexed expression and shrugged his shoulders. Master Ah Chung smiled and nodded. He said that the elders were functioning true to form. They hadn't quite finished feasting on the shank of their deliberations. The importance of the occasion, and the ramifications for the future of their community, justly demanded that they dissect every fiber of the argument. They were well aware that their civic reputations might suffer the possible charge of laxity or malfeasance. Whether they would ultimately agree to the arrangement was still very much a matter for speculation. Not even Master Ah Chung could dare predict what their eventual decision might be, but he did observe that they would take their time; their prerogatives were considered above criticism or comment.

When they exited the tong hall, Dr. Lao-Hong asked his host if it would be possible to find and visit the residence of Dr. Charles Gilbert, a professor at Hopkins Marine Laboratory. Master Ah Chung said he could find it, but it might be best if they just took the buggy out to Hopkins Laboratory and asked. Dr. Lao-Hong agreed, and off they went.

A half hour later they arrived at Hopkins, where Dr. Lao-Hong introduced himself to Professor Ray L. Wilbur. Saying that he was an acquaintance of Dr. Gilbert, he asked if it might be possible to arrange for an appointment with the professor. Dr. Wilbur, who was obviously surprised that this well-dressed Chinese gentleman spoke perfect English, said that Professor Gilbert had recently departed on a research sabbatical to San Diego. He would be gone for three months, studying southern marine migration patterns. However, if Dr. Lao-Hong wished to leave a letter, Professor Wilbur would see that it was sent on to Dr. Gilbert in the next packet of mail forwarded to him.

Dr. Lao-Hong said that his business could wait until Dr. Gilbert returned. All the same, he left his English business card as a matter of courtesy and thanked Dr. Wilbur for his kindness. The doctor and Master Ah Chung drove away, leaving Dr. Wilbur looking at the business card and scratching his nose in bewilderment.

After their interview, the doctor and Master Ah Chung went in search of the professor's cottage, where they verified with Dr. Gilbert's housekeeper that he was indeed in San Diego and would be there for some time.

Dr. Lao-Hong's relief was palpable. He now knew that even if some word of Zhou Man's treasure should leak out before the transfer to San Francisco was accomplished, Dr. Gilbert would not be present to confirm that such articles existed.

Master Ah Chung then returned his guest to Lady Yee's house, and as he took his leave, he handed Dr. Lao-Hong a round paper parcel tied with string. When the doctor asked what it was, Master Ah Chung smiled and answered that they were new seaman's togs and deck sandals made of waxed linen. He said he would return at six o'clock to escort the doctor out on the bay to watch the squid fleet at work, as promised.

The doctor had all but forgotten that he'd said he wished to go out on the bay to watch the squid fishermen by moonlight, but since Master Ah Chung had gone to so much trouble to outfit him properly, he could not find it in his heart to refuse the invitation. On the other hand, the doctor confided to Master Ah Chung that he would prefer to change his clothes somewhere else, preferably in the village, as he didn't think that Lady Yee would appreciate one of her honored guests being seen exiting her premises in such attire.

Master Ah Chung laughed out loud for the first time, and

then begged pardon for the outburst. He reminded the doctor that Lady Yee's late husband was a famous ship captain. Originally employed in the lucrative China trade, in later life Captain Hammond was known locally as a very strict whale warden, and a veritable terror to all poachers. In consequence, Lady Yee had always expressed great warmth of feeling for courageous seafaring men. Master Ah Chung then revealed that it was Lady Yee who had commissioned and paid for the expensive reliquaries that now housed and guarded Zhou Man's valuable testaments.

Suddenly, the doctor awoke to the fact that Lady Yee knew exactly what business he was set upon. And with a smile of bemused acknowledgment, he assumed at once that there were no secrets anywhere within all of Monterey that she was not privy to. He at once determined to take advantage of her judicious insights and prudence when the opportunity presented itself.

Lady Yee saw to it that there were no witnesses abroad when Dr. Lao-Hong descended from his room and exited the house dressed in the garments of a local fisherman. Master Ah Chung was awaiting him in the buggy, and they moved off to the fishing village of Point Alones just as the moon goddess began arcing over the bay. The silver web had just begun to spread once more, and the baby spiders were moving out onto the blinking silver laces of moonlight.

Master Ah Chung led Dr. Lao-Hong down to the shore, where there awaited a large sampan, half launched onto the shallow surf. The broad transom deck was crewed by two fishermen with long sculls. The sturdy little vessel had been furnished with accoutrements heretofore unseen on Chinese fishing boats on Monterey Bay. There were cushions for the doctor's place, with a small carpet laid at his feet. And in the bows, looking toward the stern, sat an old man with a shaved head who looked for all the world like a maritime Buddha. He sat facing the stern and appeared to be fanning the coals of a small, barrel-shaped clay oven set in a sandbox. The clay oven was designed to either tightly cradle a wok or support a grill. Dr. Lao-Hong had grown up seeing the same ovens on street vendors' carts in San Francisco's Chinatown. They offered everything from grilled baby octopus to stir-fried noodles dressed in every conceivable condiment.

The young fishermen sculling the sampan were obviously proud of their strength and skill; otherwise they would not have been chosen to master the vessel. As a mark of respect for their esteemed passenger, they wore brightly embroidered skullcaps and decorated vests to offset their plain fisherman's garb. Their long braided queues were handsomely dressed and oiled so that they reflected the moonlight. Dr. Lao-Hong felt a pang of pride for his sturdy countrymen as they deftly sculled the sampan out into the middle of the drifting fleet of waiting boats.

As if they'd been awaiting only his arrival, just as Master Ah Chung's sampan came abreast of the fleet, the whole flotilla lit their heavy wire fire-baskets, which were then suspended over the sides of the boats on poles to attract the rising squid. Within a few minutes the fishermen's barbed lures, which were sent down six and eight to the line, were drawing up multiple amorous squid per lure. The fishermen pulled the angry squid from the barbs and tossed them into wicker baskets. After a short while the sampan's bailer-boys were scooping squid-ink-stained bilge water over the thwarts until the little swells about the boats turned from gray-green to jet-black. But still the squid kept coming by the hundreds.

Dr. Lao-Hong found himself totally intrigued by the sights and sounds around him. Between the moon and the fire baskets, there was enough light to make out every detail of the fishermen's activities. The bounty of the harvest gladdened the men's hearts, and they happily called out to one another, making jokes and laughing like children at a dragon dance. Some men sang at their labors, and others chanted simple prayers of gratitude.

After a while Master Ah Chung had his sampan moved closer to one of the boats. The old man in the bow called out something, and in return a nearby fisherman tossed him a half dozen small squid. With practiced expertise, the old man caught them one at a time in a small handbasket. Within moments he had the catch cleaned, skinned, and washed. Then he dropped the squid into a crock of seasoning to rest while he prepared the grill over the clay oven and fanned the charcoal to life.

Master Ah Chung told the doctor the squid were now happily resting in a bath of rice wine, fresh ginger, green onions, soy, and toasted sesame oil. They both watched in fascination as their cook went about his business with simple precision, sitting cross-legged in the bottom of the bow. Everything he might need was within reach, and he could easily wash his utensils over either side. The small clay oven had two handles to make it more portable, but it was also handy in case it became necessary, from the threat of fire, to heave the oven overboard. A stout cord tied through the handles secured the doused oven, so it might be retrieved and reused if it hadn't shattered with the temperature difference.

Dr. Lao-Hong turned to Master Ah Chung and said he thought fishing, though obviously rewarding, must be a very dangerous business indeed. He asked if they lost boats and crews on occasion. Master Ah Chung thought the question odd, and possibly a little inauspicious under the circumstances, but he indulged the landsman and answered in such a way as not to anger the spirits of the dead. He said that for more than five hundred generations his people had been the finest fishermen and sailors in China. There were men and women in this very fleet who could proudly name ancestors who served under great Imperial admirals. Over the centuries those brave seamen had tasted the waves of every ocean and sea in the known world. Master Ah Chung paused. Then he spoke in a lowered voice and said that over the centuries there had been quite a few unlucky souls who had gone to their venerable ancestors by virtue of their trade, for as his guest had so aptly pointed out, working on water was a dangerous business.

Dr. Lao-Hong took the hint and said no more. He instantly perceived that discussing such matters while engaging in the practice at hand was obviously considered unlucky, or at the very least insensitive. He immediately attempted to apologize for his rudeness, but Master Ah Chung quickly interjected that he was quite sure no offense was intended or taken.

Still, though he kept it to himself, the thought of drowned ships began to unsettle the doctor's thoughts. The Three Corporations had lost a very valuable cargo in that manner only the year before. And though the goods were fully insured, the loss of so many lives was considered very bad joss indeed.

Master Ah Chung tapped the doctor's knee and pointed to the bow. The old man had begun to prepare the smaller squid, tentacles and all, over the hot grill. Every few moments he would turn them over with chopsticks to avoid scorching. Soon the squid began to make gentle sizzling sounds, and the tentacles began to curl as they cooked. The aroma that drifted back along the boat was truly intoxicating, and even the men sculling the sweeps began to make appreciative comments and nods. The doctor watched as the cook reached into a round bamboo container and withdrew generous portions of precooked, sweet sticky rice. These he formed into thick, round patties, which he seasoned with red pepper flakes. Then, using a small brush made of goose feathers, he coated the rice cakes with a light sheen of sesame oil and placed them gently on the edge of the grill to toast. They too began to sizzle away; the second piquant aroma only enhanced the first. The doctor began to salivate with anticipation and, as if reading his thoughts, the old man poured out two cups of black tea from a small cast-iron kettle. He passed these back to his passengers, and they were accepted with thanks.

The doctor watched as the cook, who had the dexterity of an accomplished street vendor, rolled two wide cones from butcher paper. They held their shape by folding over the narrow bottoms. He set these into a little stand that had two wide holes cut out to cradle the paper cones. After making sure the rice cakes were nicely browned and crisp on both sides, he placed one in each cone. The cook topped the affair by slicing two perfectly grilled squid into manageable pieces and placing them over the rice cakes. As a final touch, he sprinkled just a bit of rice wine vinegar over his creation. He retrieved two sets of chopsticks from a lacquer box kept for that purpose, placed a set into each cone in a decorative V, and then passed the whole stand back to Master Ah Chung with a slight bow of the head. Master Ah Chung returned the salute and then offered his guest the first choice. Dr. Lao-Hong took up the nearest cone and brought it close to his nose. Perhaps it was the mingling of sea air with the fragrance of the food, but the good doctor was rock-sure that, aside from the jasmine-like scent of his beautiful baby daughter, he had never smelled anything quite so magnificent in all his life. With many compliments and thanks to the cook and Master Ah Chung, the doctor turned serious attention to his food. He found he was ravenous, and what was more, the grilled squid and rice cake tasted even better than they smelled. It was only his polite modesty that prevented him from asking for more. But he needn't have bothered, for the old man had already begun to prepare two more portions.

Soon there were good-natured calls from the hardworking fishermen in the other boats. They laughed and hailed the cook to draw his boat closer so he might grill part of their catch too. At this point the fishermen were standing up to their knees in writhing squid. They would only quit fishing when their boats could safely carry no more and still make it back to shore without sinking. Greedy fishermen had been known to lose both boat and catch by misjudging their buoyancy.

As the moon rose higher, it also grew brighter. The doctor commented that one had a sense that the goddess was almost within reach of an outstretched arm. And still the fishermen labored incessantly to draw in multiple lures clustered with animated squid of all sizes. Each line gigged approximately thirty pounds of angry squid, by Master Ah Chung's estimation. He affirmed that with the right conditions and tides, the squids' mating frenzy under the light of the full moon could last for up to six hours. There were literally millions upon millions of them during this season of the year. He was convinced that with the proper care taken not to overharvest, the bounty offered up in this one bay alone could last for many centuries. It most assuredly could generate profitable work and greater wealth for many, if not poached by outsiders. By this Dr. Lao-Hong naturally assumed Master Ah Chung meant non-Chinese interests. Lao-Hong began to realize that these sturdy fishermen were a very pragmatic and conservative class in the main, and he deduced that their elders would be even more so, which gave him steep odds on failure.

As the fleet neared capacity, a small gong sounded from one

of the boats. The last turbulent lines of writhing squid were hauled aboard and the boats, now burdened to the gunwales with their harvest, doused their fire-baskets in the water and turned their bows toward shore.

But that was not the end of it. Work would not stop until the villagers had set out the complete catch to dry on raised racks, big rocks, or any other flat surface available. It would take all hands many hours of constant labor. The smaller children were given light bamboo poles with small red flags tied to the ends. The flags had big predatory eyes painted on them in black ink. Thus armed, the children were employed to run around the drying racks and chase away the always voracious and devious seagulls. This labor was an absolute necessity, but the children had transformed it into a wonderful game, and one inspiring the formation of teams, the election of captains, and the constant invention of cunning tactics slated to defeat and humiliate their ravenous avian adversaries.

Because it was lighter and swifter, Master Ah Chung's boat reached the shore first. The doctor even lent a shoulder to the job of pushing the vessel over crude rollers up onto the dry beach above the tide line. Once everything was secure, the doctor presented the two boatmen and the old cook with a ceremonial gift of five silver dollars each for their efforts and time.

Even though it was past midnight, Dr. Lao-Hong insisted that he wasn't tired. He asked his host's permission to stay on for a while and watch the boats unload their catches. The doctor said he wished to indulge a clinical curiosity, for he wanted to get some sense of the size of their harvest in one night.

Master Ah Chung pointed to a small, three-walled noodle shop not far away. He said it stayed open at night to serve the returning fishermen, who were always hungry after a hard night of working their backs into knots. He said they could watch the whole process from up there while enjoying a bowl of grilled fish and noodles, and be in no one's way. He added that old Mrs. Chu Yung and her husband, the proprietors of the noodle shop, also owned two of the fishing boats. On nights when the catch was good, they were very generous with their noodles and their rice wine.

Dr. Lao-Hong insisted on playing host this time, and so purchased two steaming bowls of fresh-made noodles with steamed mussels, sea urchins, and green onions, and a small jug of rice wine to wash it down. Then the doctor and Master Ah Chung found a place on a bench made of driftwood overlooking the beach. They sat down to enjoy their food and watch the procedures yet to come.

When the heavily laden boats were still fifty yards offshore, a gong was sounded somewhere in the village, and suddenly people began to appear from everywhere. One of the first to arrive was an old man carrying an iron tripod that he set down in the sand. Within seconds he had a bright little bonfire going. Some of the villagers who followed carried torches mounted on bamboo poles, or small fire-baskets lofted the same way. These they set alight at the tripod, and then drove them into the sand to illuminate the beach. In no time at all, the whole scene took on a very festive air, but the torches were there only to ease a long night of hard labor.

The approaching fleet was too deeply burdened and low in the water to beach, so they secured themselves to the shore with long ropes. A third gong sounded, and suddenly every man, woman, and child in the village strong enough to shoulder forty pounds of squid came down to the shore carrying broad, shallow baskets. They walked out through the shallow surf to the awaiting boats to exchange their empty baskets for ones full of squid, which they either shouldered or carried on their heads, back up the beach to the drying yards. The operation soon settled down to an efficient train of people coming and going.

As the boats unloaded their cargos, they rose higher in the water, and were then drawn closer onto the beach to ease the labor of off-loading. When the work was well under way, the boat captains released parts of their crews to refresh themselves. These men came up to the noodle shop and ordered food and hot tea.

Dr. Lao-Hong was slightly amused to notice that the fishermen, who normally rolled their pants up above their knees when they were fishing, were all stained blue-black by squid ink from the waist down. As tired as they were, the abundant harvest of squid had put them in a good mood, and they laughed and joked as they ate. When they had finished their noodles and tea, they returned to their work, and another batch of men were released to do the same.

It was now approaching two thirty in the morning according to the doctor's watch, and he began to feel the exertions of the day. The work on the beach had continued without letup for two hours, and still the boats were unloading squid. Master Ah Chung suggested that perhaps it was time to take the doctor back to Lady Yee's house. There might be a verdict from the elders at any time, and Master Ah Chung believed his guest should be rested enough to keep his wits sharp for the coming interview. The doctor agreed, but before following his host through the village to retrieve the buggy, he purchased a basket of fingerling squid, always considered a great delicacy, as a present for his generous hostess.

Once he was back at Lady Yee's home, a sleepy-eyed houseboy

answered the doctor's gentle knock. The houseboy took the basket and gave the doctor a lamp to light the way to his rooms. Once there, Dr. Lao-Hong stripped off his borrowed clothes, washed himself thoroughly at the commode, and then went to bed. Toward sunrise, he became entangled in the strands of a distinctly frustrating dream that focused on a disastrous but somehow predictable shipwreck, and the mountains of lost cargo set adrift across the waves. Every attempt he made to gather up the widening spread of bobbing cargo and bring it back into the wounded ship failed miserably. The dream, which he later recalled in some detail, left him feeling thwarted, angry, and incompetent.

In quite a departure from his normal schedule, the doctor didn't awaken until almost nine thirty in the morning. He rose at once, rang for tea, and then quickly washed and dressed. When the maid arrived with his tray, she announced that Master Ah Chung was waiting below. He had been there for over an hour. Dr. Lao-Hong requested that his guest be sent up.

A few minutes later Master Ah Chung appeared at the doctor's door and was invited to enter. Master Ah Chung was obviously troubled by something, and so the doctor offered him a seat and some tea. The master said he had already had enough tea, and that he had come about their mutual business. With an air of sad resignation, he told Dr. Lao-Hong that he had been reliably informed that the elders' vote would most likely go against any agreement to transfer Zhou Man's treasure to the care of the Three Corporations.

Master Ah Chung went on to say that he wished the doctor to understand that his people honestly felt themselves to be the true heirs of Zhou Man's legacy. After all, it was their ancestors who had manned the great treasure fleets, and they now believed it would be an unpardonable sin to allow their inheritance to leave the area. They believed that the presence of the treasure had brought great good fortune, as attested to by the abundant harvests of fish and squid that appeared after the village tong had taken possession of the artifacts. It had changed all their lives for the better, and they would not surrender the treasure without a serious resistance. He begged Dr. Lao-Hong to understand that just as he could not possibly sell the bones from his father's grave, so too the village elders felt a pious obligation to protect their patron's ancient legacy. It was all they had to unite them with their noble past, and made them feel as though they had not been altogether lost from the sight and blessings of their ancestors in this strange and angry land.

Dr. Lao-Hong voiced his sympathy for their predicament, but he reminded his host that the elders' decision would not be the end of the matter by any means. To have their generous offer thrown back at their feet would mean that the Three Corporations, the most powerful Chinese trading house in California, would lose face. But on the other hand, he also acknowledged that for the village to relinquish their interests under pressure would mean that the tong, the village elders, and the villagers at large would also lose face. There had to be another solution to the problem that would not entail public embarrassment for either party, and yet still secure the treasures for the benefit of those people whose lives were sincerely bound to the importance of its presence among them. The stones had the power to secure good fortune and prosperity. Nothing else was important as far as they were concerned.

Frustrated to the point of distemper, Dr. Lao-Hong searched his thoughts for some vehicle of mutual salvation. Indeed, he even went so far as to confide in Master Ah Chung that he hadn't the heart to return to his uncles with a notice of disappointment. The fact that one might lose face, and perhaps much more, was an unspoken possibility in every sphere of exchange, and both men knew it by custom and tradition; every nuance reduced to a nod or a gesture.

The two men sat quietly for a while looking out the window at the fishing boats on the bay. It appeared to the doctor that Master Ah Chung, who was well aware that his guest had been totally honest about his own position, was just as disturbed as he was by the possible consequences, and how they would affect future events for everybody.

As Dr. Lao-Hong quietly sipped his tea, his wife's wise voice came back to him like a sweet, distant wind chime and suddenly an idea came into his head that was as audacious as it was dangerous. His imagination immediately spun out with all the darker ramifications, while at the same time he judged the purpose pure and the motive honorable. He also realized that the greatest hazard, and one that might defeat the plan, would come to pass only if too many people knew of the scheme.

Master Ah Chung was surprised to notice a smile light up his guest's features. He waited politely for a moment or two. The doctor set down his cup, pressed his fingertips together as if in prayer, and confided that he believed he might have a solution, but one entailing great personal risk, possible loss of reputation, and worse. However, he would only divulge it if he could be assured that his host would take a blood oath sworn before his ancestors that he never reveal the device, or the doctor's part in the scheme.

Suddenly a conspiratorial twinkle came into Master Ah Chung's eye, and his mood lightened appreciatively. He at once persuaded the doctor that he would swear to any oath if it would resolve their present difficulties without bringing shame on his family, his tong, or his village. The doctor said he could make no binding promises in that regard, since karma and joss played such an engaging role in human affairs. Nonetheless, he agreed to reveal his thoughts, but he warned that events might require some sacrifices along the way, but hopefully nothing the village could ill afford to lose in light of what it might gain. Even so, Dr. Lao-Hong further admonished his host that he could do nothing to protect the village if the village elders neglected to protect him in turn, so he would require their written vows of silence as well.

The doctor went on to say that he thought it best if Master Ah Chung went to the elders alone and on his own behalf to present the design, so that later no one could honestly testify that it was the doctor who had either originated the scheme or put it into practice. In fact, he said he hoped to be far away when the final business was transacted. Only when conditions had been agreed to, and signed by all parties, would Dr. Lao-Hong divulge his plan, but even then only to those who really needed to know. All others were to be kept completely ignorant of the scheme for their own sakes. No one, he said, could be forced to divulge something they knew nothing about. And credibility, in this instance, depended upon not only the illusion of sincere disinterest, but also the innocent participation of honest men who could not be told the truth. That was a heavy burden for the soul to carry.

Ah Chung nodded silently and rose to depart. He turned at the door and formally bowed and thanked the doctor for his wisdom, discretion, and empathy. He promised that word would be sent along as soon as possible. With that he left, and Dr. Lao-Hong sat quietly and paused for a while to arrange his thoughts.

———

THE DOCTOR HEARD THE HOUSEBOY'S gong announcing lunch. He slowly arose, looked himself over in the bedroom mirror, and decided he appeared somewhat haggard, so he combed his hair, adjusted his waistcoat and cravat, put on his suit coat, and went down to lunch. All the while he cradled the abiding hope that in sharing his thoughts with Master Ah Chung, he hadn't slipped the proverbial hook through his own lip. But one way or another, like a bird released, it was all out of his hands now. He had learned in history class that a very simple idea can often have a tendency to take on a complex life of its own, especially when inspired and empowered by a perceived act of group survival.

Dr. Lao-Hong arrived at the table and was surprised to find Lady Yee, beautifully appointed in garments worthy of a court personage of high rank. He was even more taken aback when Lady Yee invited him to sit at her right side, always a place of honor for a guest.

After the maid poured tea, Lady Yee cast her eyes downward in regret and said that unfortunately this would be the last meal they would share together for a while. That very afternoon Lady Yee had been honored by an invitation to visit her husband's cousin, who was now quite infirm from years at sea. He lived in Carmel Valley on a small ranch by the river that her husband had purchased for him after he'd been crippled during a violent storm.

Lady Yee revealed that the poor man had been struck by a falling yardarm when outward-bound from Canton. He might have heeded the bosun's warning in time if he hadn't been under the influence of opium. She confided that he had always shown a preference for opium over women.

The hostess rang a little table chime, and in an instant her cook, now dressed in his finest and sporting a grin that featured a fine gold incisor tooth, entered with a covered silver platter. After placing it proudly before Lady Yee, he lifted the silver dome to reveal a phalanx of fried baby squid stuffed with sweet Chinese sausage, grated ginger, and chopped wild mushrooms. They were presented on a bed of steamed rice decorated with cunningly sculpted vegetables that made the whole presentation look like an exotic seascape.

The doctor was truly impressed, and it took a few moments for him to find the appropriate compliments worthy of the cook's care and artistry. Lady Yee took no notice at all and simply waved her cook back to his kitchen. However, the doctor caught the cook's eye before he left and made a slight formal bow of the head in recognition and appreciation. The cook's grin suddenly broadened, and he bowed his head in return for the kind acknowledgment.

With thanks for his gift of the night before, Lady Yee served her guest with her own hands, which was in itself a great mark of honor. His hostess then bemoaned the fact that she would not be present to bid her guest farewell the following morning. At once Dr. Lao-Hong wondered how she knew he would be leaving at all, much less the following morning. He didn't even know his own time of departure, particularly since he expected no word from Master Ah Chung for quite some time.

To alter the subject for a moment, Dr. Lao-Hong asked how Lady Yee wished to be recompensed for her hospitality. He then smiled and said that he would most assuredly secure the debt in silver if she wished.

Lady Yee at once assumed the pose of one slightly offended. She proudly declared that she never had, and never would, accept remuneration for her hospitality. It was a matter of family honor. However, if her esteemed guest wished to show his appreciation, he might reward her servants; this she would not take amiss. The doctor happily agreed to her terms and praised her munificence and patrician hospitality.

In turn, Lady Yee said that if the doctor's departure was delayed for any reason, he should remain her honored guest for as long as he required; her servants would see to all his needs upon pain of her darkest displeasure, which the doctor readily assumed was not a viable option for any of them.

Lady Yee departed soon after lunch, and Dr. Lao-Hong, finding he had time on his hands, decided to take a long walk to clear his head. Like everyone else with nowhere in particular to go, he gravitated toward the bay and the nests of activity that gathered along its shore. A steady breeze blew in off the water, carrying occasional hints of those labors. As he drew closer to the shore, the bracing fragrance of desiccating squid and seaweed became subtly intermingled with the damp tang of drying nets and the firmly domestic aromas of peasant cooking. In the distance, sails and steam moved commerce here and there, while smaller fishing boats rose and sank on the swells like resting seagulls.

The doctor's attention was soon drawn to the fishermen working on their boats. Other people mended nets or strung them up to dry, while the older, more experienced men sorted the morning catch for various markets. Female relations orbited almost everywhere and assisted in many aspects of these labors. However, at the first opportunity they migrated to the sorting boxes and deftly chose, within reason, the freshest morsels for their own kitchens. Family first, markets second, in all things.

The encompassing atmosphere of harmony and industry

moved the doctor to sincerely hope the village elders might
see their way toward an enlightened solution to their mutual
dilemma, though in his heart he feared that he might be grasping at smoke rings. He could well understand how the elders
might take a stand on principle. After all, honor is a stubborn
and inflexible mistress, and often driven by bruised vanity. But
the doctor also knew the call to honor had often transformed
a forlorn hope into a real and moral victory, but only in the off
chance that one outwitted and survived one's adversaries. It
had been done before, of course, but not by simple fishermen
with little or no understanding of the intricate machinations
that might be brought to bear on their refusal to comply with
the wishes of the Three Corporations. But either way, he was
confident that he had done his best to help all concerned. Now
it was up to the village elders to help themselves.

With that in mind, the doctor returned to Lady Yee's house
in the late afternoon and went up to his rooms to pack. He
would leave in the morning and take the six fifteen train north.
It would be a long day in the coaches, but more than worth the
effort and discomfort knowing that Mui Choi and the children
would be waiting to welcome him home.

Dr. Lao-Hong had no idea how he was going to explain his
failure to his uncles, but at least he'd have plenty of time on
the train to think of something viable, if not altogether truth-
ful. Whichever way the coin fell, his biggest concern remained.
What would the Three Corporations do to save their collective
reputations in the face of a polite but adamant refusal to cooperate with their wishes? The doctor had no desire to see anyone
hurt or humiliated, but his own influence in the matter was
negligible at best. For all intents and purposes, his role in the
affair would end with his report of failure. And to that end he
now applied himself.

After being served tea, Dr. Lao-Hong retired to Lady Yee's magnificent garden, where he sat in the afternoon's warmth and wrote pertinent notes in his business journal. With these he hoped to flesh out a report that might ameliorate the circumstances somewhat. Grasping at straws, Dr. Lao-Hong hoped that his uncles might appreciate the depth of commitment expressed by the village elders; perhaps then they might see their way clear to forgive their response, and let the matter drop out of sight. He didn't really hold out much hope for this eventuality, but he would do what he could to save face for all concerned, even if it meant appealing to the highest authority, which in this case meant the chairman of the Three Corporations, Grand Master Shu Ling Woo. The doctor had never spoken to this venerable gentleman. In fact, he'd seen him only twice in his life, but the doctor had heard things that led him to believe the chairman was a man of modesty and compassion. It wasn't much to go on, he had to admit, but it was better than no alternative at all.

By the time dinner was announced, Dr. Lao-Hong had still heard no word from Master Ah Chung. As the hours passed, the doctor's withering optimism waned. Before sitting down to his meal, the doctor called on Lady Yee's houseboy and asked him if he knew Master Ah Chung on sight. When the boy answered in the affirmative, the doctor wrote out a short note explaining that, regardless of the elders' verdict, he would be taking the morning train back to San Francisco. Then he gave the houseboy a silver dollar and asked him to deliver his message as soon as possible.

An hour after dinner the houseboy returned, saying that he had delivered the doctor's note, but Master Ah Chung had offered up no response. As far as the doctor was concerned, the signs were hardly propitious. And, sadly, there was nothing further he could do to influence matters one way or another. But since that bird had flown, Dr. Lao-Hong decided to put the matter behind him and concentrate on his situation, which was relatively precarious on its own merits.

By the time the doctor retired to bed, there had still been no word from Master Ah Chung. Dr. Lao-Hong shrugged off his failure and went to sleep early. The next morning, as per his request, the maid woke the doctor with a tray of tea. As soon as he'd finished his packing, he went down to breakfast. After enjoying a light meal, he distributed five small packets of money to Lady Yee's servants and asked the houseboy to carry his valise down to the station. He would follow on foot shortly.

The houseboy did as requested, but returned twenty seconds later to say that Master Ah Chung was waiting in a buggy to take the doctor to the station. Dr. Lao-Hong's surprise was palpable, but he kept his emotions in check and went out to greet his erstwhile host.

Master Ah Chung was standing next to the buggy when the doctor joined him. The master bowed politely, as did the doctor, but just as he was about to ask Master Ah Chung why he hadn't answered his note, the master smiled broadly and pulled two wax-sealed envelopes from his sleeve and presented them to the doctor. Ah Chung said it had almost taken a full night of sharp deliberation, but knowing that time was of the essence, they had at last come around and agreed to acquiesce to the handsome offer put forward by the Three Corporations. The first envelope was addressed to the venerable uncles of that esteemed company, but the second envelope was marked with two characters only. Translated, it said "Binding Pledge."

On the way to the depot, Master Ah Chung explained that the second communication was a binding assurance of secrecy, pledged to the doctor, and sworn to with oaths of everlasting fidelity by every elder in the tong. Their names were all affixed to the document, which would mean their heads would roll should the doctor betray their part in the agreement. They knew that this was hardly likely, since it would be the doctor, regardless of his family connection, who would suffer the first axe to fall.

Master Ah Chung went on to say that the letter to the Three Corporations contained three unalterable conditions. First, no exchange would take place until all the promised funds were delivered in cash. Second, the receiving party must show proof that the items in question had been adequately insured against loss or destruction. And third, the elders required that the Three Corporations send a trusted courier to witness the packing of the goods, and to escort the artifacts personally to their destination. For their part, the tong elders would see to it that the goods and the courier were transported by steamer to Santa Cruz, where they could make connections with the coastal mail packet bound for San Francisco. In this way they could avoid using the railroad, which, for obvious social reasons, was no longer really trusted by the Chinese community in Monterey. However, if the Three Corporations chose to complete the trip by rail from Santa Cruz, they would have to bear the responsibility for the security of the artifacts themselves.

Master Ah Chung asked if the uncles would agree to those stipulations. Dr. Lao-Hong thought for a moment, and then said he could see no reason why they shouldn't, since all necessary documents would have been signed and notarized with the package in question technically in their possession once the exchange had been made. Master Ah Chung sighed in relief.

———

WHEN THEY ARRIVED AT THE depot, the train was already waiting and loading passengers while the engine rhythmically panted steam in anticipation of departure. Dr. Lao-Hong thanked Master Ah Chung for all his efforts, and especially for the excursion out on the bay to watch the fishermen. He said he didn't know whether he would be coming back with the courier, but he doubted it. He said the rest of the journey was now in their hands. Master Ah Chung understood the meaning of the last remark and heartily thanked the doctor for all his patience, wisdom, and sympathy.

As if on cue, a deputation of three tong elders suddenly appeared. They had come, they said, to wish the doctor a safe journey, and to present him with a small token of their sincere appreciation for all his efforts on their behalf. The senior member present bowed and handed Dr. Lao-Hong a small polished rosewood case secured with a dark blue velvet ribbon. The conductor then called for all passengers to board the train, so the doctor quickly bowed and bid Master Ah Chung and the other tong elders farewell. As he mounted the steps to his carriage, he turned and said he would pray for a successful outcome to their endeavors. Master Ah Chung said they would do likewise for him.

As the train departed the depot and slowly rolled north along the bay, it once again entered a low, dense fog bank that obliterated the landscape in all directions. Dr. Lao-Hong took the opportunity to close his eyes, and within moments he was drifting in a half dream, lost in a thorny miasma of uncomfortable reflections. He realized, and not for the first time, that he had instigated either something very fine and good, or something very calamitous. However, the doctor was fair enough to acknowledge that only the final verdict of history counted for anything. But for now, he felt far too close to the situation to have any accurate perspective at all. The best he could do was to pray sincerely that in the end, history would take the side of the poor villagers who had suffered perennial indifference from all quarters, even from their more successful countrymen. And despite all hazards, they endured and prospered reasonably well, relying solely upon their own skills, courage, faith, and endurance—and all that without the least assistance from their white neighbors.

THE DOCTOR AWOKE FROM HIS daydreams with the bright morning sun flashing off the window glass and into his eyes. The train had moved out of the fog as it climbed away from the coast. Dr. Lao-Hong shaded his eyes and looked down to avoid the glare. He caught sight of the tong elders' gift resting on the seat next to him. He picked it up, placed it on his lap, and carefully removed the ribbon. When he opened the little chest, what he saw almost took his breath away. There, nestled in a molded bed of plush blue velvet, was one of the most beautiful cup-and-saucer sets he had ever seen. The items were fashioned from flawless, white bone china so thin and delicate that one could almost read print through the translucent glaze. Around the body of the cup and the rim of the saucer, elaborate Chinese characters had been delicately pressed into the damp medium before it had been glazed. Like a watermark, the characters only appeared when light passed through the delicate opalescent glaze. The doctor held up the saucer to the light and read the inscription: "Mankind poses questions for which there are no answers. Without devotion chaos ensues."

Upon his return, Dr. Lao-Hong attended upon his uncles,

who were truly delighted to hear his report. They praised his efforts and rewarded his services with a purse of Mexican gold pesos valued at five hundred dollars. The doctor politely accepted the purse and said he was pleased to be of service on such an important mission.

The hardest aspect of Dr. Lao-Hong's return home was the fact that he was barred from divulging the slightest detail of the negotiations to Mui Choi. Perhaps one day he would unburden his soul, but he doubted it. The doctor instinctively knew he was now shackled to the consequences of his actions to the grave and beyond.

TEN DAYS LATER HIS UNCLES summoned the doctor once again, and this time he was informed that all the arrangements, both financial and practical, had been set in motion. In accordance with the agreed stipulations, the Three Corporations were going to send their chief clerk, Master Chow Eng-Shu, to supervise the packing and shipping of the goods. But that aside, the doctor was still the only person who had viewed the treasure in some detail, and could justly verify that the items to be packed were the same ones that he had seen. Therefore, it was deemed a necessity that their astute nephew should accompany Master Chow Eng-Shu back to Monterey, make the necessary introductions to the local tong elders, and see that all proper arrangements were set in place. After that, he was free to take the train back to San Francisco at his leisure. His uncles promised that this important task, once accomplished, would be handsomely rewarded.

Dr. Lao-Hong saw no way to avoid this last mission, and so

resigned himself to honor his uncles' wishes, even though it placed him in an awkward position. With all eyes on him, and without the least hesitation, the doctor obediently agreed. Any other response would have been noted with some suspicion.

FOUR DAYS LATER THE DOCTOR and Master Chow Eng-Shu arrived back at the depot in Monterey at five o'clock in the afternoon. Word had been sent ahead, so Master Ah Chung and a delegation of tong elders were at the depot when the train arrived. The doctor was treated with the greatest respect, as was Master Chow Eng-Shu. They were taken to Lady Yee's house to refresh themselves, share a light meal, and take tea with their hostess. Lady Yee was delighted to see the doctor again so soon, and she promised her esteemed guests that a fine feast would be waiting when they finished the day's business.

Later, the doctor and his clerk were escorted to the tong hall, where they were reverently shown the altar and Zhou Man's stone plaque and the jade seal. The plaque had been carefully cleaned and the relief decoration polished so the whole stone reflected a deep brilliance; even the gold inlaid characters twinkled like stars. The great giraffe seal of pink jade was also displayed to advantage. It shimmered to its depths, as though it had been carved and polished only recently. The Imperial power and majesty the jewel implied were tangible for everyone who gazed upon it.

Master Chow Eng-Shu, who was a man of considerable education, was truly impressed with what he saw. He was, unlike the doctor, capable of reading the Chinese inscription in its entirety, which impressed everyone. The text was set down in characters that had been much modified over the centuries. It was therefore difficult to read by those who were not trained as scholars, and even then it would have required some research and study. However, Master Chow Eng-Shu, who was accustomed to reading and evaluating older documents, appeared to have no trouble deciphering the text.

He then closely examined the beautiful jade seal and pronounced it authentic, barring further study. He pointed to a character surmounting the admiral's personal chop and said that in modern Chinese it might be incorrectly translated as "head of the dragon." But in fact, in ancient Chinese texts it represented a sign meaning that the bearer was the personal servant of Emperor Zhu Di. Only high-ranking officials of the Imperial Court were allowed, nay required, to include this character surmounting their personal chops.

Dr. Lao-Hong was very impressed with Master Chow Eng-Shu's scholarship in these matters, but he was also quite relieved when the clerk declared that the artifacts appeared authentic in every detail. It was only then that the doctor realized just why his uncles had assigned Master Chow Eng-Shu to supervise the exchange. If the stones had indeed been forgeries, they would not have passed such close inspection. Simple fishermen hadn't the skill or scholarship to create such artifacts. Add to that the fact that Zhou Man's seal was carved from a rare piece of pink jade of such unusual size and purity that one could not but believe that its authenticity was beyond question. The clerk took the doctor aside and, in a low voice, said that the jade seal alone, even if it only had once belonged to a middling court official, would be worth ten times the price offered for the whole lot.

THAT NIGHT LADY YEE AGAIN entertained her guests in grand style. Master Chow Eng-Shu was very impressed with her hospitality and her cook's formidable skills. The doctor also discovered that Master Chow Eng-Shu, not to put too fine a point on it, rather enjoyed his wine, for he consumed a goodly portion and consequently went to his bed much affected by its potency. The doctor filed this knowledge away for future use.

The next day, somewhat worse for the wear, Master Chow Eng-Shu accompanied the doctor and Master Ah Chung back to the tong hall to supervise the packing of the artifacts for shipment. The process proved rather complex, but Master Chow Eng-Shu, despite the pounding in his head, paid very close attention. First, the artifacts were wrapped in several layers of soft linen. Then, the stones were wrapped again in two layers of heavy waxed silk, which was in turn painted with a thick coat of melted beeswax thinned with turpentine. As it slowly cooled, Master Chow Eng-Shu and Master Ah Chung pressed their chops into the wax coating at several critical points. Any distortion to these marks would indicate that the contents had been tampered with. Finally, the packages were bundled in small quilted blankets, and then placed into a wooden tea chest and cushioned with tightly packed straw all around so that they could not move about within the chest. Lastly, the chest was tightly bound all about with a heavy cord. When the ornamental knot was secured to everyone's satisfaction, Master Ah Chung poured hot red sealing wax onto every intersection of the cords and also upon the knots. Into each, Master Ah Chung pressed the tong's chop to mark the final seal.

Once this was accomplished, a stout chain was wrapped in two directions around the chest. The chain was then looped twice around a strong pillar at the back of the hall near the now empty altar, and secured with a large padlock. The senior elder took the key, turned, bowed toward the altar, and then ceremoniously presented it to Master Chow Eng-Shu. He politely informed Master Chow Eng-Shu that two of the strongest men available had been armed and told to guard the chest until they were relieved.

Just then a side door opened, and three men entered carrying furniture. The first two hefted a simple Chinese-style bed, and the second entered with a low table and cushions. These they placed near the chained tea chest in front of the altar.

Master Ah Chung turned to Master Chow Eng-Shu and said they appreciated that the esteemed Three Corporations required their own guard to oversee the security and protection of the treasure. To that end the tong was only too happy to accommodate Master Chow Eng-Shu until the steamer departed the following day. They would also send a cook to attend to his meals. In that way he could keep an eye on the treasure and be comfortable at the same time.

Dr. Lao-Hong watched the master clerk out of the corner of his eye, and he knew at once what was going through his mind. Master Chow Eng-Shu could either accept the tong's Spartan hospitality, or return to the obvious pleasures and stately affluence of Lady Yee's home. As the doctor expected, Master Chow Eng-Shu took no time in making up his mind. He bowed to Master Ah Chung and said there was no need for him to guard the treasure personally. The tong had done very well in that respect for quite some time. He bowed again and said that he had every confidence the treasure would be safe in their hands.

Dr. Lao-Hong knew that Master Chow Eng-Shu was quite confident of the chest's security, since the funds and documents he had brought in exchange would not be handed over until the treasure was safely placed aboard the steamer. Only then would he officially take possession in the name of the Three Corporations. A Chinese notary would be present to witness the contracts signed, and the funds counted out and handed over.

THAT NIGHT LADY YEE AGAIN entertained her esteemed guests with a lavish farewell feast, and again Master Chow Eng-Shu enjoyed a surfeit of excellent wine. The doctor took note of this and suspected the master clerk might pay dearly for his overindulgence the following day. For those not used to the experience, the motions of a ship at sea would only enhance the discomforts awaiting one who overindulges. But it was not the doctor's place to criticize. Master Chow Eng-Shu would have to plumb those depths for himself. Besides, the doctor was already experiencing his own catalog of disquieting symptoms, but his could easily be traced to an unsettling phalanx of tormenting preoccupations.

Dr. Lao-Hong could not help but reflect upon the complex Imperial ambitions and vast heroic accomplishments commemorated by those two stones, and by what strange chain of events they would now undertake another fateful voyage. Whether they found their rightful place of repose, or were sucked into the maw of greed, power, and jealousy, which in itself was a kind of oblivion, only time and fortune would determine.

Dr. Lao-Hong was quickly learning that it was a tasking burden to shoulder another man's honor, not to mention his mortality; lives were at hazard, families and clans imperiled. The doctor had done the best he could for all concerned. He prayed that it wasn't too late.

———

THE NEXT MORNING THE GUESTS bid their generous hostess a respectful farewell, a formality that included the doctor presenting Lady Yee with a beautiful and intricately pierced ivory fan, inlaid with mother-of-pearl and amber. And though it wasn't exactly the truth, he said the Three Corporations wished her to accept the gift as a mark of their respect. Lady Yee was delighted with both the fan and the recognition.

A half hour later the concerned parties again met at the tong hall. Everything was just as they had left it the night before. Even the same guards were in attendance. A table and chairs had been arranged for the signing of contracts and the counting out of the agreed payment. This was made in small gold bars called teals. Each was weighed carefully, stamped by the notary, and entered on a receipt. Only after all the necessary documents had been signed and exchanged, and all financial formalities accomplished in good order, would the sealed chest be transported to the pier and loaded aboard the little hired steamer.

Master Chow Eng-Shu was formally presented the tong's key to the padlock. The treasure was duly released from its bonds, and the two guards then slung the chest from a stout pole, which they carried away upon their shoulders. With the tong elders in informal attendance, the procession made its way to the pier. There the chest was loaded down into the stern cabin of the steam launch that would take it to meet the mail packet in Santa Cruz.

The chartered steam launch was fifty feet long, and had started life as an excursion boat for the guests of the famed Hotel del Monte. After the hotel burned down in 1887, the launch had been sold to a merchant, who put it back into service as a tour boat. Though of heftier construction, it had been built to the standards and lines of an English lake steamer. The brass-trimmed engine and boiler sat amidships, and a tall carriage cabin with large windows all around surmounted the aft third of the vessel. The cabin was furnished with plush upholstered benches on both sides, and even boasted an enclosed toilet for the convenience of the passengers. For the sake of security, the tong had insisted on manning the steamer with its own seamen. Only three men were necessary: a helmsman, a stoker, and a deckhand.

Heavy swells and a stiff chop of whitecaps troubled the bay, and the doctor noted that as soon as Master Chow Eng-Shu boarded the vessel, his previous overindulgence began to register as an evident change in complexion. Dr. Lao-Hong, who wished no creature harm, felt guilty that he had not made a finer point of cautioning his colleague the night before about the discomforts awaiting those unused to traveling under such conditions.

After parting salutations and compliments, the little steamer pulled away from the pier. A towed jolly boat skipped attendance at the stern. The party waited a short while watching the steamer move off, and then returned to the tong hall to have tea and discuss events.

Later, Master Ah Chung took the doctor to meet the three o'clock train north. Before parting, Dr. Lao-Hong presented his host with a gift of a fine gold pocket watch made in France. The case bore a small but exquisite enamel painting of a floating swan wearing a gold crown, and the dial face was surrounded by seed pearls to mark the hours. Master Ah Chung was much surprised and very pleased with the gift. He promised to think of his friend and benefactor every time he read the hour. They parted with deep respectful bows and salutations. The doctor was moved to see a mist of gratitude in his friend's eyes.

DR. LAO-HONG WAS OVERJOYED TO be back with his family, and he promised Mui Choi that he would do no more traveling for quite some time, if at all. However, he felt that he might have spoken too soon, as on the fourth day after his return he received an urgent summons from his uncles to come to their offices at once.

When he arrived, it was to witness a scene of great distress. He was told at once that there had been a terrible accident. The steamer carrying the treasure to Santa Cruz had suffered an explosion, caught fire, and was lost. Happily, there were no fatalities, though the deckhand and stoker had suffered minor burns, but it was no less a tragedy for all that. If it hadn't been for the courage of the helmsman and stoker, Master Chow Eng-Shu might have lost his life. For at the time of the accident he was suffering from a bad case of seasickness, which rendered him all but helpless to save himself. The seamen had to break out the cabin windows to help him escape, but by then the fire had grown so intense that it proved impossible to go back for the chest.

Lao-Hong was relieved to hear that the four men had escaped to the safety of the jolly boat, and were soon rescued by a passing schooner that had seen the smoke from several miles away. The doctor was told that Master Chow Eng-Shu had only just arrived that very morning with the terrible news. The poor man had been so thoroughly traumatized by the whole experience that he was contemplating taking the robes of a Buddhist monk and retiring to a monastery. Barring that, he had taken a solemn vow never to set foot on a steamship again. He was devastated at the loss of the treasure, felt he had failed his masters, and knew not how he would survive his disgrace.

Dr. Lao-Hong took great pains to convince his uncles that Master Chow Eng-Shu was far too valuable a servant to discharge over a matter of chance, and since the loss was well insured, he should be exonerated of all blame. Indeed, the tragedy must be attributed to bad joss, and not any failure on his part. The doctor reminded his uncles that the fates had determined that Zhou Man's treasure, which had been raised from its guarded obscurity in the earth by mere chance, should now return to the guarded obscurity of the sea in like manner. Perhaps the long-revered and powerful spirit of the venerable Zhou Man had taken a hand in the matter. Who could tell?

Again the doctor was presented a purse of money for his services, but he politely refused it on the grounds that all concerned should share in the loss of the treasure. It was only just and right that he not gain where others had sacrificed. He went on to suggest that the money might be given to Master Chow Eng-Shu, for it was he who had almost surrendered his life in faithful service to the Three Corporations. The uncles were quite impressed with their nephew's worthy suggestion. He gained great face with the gesture, and Master Chow Eng-Shu became his loyal friend for life.

As Dr. Lao-Hong made his way home through the busy streets, he was drawn to one interesting but totally unimportant question: How much would his uncles settle on the owner of the lost vessel? Then he smiled and put the question aside. It was none of his business anyway. Everyone had lost something in the bargain, everyone except perhaps Admiral Zhou Man.

That intrepid explorer had long since secured his place in the Chinese pantheon of great men. In the eyes of most scholars, the loss of the seal and stone would hardly affect his brilliant reputation one way or the other. There remained the improbable chance, of course, that in the future some enterprising salvage diver might find the sunken launch and recover her cargo. But it was highly doubtful that eventuality would come to pass. The great Imperial explorer Admiral Zhou Man was beyond all that now. He was at rest under the sheltering devotion of his people.

AND THE SEA SHALL
GIVE UP ITS DEAD

"Wisdom is not a birthright, it is a treasured inheritance."

—CHINESE PROVERB

NINETEEN NINETY-EIGHT WAS A TROUBLING year for young Charles Lucas, known as Luke to his family and friends. He had shown himself to be an indifferent C student for the first two years of high school, and his lack of application had troubled his parents exceedingly. Luke's parents had both been honors graduates of Stanford University, and they felt they had somehow failed their son. More so since Luke had always tested in the top five percent of every intelligence test he had ever taken. There were even those who believed, once upon a time, that Luke would most likely be inducted into Mensa by the age of fifteen. But such was not to be, for an ironbound, teenage streak of rebellion set in like a Siberian winter, and he refused to be influenced by any reasoning not his own. As if to pour acid on his poor parents' wounds, he developed a full-blown obsession with surfing that seemed to occupy almost all of his time, attention, and money.

Unfortunately, Luke, being a normal teenage boy, possessed little or no abiding sense of personal direction whatsoever. He floundered at everything remotely academic, which only made matters worse for his long-suffering parents. Their daughter, Beth, five years older than Luke and thriving with honors back east at Princeton, had never been a real problem. At least that was how they liked to remember her.

Luke thought his sister was a thoroughgoing cow, a shameless suck-up, and a bullying snitch. He was subsequently transported on the wings of heavenly delight the day she moved east. Beth departed with tears in her eyes, a low-mileage BMW station wagon, and a stack of credit cards that could choke a goat. Luke was almost giddy as he hugged his sister good-bye and snickered at her departing tailpipe. It was all he could do to keep from jumping madly into the air, arms arched upward in triumph, while screaming at the top of his lungs, "Eat my shorts, Spooky!" Luke delighted in calling his older sister "Spooky" because she hated it so much.

Luke's limited curiosity about academic matters continued to hobble along in a halting fashion, while his parents tore out their hair. Then suddenly, just in the middle of his sophomore year, his biology teacher, a brilliant educator with the improbable name of Mrs. Tallulah Entwhistle, took Luke in hand. With skills his parents could not possibly invoke or duplicate, Mrs. Entwhistle somehow turned her rebellious pupil completely around. It didn't hurt that she looked like an Italian movie star, but that didn't disguise the fact that she was a hard-core polymath, and possessed an encyclopedic mind and a memory only rivaled by her laptop. Luke was once quoted as saying that "the Intrepid Tallu" could spot sham work and BS through a brick wall and, like she did her dead frogs, publicly dissect the offending student in moments. Nothing got by Mrs. Entwhistle, but she tempered her occasional disappointments with understanding, humor, and compassion, which only made Luke work harder to please her.

Within a half semester, Luke was suddenly making straight A's in all his courses, and in some subjects, like biology, mathematics, geology, and history, he was adjudged either first or second in the class. This pattern continued and increased in energy through his junior and senior years. In fact, Luke's quantum leap from disinterest to total absorption was so remarkable that his amazed parents tried to persuade him to undergo a more advanced battery of computer-aided intelligence tests so they could calibrate the remarkable change in his development.

Luke correctly figured that they just wanted something to boast about to their friends and coworkers, so he told them, as politely as he knew how, to kiss that idea good-bye. And he issued a threat, thinly veiled as humor: if they ever brought up the subject of IQ tests again, he'd start doing serious drugs and begin dating a thirty-year-old lap-dancing pickpocket named Bubbles. It worked. Luke's parents never mentioned the subject again.

By the time he graduated, Luke was rated the most accomplished student in the school. Two of his papers on biological variation had been published in respected scientific journals, and he was subsequently made valedictorian for his class—an honor he would have preferred to dispense with, as he hated public speaking above all else.

Even before his graduation, four universities had approached Luke. Each vied for his consideration with offers of scholarships and living allowances. This news thrilled his parents, who were already financially stretched to the limit by a daughter at Princeton who seemed to be majoring in expensive tastes.

Luke at last decided to take advantage of his parents' connections, and appreciatively accepted a generous offer to attend Stanford. It was only thirty minutes from his home, so he wouldn't lose touch with his friends, or his parents' refrigerator and laundry room. Stanford was also close enough to the Pacific to allow him to surf whenever he could find the time. Happily, Luke's girlfriend, another compulsive A student named Rosie Hall, had also been accepted at Stanford, so life would continue much as it had, or at least that was what Luke wished to believe.

During his freshman year, Luke once again floundered. Not in his grades, but in his course choices. His counselor noted that Luke's schedule included French, astronomy, chemistry, biology, and a broad introduction to engineering. He had also elected to assume extra courses in geology, anthropology, and, of all things, South American history. Luke's counselor pointedly suggested that he was spread too thin for his freshman year. And though his grades were excellent, his counselor believed the stress of carrying such a weighty course load would ultimately prove detrimental to his health. He'd seen other gifted students literally wither under the pressure of their ambitions, and he told Luke to slow down. After all, he had years to focus his interests and find himself. Even Mrs. Entwhistle, who had made a point of staying in touch with her most gifted pupil, warned Luke against pushing himself too hard in his first two years. She laughed and said there was still plenty of time to kill himself in postgraduate school.

Perhaps it was his love of surfing and the ocean that finally turned Luke's interests toward marine sciences, but his choice was certainly buttressed by all the great Cousteau documentaries he had loved as a boy. So at the beginning of his junior year at Stanford he decided to focus all his efforts toward degrees in marine biology, maritime engineering, and world maritime history, the last being a subject he elected for the sake of pure distraction.

Luke had shown so much promise in his work that in 2008, at the beginning of his senior year, he was invited to study marine biology and related subjects at the prestigious Hopkins Marine Life Observatory in Monterey.

Like his parents, Luke had always loved Monterey. His folks had taken him to see the Monterey Bay Aquarium when he was fourteen, and it was all they could do to drag him out of the building when it closed for the night. He had returned every time they came to Monterey for the weekend, and at one point he'd even been introduced to the aquarium director, Julie Packard. Luke told her that he wanted to work for the aquarium one day, and Ms. Packard indulged him by saying that he should come back after he had finished college, and she would see that he got his wish.

LUKE'S MOM HELPED HIM FIND a small but decent apartment high up on David Avenue. Its best feature, as far as Luke was concerned, was that it had an unobstructed view of the bay from the living room window. With the help of his war-surplus Russian binoculars, Luke could just make out the surfing conditions at Lover's Point when he got up in the morning. He also enjoyed being able to coast his bike downhill all the way to Hopkins. Getting back up David was another matter, and Luke soon developed a set of calves like steel springs.

Using his attendance at Hopkins as an introduction, Luke went back to Julie Packard, and asked for a part-time job to help cover his expenses. She remembered him from years before and, having perused his exceptional academic record from Stanford, was pleased to be able to keep her promise, even though he hadn't yet graduated.

Luke was offered a job in the aquarium's complex and extensive water treatment facilities, which he rather enjoyed because he got to work with qualified scientists and engineers and not the general public. It was also just a skip and a jump from Hopkins, which cut down on travel time.

The best part of being in Monterey was its proximity to Stanford, so Luke's girlfriend, Rosie, could drive down to see him every other weekend, class work and exams permitting. And since they text-messaged each other at least eight times a day, their separation was easier to bear than might be expected. Happily, Luke's father was footing the phone bills, and doing so without complaint.

Then, one bleak and foggy day, Luke's hydrology professor asked some of his students to help him clear out the old storage vault. This room had been a catchall for at least twenty years. Among a vast assortment of oddities, it housed scores of old specimen jars containing long-dead marine exhibits, and crates of antiquated and disused laboratory paraphernalia. But by far the greatest clutter consisted of boxes and boxes of papers that had evidently never been sorted or cataloged or thrown out. The job of sorting and organizing the chaos paid little or no money, but it did put Luke in the position to go rummaging around in Hopkins's attic.

Old attics stacked with long-forgotten mementos had always sparked Luke's fertile imagination. His first taste of an attic safari came as a childhood adventure while visiting his grandmother's old Victorian house in Watsonville. Thus, long after his fellow students had lost interest in the job and found excuses to quit, Luke continued on sorting through the trash, most of which was destined for the Dumpster. And then, one Sunday morning in April, Luke came across something that would completely change his life.

Under a stack of old cardboard file boxes at the back of the vault, Luke discovered a small, antique-looking, leather-bound trunk stamped with the name of Dr. Charles H. Gilbert. It was very like the trunk he'd found and explored in his grandmother's attic. That one had contained hundreds of old photographs that his grandfather, an enthusiastic if somewhat untutored shutter-bug, had taken over the years and stored away before his death. Luke's grandmother had totally forgotten about the trunk, and Luke and his grandmother had spent many happy hours going through the photographs. She seemed to bloom again as she recalled every detail depicted in each picture. It had inspired Luke to rummage further, and he went on to also discover a large mahogany case of very fine English silver flatware that his grandmother had been given as a wedding present sixty-six years before. Being a modest creature at heart, she had never found occasion to use it, preferring her mother's simple flatware pattern instead. However, when Luke's grandmother decided to sell the silver at auction with Butterfield & Butterfield, she was stunned to find that it had gone out the door for $7,800. Far more than she had ever imagined it was worth. With this youthful experience to inspire him, Luke took to rummaging with a passion. Show him a cluttered attic, and he was off to the races.

The leather trunk Luke discovered in the Hopkins vault made him think that perhaps he was at least onto something interesting once more, but he was disappointed at what he found. The bulk of the contents appeared to be the property of a long-departed Hopkins professor. It consisted mostly of old scholastic papers, numerous notebooks, and scientific journals. There was also a box of fading antique photographs that included several labeled pictures of Hopkins when it was just a plain, wooden, two-story building perched on Lover's Point. There were even some old pictures of the previous owner, Dr. Gilbert, standing with colleagues and students in front of the first Hopkins Laboratory in 1894. All of this tickled Luke's sense of history, and he knew the Hopkins administration would love the photographs.

But it was the large package at the bottom of the trunk that drew Luke's greatest interest. It was neatly wrapped in brown paper and secured with string and sealing wax. When Luke pulled it from the trunk, the rotting string parted and fell away, and when he removed the wrapping paper he discovered a leather-bound print folio and a journal. Luke opened the folio and found it contained some large sheets of folded rice paper, which at first glance appeared to be something like Chinese gravestone rubbings. Next, he found some odd photographs of a flat, black stone with engraved Chinese characters, and a half dozen pictures of an object that looked something akin to a stylized giraffe, but resting on its knees like a camel. Lastly, he examined a handwritten journal with Dr. Gilbert's name inscribed on the inside cover. Since there was no one around to monitor his activities, Luke decided to let his natural curiosity take point. He indulged himself with an early lunch break and read the journal, if only to find out what the other documents and photographs depicted.

What Luke soon discovered in the journal's pages set his pulse racing. He couldn't believe what he was reading. If it was true, and he had no reason to doubt Dr. Gilbert's account as yet, then out there somewhere was solid, incontrovertible evidence that the Chinese, not the Spanish, had been the first foreigners to discover California. And if this was true, the Chinese, to judge by all the standards of European history at that time, possessed a prior claim to California, and perhaps parts of South America as well.

Luke could barely catch his breath. He had hit the mother lode, the apogee of the rummager's art: this was a discovery that could literally change the history of the Western world, and Luke knew it. Though he felt himself to be scrupulously honest, Luke had been around university dons long enough to know that they'd do just about anything to get their hands on something like this; and of course, they would also claim the right of discovery. One of Luke's roommates at Stanford had once joked that he could judge the level of success of a tenured professor by the number of stab wounds in his competitors' backs. Luke was not about to reveal his discovery until he knew enough to secure those credentials for himself.

On the other hand, Luke knew that he never wanted to be accused of theft from the university archives, so removing materials from the Hopkins vault was out of the question for the moment. Instantly, Luke knew what must be done. He would have to copy all the relevant material, pack it all back in the trunk just as he found it, and then hide it again under the clutter in the back of the vault, where it would not be discovered without his notice.

As it was a Sunday, nobody was really around to ask uncomfortable questions. So Luke took the rubbings, the faded photographs, and Gilbert's journal and left to use the office's broad-plate copier. He duplicated everything in the folio, and then carefully returned the documents, rewrapped in the original paper, to the trunk just as he had found them. He also included the moldy string and wax seals. At first Luke regretted that he had not thought to use specimen gloves when looking through the papers, but he later determined that if provenance were required in the future, his would be the only new fingerprints on the documents, thus giving weight to his claim to prior discovery of Dr. Gilbert's papers without opening him to charges of theft of university property.

After work Luke went home and immediately fired up his

laptop. He was surprised to find quite a bit of information concerning fifteenth-century Chinese maritime history on the Internet. He discovered at least three books, one of them a bestseller, and numerous articles on the subject. He also found references to three television documentaries, and a plethora of newspaper articles from all over the world. Luke ordered the books and documentaries and downloaded all the newspaper articles he could find. Then he scanned Dr. Gilbert's journal and, when it was practical, returned to the vault, retrieved the rubbings, and had them copied full size at a blueprint shop in Salinas. The printers also scanned the rubbings onto a disc with exceptional detail. Then he returned the material to the trunk and covered his tracks.

OVER THE NEXT TWO MONTHS Luke became more and more obsessed with his search. He remained diligent in maintaining silence on the subject to everyone, including his girlfriend. He spent every free hour scanning research on the great Chinese admiral Zheng He and his treasure fleet, and this led to finding references to one of his subordinate officers, Admiral Zhou Man, who, according to several qualified references, had sailed north along the coast of the Americas around 1422.

Luke found it impossible to believe that Zhou Man's giant, ten-masted ships and his many hundreds of sailors never landed to refresh their water supplies, or to hunt and fish to restock their larders. It seemed to Luke that these necessary forays would have required establishing at least temporary settlements to hunt, butcher, and preserve meat, catch and dry fish, gather other available foodstuffs, and perhaps do a little trading with the native peoples. And though Luke was persuaded that incidental trade must have been established with the few indigenous tribes they encountered, historical evidence to back his supposition would not be found, since the coastal peoples lacked a written language and depended on oral tradition alone.

Without hinting at the evidence in his possession, Luke began to send e-mail inquiries to all the Chinese historical societies in California regarding artifacts that might have been left behind by Zhou Man's fleet, but again he came up empty. And though many respondents were of the opinion that Zhou Man had indeed explored the western coast of North America, none could point to any evidence that he had left behind as a sign of his visit.

Luke discovered there were stories floating around that a few remnants of a giant sternpost and transom of an ancient ship had been discovered the previous century, buried somewhere along the banks of the Sacramento or American river. However, there was no substantial proof that the ship was even Chinese, and a few supposed experts said it looked Spanish. And since the river and the dredgers had long ago swallowed up the wreckage, it was hardly feasible that such evidence would ever be found.

One of the more interesting books Luke had ordered was authored by a retired British naval officer who made broad but well-founded claims that Zhou Man had indeed visited the West Coast of North America. The author buttressed his theory with quite a few remarkable references, and though the author admitted it was difficult to present solid physical proof that could determine the location of the landfalls with any certainty, there was a most compelling body of zoological and botanical evidence to support the premise.

Luke contacted the author through his e-mail address, and though the gentleman was glad to share all he knew, Luke still found himself strapped with more questions than answers. But even with these hampering details, he was coming to realize that there was a good chance that he was nesting on a sizable historical bombshell. If his discovery was correct, and if Dr. Gilbert's journal, rubbings, and photographs could stand up to close scientific scrutiny, then Luke was in possession of the only existing substantiation ever found that the author's hypothesis was correct.

But even that was not quite enough for Luke. He was slowly coming to the question, if such artifacts still existed, and had not been returned to China as Dr. Gilbert presumed they had, then where were they now? The discovery of their whereabouts, if at all possible, would set Luke's reputation in both the scientific and historical communities. He presumed the success of a master's or doctoral thesis on the subject would be a foregone conclusion. But for the moment Luke had come up against a blank wall. There was simply no trace anywhere of the existence of such artifacts.

As an afterthought, and without revealing his own evidence, Luke e-mailed several museums on mainland China in the hope that some Chinese scholar might shed light on the subject. In return, he was informed that articles similar to the ones he described were known of, and there were a few examples of marker stones and seals housed in various museums, but nothing that corresponded directly with the items Luke described. The end of one of these communications politely inquired if Mr. Lucas had any personal knowledge that such artifacts actually existed in the West. Luke wrote back and, sticking to the truth as it stood at that moment, said that he did not.

However, Luke had found out something that Dr. Gilbert never suspected. If Zhou Man's plaque and seal had been returned to the Chinese government around 1907, or soon thereafter, there was no record of it, and assuming that Chinese scholars would be very particular in matters of this kind, Luke could only believe the artifacts had never left California. Either that, or they had been lost due to a shipwreck or some other unforeseen misadventure. But one way or another, Luke would have to do a great deal more research to find the truth, if in fact there was any truth to be found. The trick was to search out the proper resources, but Luke hadn't a clue where to start looking for them without revealing what he knew, or showing someone his copy of Dr. Gilbert's evidence.

This suddenly posed another sticky problem: What if someone else at Hopkins decided to look through Dr. Gilbert's trunk? Luke would have to somehow secure the doctor's papers against that eventually, and without actually keeping them in his personal possession.

The following day Luke found his way back to the vault under the pretext of doing more sorting. He was relieved to find the trunk still undisturbed beneath the stack of file boxes just where he'd stashed it. He suffered only minor qualms about removing the papers from the vault, since he had every intention of returning the property before word got out about his discoveries. When everyone left for lunch, Luke again removed Dr. Gilbert's folio and journal from the trunk. He wrapped the items in new paper, packed them in a sturdy corrugated box with tissue paper, and sealed the package with heavy packing tape. He printed out a label addressing the package to himself in care of his grandmother in Watsonville. And after visiting the post office, where he registered and insured the package for a thousand dollars, he mailed it priority parcel post. That done, Luke called his grandmother on his cell phone and told her to expect a package addressed to him. She was to put it away in the attic until he called for it. Luke's loving grandmother was more than happy to oblige. Luke had debated with himself whether this might be considered theft, but he knew there was a good chance that someone else might just throw out the old trunk as mere junk, and so he went ahead under the banner of preservation, with every intention of setting the matter right at a later date.

THAT JUNE LUKE GRADUATED FROM Stanford with top honors. He immediately requested to be enrolled in a master's program, but only if he could continue his studies at Hopkins. He chose a relatively new area of study, specifically the effects of global warming on deep submarine deposits of carbon dioxide, methane, and other trapped gases. The proximity of the cavernous Monterey marine trench, practically at Luke's front door, made this a reasonable field of research to accomplish at Hopkins, and so his request was granted. Luke also ferreted out another scholarship, much to the relief of his parents, who were now saddled with Beth's insistence that she go to Paris for a graduate studies program at the Sorbonne.

After graduation it was an ecstatic young man who returned to Hopkins wreathed in glory. Luke had come to love Monterey more than his own hometown, tourist trade notwithstanding, and he had no desire to leave. Besides, Monterey was where the trail of the Zhou Man artifacts had gone cold, and he instinctively felt that the thread leading back to it lay somewhere nearby.

After graduation Luke was offered a more responsible position at the Monterey Bay Aquarium doing work in the field of ichthyologic diseases unique to aquarium-maintained specimens. His previous experience in water purification and maintenance proved invaluable in this regard. The fact that he also had access to Hopkins's research laboratory only added to his value in that capacity. He was dedicated to his work and enjoyed it as much as anything he had ever done. But there was that one fixation that haunted him every day regardless of whatever else he was doing: he couldn't shake free of his abiding passion to find Zhou Man's plaque and seal, and this obsession would engage more and more of his attention for some time to come.

Rosie still came down to visit every other weekend when her heavy premed schedule permitted. She would not graduate Stanford until the following June, and her choice of a medical school was predicated on her grades. For as long as she could remember, she had wanted to be a doctor like her famous father.

Luke had always supported her in that ambition, and never pressed her to give him more time than she could comfortably spare from her studies. On the other hand, Luke wasn't exactly wallowing in free time. Between his work at the aquarium, his graduate studies, and his private research, it was all he could do to find time for a little surfing now and then. His enthusiasm for that pleasure had waned slightly since a fatal white shark attack had taken another surfer off Lover's Point three months earlier. Luke had seen the surfer's board on the news. The shark had not only cut the surfer almost in half, it had also taken an identical bite out of his board at the same time. From the width of the bites, one of the biologists at the aquarium estimated the shark at sixteen to eighteen feet long. Luke had no desire to make the acquaintance of that particular fish, so he'd hung up his own board until he could find a safer set of waves farther down the coast.

As far as his Zhou Man research was concerned, Luke had decided that it was time to get the inscription on the marker stone translated. The question remained as to how to accomplish this without either giving away the game or showing his evidence prematurely. To that end, Luke worked up some computer magic. He isolated the Chinese portion of the plaque, which, because it was a rubbing, showed the inscription as white against black, like a photographic negative. He reversed the tones so that the text came out black against white, and then he enlarged and printed the image. After close examination, Luke believed it would be quite impossible for anyone to determine where the text came from, or how it had been executed.

Luke called one of his old Stanford history professors, Dr. Lane, and asked if he could recommend someone who could translate old Chinese texts. He said it was for a paper he was writing. Dr. Lane said he would ask around and get back to him when he had a contact. But he warned Luke not to hold his breath, as real talent in that arena was hardly commonplace.

It was almost a week before Dr. Lane called back with a name. He said that a colleague had recommended one of his star pupils, and as luck would have it, the person in question was working on his second doctoral thesis at Stanford. His name was Dr. Robert Wu, and he was considered a linguistic genius. Dr. Lane said he was told that Dr. Wu could speak, read, and write in nine languages, including Greek and Latin, and that he spoke both Mandarin and Cantonese with equal skill. Dr. Lane gave Luke Dr. Wu's e-mail address and wished him luck with his paper.

Luke e-mailed Dr. Wu at once, introduced himself, stated his business, and asked for an appointment. Three days later Luke got a response. Dr. Wu wrote that the only time he had marginally free was the following Thursday between two and five in the afternoon. He indicated that he could be found at his office in the language lab. Unfortunately, if that proved inconvenient, Mr. Lucas would have to wait for another six weeks, as Dr. Wu was departing for Taiwan the following morning. Luke wrote back thanking him, and confirming that he would be at the lab promptly at two o'clock on Thursday.

On the appointed day Luke arrived at the lab on campus and asked for Dr. Wu. He was directed back to a tiny office that looked like it had once been a large coat closet. There was a messy pile of books on the desk, many of them left open to marked pages. A leather motorcycle jacket and helmet hung on an old coat rack in the corner, and an open briefcase stuffed with papers sat on the floor beside the desk. But there was no Dr. Wu in sight. Then a voice spoke from behind him and said, "Can I help you find something?"

Luke turned and found he was looking at a fellow who appeared approximately his own age, or perhaps a little older, he couldn't quite tell. The young man looked as though he might have been Chinese, but Luke couldn't be certain since the young man was wearing dark glasses and had his black hair tied in a ponytail. He wore crisp tailored jeans, penny loafers sans socks, and a T-shirt that sported the slogan "Will Think For Cold, Hard Cash."

"Why, yes," said Luke, "I'm looking for Dr. Wu. I have an appointment."

The man lifted his dark glasses to the top of his head and smiled. "Well, you've found him. What can I do for you?"

Luke smiled. "I'm Charles Lucas. I wrote you last week asking for an appointment."

"Well, well, so you're Mr. Lucas." He smiled again. "Should I address you as Mr. Lucas or Charles?"

"My friends all call me Luke. I hate Charles. My sister calls me Charles when she wants to tick me off."

Both men laughed and shook hands, and Dr. Wu gestured for Luke to enter the office.

"I hope you're not claustrophobic. I apologize for the mess, but I have a full plate at the moment. I'm up to my knees in travel nonsense, and I'm still getting ready to leave tomorrow morning. I have a tendency to procrastinate now and then. This time it caught me off my game." Dr. Wu gestured for Luke to take a seat on an old metal folding chair. He continued. "This isn't really my office, you understand, I'm just using it while Dr. Heinemann is on sabbatical in Turkey. I don't know how he handles working here. I know I couldn't take it for long if I wasn't so pressed for space at home." He smiled at a private joke. "So, what can I do for you, Luke?"

Luke reached into his jacket pocket and handed Dr. Wu a folded piece of paper. "Do you think you can translate this for me?" Luke grinned. "Unfortunately, I don't read Chinese, and I think I need a hand up on this one."

"I'll do what I can." Dr. Wu took the paper, opened it, turned it right-side up and looked more closely, and then he pulled a large magnifying glass from a cluttered desk drawer and looked again. After a few moments he whistled in surprise and looked up. His manner quickly altered from light and conversant to somber and serious. "Just where did you get this text?"

Luke kept as neutral an expression as he could muster. "I found it among some old papers in a steamer trunk. That's just a copy, of course."

"I surmised that, but do you have any idea what this says?"

"If I did, I wouldn't be here. But certain other documents I've come across lead me to believe it has something to do with a fifteenth-century Chinese admiral named Zhou Man."

"You can bet hard cash on that, Mr. Lucas. Some of the characters are a little obscure and arcane, to be sure, but in short this appears to be a formal declaration stating that Admiral Zhou Man takes under his protection the lands neighboring someplace called the Bay of Whales. He does so in the name of his Imperial Master, the Emperor Zhu Di."

Dr. Wu looked up from his reading to explain. "Zhu Di was the third Ming emperor. It was he who commissioned the building of the great treasure fleets that were placed under the command of Admiral Zheng He. Zhou Man was his subordinate, and some say he explored the western coasts of the Americas. I've been told there seems to be some evidence for a claim of Chinese presence on the west coast of Mexico. But I wouldn't know. That's not in my field exactly. But either way it makes a whopping good story . . . Where did you say you found this again?"

"In an old trunk with some other papers."

"Was there anything else in that trunk worth mentioning?"

Luke could feel his face redden. He wasn't really very good at prevarication. "Just some odds and ends, nothing worth mentioning at the moment."

Dr. Wu smiled. "Not worth mentioning, or not willing to mention? Remember, we Chinese invented inscrutability. But tell me, was there anything else on the same page that you haven't shown me?"

Luke smiled. "Perhaps."

"Perhaps yes, or perhaps no?"

"Just perhaps."

Dr. Wu laughed. "Okay, we'll do this your way and I'll tell you what else was on that paper, and why."

Luke grinned, but his expression signaled serious doubt. "Really. Do you think you can?"

Dr. Wu leaned back and nodded. "When the various admirals of the treasure fleet discovered something important, they'd mark it with a stone. They commissioned them in all sizes. Admirals like Hong Bao, Zhou Wen, and Zhou Man carried predressed stone plaques of different sizes in the holds of their ships. When they came upon a place of interest or profit, they'd land and explore the surrounding area and possibly set out a marker. Sometimes, on well-traveled routes, they set the larger stones where everyone could find them. Other explorers felt their plaques would be disturbed, so they did something quite unique and very Chinese. They would bury their markers on some prominent piece of ground easily seen from seaward. It's said that sometimes they also interred an Imperial token of some kind to verify their claim. Then they'd plant and cultivate some long-lived vegetation, preferably cypress trees, over and around the sacred spot. These locations were generally established near the shore where their forestation efforts could be spotted from the sea years into the future." Dr. Wu smiled with pride. "We Chinese not only invented the compass, the rudder, watertight bulkheads, and fully battened sails, but we also invented living navigational aids."

Luke appeared slightly incredulous. "Really? How'd they manage that?"

"Simple. The trees and plants they used were all primarily indigenous to China, like the tuberose or the silver cypress, things like that.

"The marker stones were usually carved in three languages,

primarily because there were three important elements of those cultures involved in Zheng He's treasure fleets. The uppermost script was court Mandarin circa thirteen to fifteen hundred. The one below that would be Persian of the same period, and the last is Tamil."

Luke was more than a little impressed, but he was also confused. "Why Persian? And what's Tamil?"

Dr. Wu went on. "Ornate, scripted Persian of the period is simply a courtly written form of Arabic. Many of the fleet's navigators were Arabic. And Tamil, in one form or another, was the common tongue for almost all the coastal populations of southern India and Sri Lanka. So tell me, Mr. Lucas, am I right?"

"Perhaps."

"Are we back to that?"

"Perhaps."

"It sounds like you're bucking to become Chinese."

Luke smiled. "I don't have the chops, if you'll pardon the pun. Besides, my ambitions fall into a different category altogether. But yes, you're right, or at least I think you're right."

"Well, I suppose that's better than nothing."

Luke took on a serious tone. "If you don't mind my asking, Dr. Wu, how do you know all this? I was told you were a linguist, not a historian."

Dr. Wu sat back and smiled. "I grew up in museums. My grandfather used to be the documents curator for the Chinese Historical Society in California. My father was one of his pupils, and I grew up on stories of Zheng He and his treasure fleets. But to tell you the truth, I liked stories about Chinese pirates better, and believe me, we had some real corkers. One of our most successful pirates commanded an entire fleet of ships, and believe it or not, it was a woman. Her name was Ching Shih.

In fact, she ran a very powerful and extensive crime syndicate. Even the mighty triads bowed to her wishes."

Luke took on a slightly wistful expression. "Yeah, I used to like pirates too. My favorite was Henry Morgan. You don't find many buccaneers with enough brass to talk themselves out of execution and then become royal governors."

Dr. Wu grinned. "Maybe not then, but today it's almost a prerequisite for the job." Dr. Wu paused, and when he spoke again there was no humor in his voice. "But now I'd like to ask you a serious question."

"Shoot. I'll do the best I can."

"Do you know where this marker stone is now?"

Luke paused for a second and smiled. "To tell you the truth, Dr. Wu, I don't know where the stone is now. But to even begin a search, and not waste years on fruitless speculation and false claims, one would have to know where the stone isn't." Luke shook his head. "I work on the principle of diminishing perspectives. One small step leads to another, and another. Perhaps I'll get lucky, but as far as I can see, the odds aren't in my favor at the moment. I've hit a dead end for sure, but the maze still presents lots of other possibilities." Luke shrugged with an air of disinterest. "But for now, I've got a master's program to complete, and after that I'd like to take a stab at a doctorate. Zhou Man's stone and the mystery of its whereabouts are little more than a speculative avocation right now. I suppose if I should come across a promising lead I would delve into it further. Besides, you were right, everyone loves a whopping good mystery, and this one has real legs from an academic point of view. Don't you agree?"

"I'm Chinese, for Pete's sake. Our whole existence is based on unsolved mysteries. As a matter of record, we invented the mystery story. But tell me, Luke, have you spoken about this material with anyone else?"

"No, not even my girlfriend."

"So you're going on this quest by yourself?"

"For now, yeah. I don't dare trust anyone else just yet. Why do you ask?" Luke gave out a curious smile. "You wouldn't be volunteering yourself by any chance, would you?"

"Of course I'm volunteering. Who could pass up a thing like this? A chance to rewrite history doesn't come along every day. Besides, you're going to need someone like me along."

"And just why is that?"

"Well, unless you think you can master at least three dialects of Chinese in a few months, there's no reason at all. Besides, you've already told me a great deal, and I don't think you would have done that unless you suspected that I could be trusted. Remember we Chinese love secrets, and I truly believe I can find out a few things that you could not. Especially when it comes to dealing with the natural reticence of my people to answer questions posed by westerners. For instance, have you made any inquiries with any Chinese scholars at the important institutions on the mainland, or anywhere else?"

Luke nodded. "Yes, but the effort hasn't proved very helpful so far."

"So who have you contacted so far?"

Luke listed the various museums he'd e-mailed. "You see, I have reasons to suspect that there might have been a plot afoot to secretly return the stones to China sometime around 1906 or '07. But all the Chinese institutions I've contacted say there's no record that was ever the case. And since you Chinese have a tendency to be meticulous about such things, I'm half-persuaded that the stones are still somewhere in California."

Dr. Wu looked puzzled and surprised. "Stones? You mean there's more than one?"

"In a manner of speaking, yes. There was something else buried with the stone tablet, but I'm not at liberty to discuss that just yet. If you are still interested in putting your oar in the water when you get back from Taiwan, come and see me."

"Oh, I'm interested. There's no doubt in my mind about that." Dr. Wu waved the paper. "I'd like to take this with me if you don't mind. I'll be going to mainland China as well, just to visit with relatives, you understand. I might be able to run down a few rabbits while I'm there."

Luke thought for a moment. "You may borrow the paper if you'll sign a receipt, but it's not much good without the rest of the inscriptions. Like I said, if you're still interested when you get back, contact me." Luke pulled a business card from his coat pocket. "You can reach me at these numbers. My e-mail address you already have." Luke noticed the time, rose from his seat, and put out his hand. "I see that it's getting late, and I'm sure you've a lot to do, so I won't take up any more of your valuable time. Thank you for all your help so far, Dr. Wu. I look forward to hearing from you again."

Dr. Wu got up, looked at the business card, nodded, and then shook Luke's hand. "Not at all, quite the contrary. I'll e-mail you if I stumble over anything interesting while I'm gone. But up, down, or sideways, you'll be hearing from me again. And by the way, you can call me Robert if you like. Dr. Wu sounds so sentimental."

Luke laughed at Dr. Wu's choice of words. "And you can continue to call me Luke. Charles sounds so majestic."

———

ROBERT WU WAS AS GOOD as his word, and every week or so Luke would get a progress report, which in every case indicated that Robert had come up empty. But it was through these e-mails that Luke discovered his new friend possessed a wonderfully bizarre sense of humor. Whenever Robert visited a noteworthy location, he'd shoot an eight-second video stream of each landmark. In the center of every picture Robert would set up an orange windup toy kangaroo that wore blue boxing gloves. When placed into action the boxing kangaroo would slowly lean forward, and then suddenly leap backward into the air, flipping over and magically landing on its feet once more. To this stunt Robert had added a canned drum roll that ended with a crash of cymbals as the kangaroo successfully completed the trick. The toy's action, when set against something as austere and serious as the Great Wall, or Tiananmen Square, or the Forbidden City, was intrinsically funny. One or two of these little performances would show up on Luke's e-mail every week or so. Usually with an accompanying note that just said, "Nothing yet. The mystery grows apace, but I'm hopeful still. All my best, Robert W."

It was because of the leaping kangaroo that Luke and Robert, for the sake of security, began to refer to the objects of their search as "the toys." Then, five weeks into his trip Robert sent another e-mail. This time the kangaroo was posed in front of a large stone tablet that was surrounded by ornate carving. The stone was covered with engraved texts that were difficult to make out on the video. Once again there was a drum roll, a leap, and a crash of cymbals. The e-mail simply said, "Look familiar?" Luke wrote back with one word. "Perhaps." The word "perhaps" had become part of Luke's code as well. It meant "yes."

The next day another e-mail photo arrived. The kangaroo was noticeably absent this time. The e-mail shot was a picture of a Bactrian camel carved from a single large piece of dark green jade. Luke noticed at once that the camel was resting on its knees just like the pink jade giraffe in the old photograph in Dr. Gilbert's folio. The attached note said, "Does this look anything like one of the toys?" Luke signaled back one word: "Perhaps."

The following day Luke received another e-mail from Robert. The attached video stream showed the toy kangaroo set on a restaurant table surrounded by exotic-looking platters of Chinese food and glasses of beer. This time the kangaroo repeated his leap four times in a row, with drums and cymbals accompanying each repetition. The accompanying note said, "Due back in USA this Thursday. I should be in Monterey on Saturday around 4:00 p.m. We must talk. Can you spare the time?"

Luke e-mailed back, "Absolutely! Come to Hopkins when you get in. Anybody can tell you where to find the lab."

THE FOLLOWING SATURDAY MORNING FOUND Luke at Hopkins Laboratory in the dissection room. Professor William Gilly was showing him and two female students how to inject dyes into the venous system of a whopping eight-foot-long Humboldt squid that recently had been donated to the lab by a local fisherman who had discovered the angry, ink-spitting beast in his nets.

Out of the corner of his eye Luke caught sight of someone standing at the glass viewing partition on the other side of the lab. When he looked up he saw Robert, sunglasses, ponytail, and all, standing there grinning at him. He was early by hours.

Robert was still waiting outside when Luke got out of class.

The two of them walked toward Cannery Row to get a bite to eat. Luke said, "Have you ever seen the Monterey Bay Aquarium? It's really a great experience. You have to see it. I love working there. The people are great, and when something big and tasty kicks the bucket, we have a grand barbecue."

"You're kidding, of course."

Luke grinned. "Sort of."

Robert smiled. "Yeah, I think I'd like to watch sushi in its natural setting. I'll bring my chopsticks, but first I've got to find a hotel room somewhere nearby. I intend to stay for a few days. We've got our work cut out for us, and we need to make some serious plans."

Luke winced. "A hotel room in Monterey? Save your money. You can stay at my place." Luke pointed toward David Avenue. "It's just up the hill over there. I've got a big leather couch that folds out to make a great double bed. Hell, it's more comfortable than my own bed."

During lunch Luke wrote out his address and drew a little map. Then he gave Robert his extra key and told him to make himself at home. "If you want to take a shower, you'll find clean towels and stuff in the hall cupboard. Help yourself to anything you find in the fridge. I think there're a couple of beers hiding in there somewhere."

"Thanks, Luke."

"When you've rested up, come back down to the aquarium around five o'clock, ask for me, and I'll give you a Cook's tour of the place. I think you'll be impressed."

Luke was waiting at the front entrance of the aquarium when Robert arrived. They hadn't walked twenty feet into the foyer when a dark-eyed beauty passed nearby. She greeted Luke in passing with a beautiful smile and a wave.

Robert did a double take. "Who's that stunning little creature?"

Luke looked up. "Oh, that's Lorraine Yglesias. She's from Costa Rica. She handles emerging markets for the aquarium. Pretty, isn't she?"

Robert's eyes widened with appreciation. "You can say that again, and in spades, and how convenient that I speak Spanish like a bloody native."

Luke smiled. "Don't bother, she speaks better English than you do. And besides, she's married to a lawyer and has two children."

"You're kidding. She doesn't look it."

"Well, you don't look like a doctor either."

LUKE AND ROBERT HAD REFRAINED from discussing business matters where others might overhear, so after the aquarium tour Luke suggested they get a couple of takeout cheeseburgers at McFly's up the street and go back to his place and talk.

After supper, Luke said there were a few things he thought his friend should see, but only if Robert was still interested in going into partnership on the search.

Robert quipped, "I'm here, aren't I, and I didn't come here for the scenery, though I must say it's not half bad."

Luke paused thoughtfully. "Would you be willing to sign a nondisclosure agreement?"

Robert thought for a moment and looked at his empty plate. "Only if you sign too, and we both get a copy." In a blink of an eye Luke pulled two contracts from his desk drawer. He took Robert's plate and set the nondisclosure agreement contracts down in its place. "Read that, and if you're still in the mood after reading the small print, sign them. I'll stick my handle on it after you do."

Robert quickly perused the single-page agreement, and then took out an expensive-looking fountain pen and signed. He handed the pen to Luke. "Your turn, Mr. Lucas."

Luke signed and then gave his new partner a copy. "I think we're in business now, Dr. Wu."

"Do I get a secretary and everything?"

"What are you, some kind of skirt hound?"

"I'm being serious. We're going to need someone good to handle all the paperwork. Someone we can trust to keep our secrets."

Luke nodded. "Perhaps later, but you're right. In fact, it might be a good idea to set up a small corporation to mantle our purpose with respectability. I don't want anyone thinking we're just a couple of grasping, amoral treasure hunters."

"That's right, take all the fun out of it for me. What's next?"

Luke went to his desk and unlocked the file drawer. He pulled out a folder, relocked the drawer, and handed the file to Robert. "Read this. It's a copy of Dr. Charles H. Gilbert's journal. He was a professor at Hopkins Marine Laboratory at the turn of the last century. His handwriting is a little cramped, but at least he wrote legibly. I'm off to take a long shower. I smell like formalin and dead fish."

Robert scrunched up his nose. "You're telling me."

Luke smiled and let it pass. While he shaved, Luke could hear Robert in the living room occasionally voicing what sounded like expletives of surprise. He couldn't be sure because Robert spoke to himself in Chinese, which Luke found amusing.

When Luke came out of the bathroom, Robert was just

finishing the journal. He looked up at his new friend. "This is the most extraordinary thing I've ever read. What do you have that backs this up?"

Luke took back the journal, went back to the file drawer, replaced the folder, and brought out another, fatter file. From this he handed Robert copies of Dr. Gilbert's photographs and the folded copies of his rubbings. Robert spread the material out on the floor. Luke confessed. "But you were right. There was a verifying token buried with the stone tablet. I believe it's Admiral Zhou Man's personal jade seal, but I can't be sure since I can't translate the text or the chop. See what you think."

Robert examined the numerous old pictures of the jade seal in the shape of a recumbent giraffe, and the detailed studies of the text engraved on the seal itself. The stone rubbings were full-sized and accomplished with great care given to represent the multilingual text with precision. Robert said he could read most all of the characters and he ventured that, from first glance at least, everything concerning the text seemed precise and authentic.

Luke went out to the kitchen, searched through the fridge, and found two beers. As he cracked them open he heard Robert in the next room give out with a long, expressive whistle. Then he called out, "You've hit the mother lode this time, Luke. This is, without a doubt, Zhou Man's Imperial seal. Believe me, this is going to set the cat among the pigeons, historically speaking. You couldn't find better proof of the existence of these artifacts, except, perhaps, to come up with the originals. Where do you suppose these treasures are now?"

Luke exited the kitchen and handed Robert a beer. "If I knew that, Dr. Wu, I wouldn't need you, now, would I?"

Robert looked pleased with himself. "I'd like to think we

would have come across each other eventually, but I'd rather be in on the ground floor, if you know what I mean."

Luke sat down on the couch and leaned forward. "Well, as my grandfather used to say, fortune favors the lucky. Whether we find Zhou Man's relics or not, this information is history in and of itself. But how it's ultimately released to the world, and how it's received, depends a great deal on the credibility of the people disseminating it. The slightest hint of commercial exploitation would taint all concerned, from Zheng He to Zhou Man, down through Dr. Gilbert to you and me." Luke took a long, satisfying swig of beer.

Robert sat back on his haunches and gave a wry smile. "I do hope you appreciate the fact that there is still a whole predatory tribe of blood-in-the-eye racists prowling around out there. They won't be too pleased to discover that what they thought was exclusively theirs belongs in effect to somebody else, culturally speaking. At least that's how it's ciphered in the antique framework of such things."

"What do you mean by antique framework?"

"Well, Columbus claims the Americas in the name of Imperial Spain, and with little more than a stupid flag shoved in the sand and a few peaceful Indians as witnesses. So what do they do? They kill the Indians off with nasty diseases and outright homicide, and then steal all their stuff. And the ones they don't kill, like the younger women and children, they turn into slaves and concubines. What a thrill for them."

Luke got up and walked to his desktop iPod player and turned it on. Immediately the soft strains of Purcell softened the hard edges. He looked over his shoulder and cocked one eyebrow at Robert. "And your point is?"

"Isn't it obvious? The Chinese set out with some of the

largest sailing ships ever built, and all just to explore and trade with the known and unknown world, which they seem to have accomplished before Columbus was even a glint in his father's piratical eye, so to speak. But the treasure fleet commissioned at great expense by Emperor Zhu Di didn't set sail to steal treasure, quite the opposite, in fact: they brought their own treasure to trade with others. They left behind magnificent jade seals, and multilingual stele, and beautiful Ming porcelain and exotic flowers, jungle chickens, and perhaps a hundred other wonders as yet unsuspected. But the most important fact of all: the only graves they left behind when they moved on were their own. There is no record anywhere in this hemisphere, either oral or written, that indicates any experiences of hostile conflicts with these explorers, and believe me, violence is the kind of thing people have a tendency to remember the longest and in the most detail."

Luke nodded. "With that as a given, and conflicts aside, why didn't they stay on and colonize?"

Robert flashed a conspiratorial wink. "What makes you think they didn't? The west coast of the Americas is veritably littered with Chinese DNA. The difference is that the Chinese were bright enough to assimilate themselves into other cultures without demanding that those around them adapt to Chinese standards and practices. You stay alive a whole lot longer that way. It's a Chinese principle to contribute to, and not denigrate, potential markets. After all, you can't carry on a lucrative exchange with dead trading partners. Besides, why conquer when you can rent? If you play your cards right you can end up controlling the whole shebang without firing a shot."

Luke shook his head as though he'd not heard right. "And what has that to do with today?"

Robert got off the floor and sat in the yellow director's chair by the open window. He looked out over the lights of Monterey,

Cannery Row, and the harbor beyond. The bright lights of five squid boats danced in the distance, and the perfumes of low tide drifted gently with the onshore breezes that came through the window.

After pondering the question for a moment, he turned to Luke. "Those running shoes you're wearing, or the components in your computer, your ten-speed bike, almost everything we use daily, and depend upon daily, is made in China. And as yet I haven't seen one Chinese Communist soldier patrolling the streets of Atherton or San Jose. I mean really, why bother spending the time, the expense, and the blood to conquer, when all you have to do is make your opponent a dependent client? The more you sell him, the more money he owes you; in a short while the creditor owns the whole ball of wax. The good old USA, despite its military prowess, is now suddenly just another de facto client state that owes billions, if not homage, to China. In effect, the little fish has jumped into the net of its own accord, but the wise fisherman gently puts him back in the water to grow bigger and fatter for next year, or the year after."

Luke shrugged and took a swig of beer. "To tell you the truth, Robert, I don't give a crap who sells what to whom, or what nation declares itself the progenitor of another's culture. Pure science depends upon empirical and provable truths. And whether we like it or not, the result would be the same regardless of all cultural, religious, or ethnic bias."

Robert appeared impressed with Luke's shorthand summation, but slightly confused in the bargain. "I know this is all leading to something pointed. I just can't see the target."

Luke nodded and patiently went on. "As a scientist and amateur historian my only concern is the truth. I don't care if Mickey Mouse discovered America first and everybody on the planet denied it. If I discovered proof to the contrary, and I truly believed that this fact was important to man's often illusory understanding of his own nature, I would find some way to disseminate it regardless of the consequences, because we ultimately suffer greater pains from ignorance than from the truth, even if our first exposure to the truth hurts our pride, our sense of privilege, or our quaint faith in priestly prestidigitation. Cultural envy or political jealousy should have no place in science, any more than religion plays a viable part in international commerce. If we have the least hint of the truth, it is our obligation to explore it until we can arrive at a provable resolution."

Robert sat back and grinned. "That was quite a lecture, Professor Lucas. Of course it all makes perfect sense, but you must also remember that, if anything, I have an even greater vested interest in finding out the truth than you do. I am Chinese after all, and these cultural and historical artifacts play an important role in our knowledge of ourselves, and the world's knowledge of us. But the thorny question remains, where do we go from here?"

Luke shook his head. "That's just what you and I have to figure out in the next few days."

Robert flashed another wry smile. "I'm all abuzz."

Luke and Robert sat up talking until two in the morning and slept in the next day. After a late breakfast of ham and eggs served by an indifferent waitress at a local café, Luke said he wanted to take Robert, who had never visited Monterey before, on what Luke was pleased to call a "used-to-be tour" of the locations mentioned in Dr. Gilbert's journal.

Robert was puzzled. "What is a 'used-to-be tour'?"

Luke grinned. "That's when you visit places that used to be there but aren't there any longer."

"What's the use of that?"

"Oh, just to give you a flavor of the place. Sometimes one can eke out subtle insights from locations. Besides, I just thought you'd like to see where all this history took place. Sight-seeing is just what we need right now. We'll take my Jeep. It's just the thing for where we're going."

LUKE TOOK ROBERT ON A leisurely tour of Pacific Grove and pointed out Lover's Point, where Hopkins had once been, and China Point, where the Chinese fishing village had once stood, before the fire obliterated it. He showed Robert examples of the famous Monterey cypresses, but admitted that though he knew the general area, not even Dr. Gilbert knew exactly where the original site of the discovery was situated. Luke drove out to the Spanish Bay resort, which had once been called Asilomar Beach, and then went on to see the Carmel River, which Luke believed might have been the site of one of the original Chinese encampments. His presumption was based on the fact that the river had once flowed with abundant freshwater all year long, and that, according to Luke, would have made the site an ideal place to take on that precious commodity. The river, before it had been dammed up, was said to have been fat with trout and even salmon when the season called them from the sea.

Luke and Robert walked out to where the river met the ocean. There, they sat down to enjoy the view for a while. After a few minutes of quiet contemplation, Luke turned to Robert and said, "I know it's none of my business, but Stanford isn't the cheapest school on the block."

"You're telling me?"

"So what do you do to make a living while you're acquiring

all those doctorates of yours? I hope that's not a rude question."

Robert shook his head. "Not rude at all, but the answer is rather embarrassing. In fact, I don't do anything to make money just now. Hell, I've never had to earn a living. At the risk of losing face, I must confess that my parents are very well fixed. As long as I stay in school and keep adding credentials after my name, they give me all I need or want."

"When you say fixed, just what are we talking about?"

Robert shrugged. "My natural modesty prevents me from naming a figure because I don't really know. We Chinese never discuss such things. But last year the government stuck my father's company with a twenty-seven-million-dollar tax bill. I know because he moaned about it for two whole months. You do the math. I'm terrible at finances."

When they got back to Pacific Grove later that afternoon, Luke stopped at a little bookstore and purchased a volume put out by the Heritage Society. It was a photographic history of Pacific Grove. Luke felt it would help his friend get a better feeling for the place, and what it looked like at the time Dr. Gilbert penned his journal. There was even a picture of the professor standing with his colleagues and students in front of the old Hopkins Lab at Lover's Point. Robert, however, seemed far more interested in the photos of the Chinese community.

"You know, Luke, it occurs to me that the only people who could give us a leg up on this problem are these very same Chinese fishermen."

"But they've been gone for generations."

Robert nodded. "But these people had children, and their children had children, and so forth. The Chinese traditionally pass down their family histories in great detail, either written or in a memorized oral tradition. You'd be surprised how much

they can recall about their ancestors going back many generations. To remember their people and their contributions is the
most concrete form of devotion and respect one can pay to one's
ancestors. My old man can remember the names and histories
of his family going back ten generations. He talks about them
as though he knew them all personally. My mother can do almost
as well with her family tree. And my point is that if we're going to
make any headway with this mystery, we're going to have to find
someone who recalls their grandparents or great-grandparents
having said something about Zhou Man's marker stone. Perhaps
someone who even knew the people involved."

"And how do we go about that?"

"Well, the Chinese tongs have always kept excellent genea-
logical records. Even then information was power."

"But I always thought that the Chinese tongs were like the
mafia, just big organized gangs preying on their own people for
profit."

"In some cases that was true, especially in the big cities like
San Francisco and Seattle, but in the smaller communities they
were relatively benign organizations that operated for the benefit and protection of their constituents. The tongs grew out of
the older triad system that flourished in China. But here they
became a kind of shadow government that tried to protect their
people from the depredations of national authority, just as the
triads did in China. The difference being that the tongs, which
were built on the more ancient model, kept impeccable records
of births, deaths, debts, and vendettas."

Luke looked confused. "But our Chinese and their local tong
have long since disappeared from Monterey Bay."

"It may appear that way on the surface, but I'll lay you heavy
odds that their scrupulous records, which the Chinese are

traditionally loath to destroy for any reason, are still out there somewhere. And if not the records themselves, then at least perhaps some oral tradition that may be of some help."

"And how do you propose to find those records at this late date?"

Robert smiled with confidence. "My father's influence has a very long reach within the Chinese community. His name will open doors that would be sealed to all others, especially to non-Chinese inquiries. I think I can make some use of his prestige to cast about for a few innocent facts and names. After all, isn't that why you brought me on board?"

"I hadn't thought of it in quite that light. To tell you the truth, my reasoning was far more prosaic than that."

"And what would that be?"

Luke shrugged and smiled. "I think it was, in the main, because I liked you from the first. And perhaps because I needed someone to confide in who would appreciate what I'm trying to do. Something in the back of my mind kept saying that you were sent as an answer to my dilemma." He shook his head with slight embarrassment. "I have a tendency to follow my instincts in most things, and I'm not often disappointed in the results." Luke laughed. "And besides, you're filthy rich. I'm always impressed with inconsequential things like that."

"Well, if that's all it takes, you should meet my father. He's got a wine cellar that's five times the size of your whole apartment. And he will always be richer than I'll ever be. You don't go into linguistics for the money, old son."

"I suppose not, but the same can be said for my field, but I do it for the glory."

Robert found this amusing. "Well, you see, that's something else we have in common. I think that secretly I hunger for fame more than money. But with the sincere hope, mind you, that the one attracts the other."

Robert drove back to Atherton that afternoon. He promised to forward anything promising that came his way, but he told Luke not to hold his breath, as there was one elemental drawback to researching such matters. "The older generations of Chinese," he said, "have a tendency to pretend that everything is a secret, when in fact the secret simply covers their complete ignorance of the subject at hand. It gives them a sense of power and importance that would otherwise be denied them."

THOUGH LUKE AND ROBERT COMMUNICATED two or three times a week by e-mail, and sometimes by phone, nothing of any value had come to light. The weeks passed into months and still neither one of them could discover any trace of information concerning the objects of their search. Luke was beginning to believe that the "toys" had disappeared off the face of the earth forever.

On the other hand, Luke had found plenty of time to finish his master's thesis, which was very well received, and he was subsequently awarded his degree. However, he decided not to apply for a doctoral program until he'd made some progress in his private search for the Zhou Man artifacts. He believed the subjects of his search, if discovered, would make one hell of a doctoral thesis, and in this Robert concurred completely. Robert even owned up to having some ambitions of his own along those lines. He suggested that a paper authored by them both would have a remarkable impact on their careers.

Then one day in late December Luke received an e-mail

message from Robert. It asked, in the most insistent terms, if it was possible for Luke to take a few days off and visit him in Atherton. He even e-mailed a map showing how to find his house. Luke e-mailed back and asked what the urgency was all about, but Robert demurred and said he'd rather speak to Luke in person, as the matter was of some importance and required security for several valid reasons. He requested that Luke bring all his files on the "toys." Then he added, "Do you own a presentable suit and tie?"

Luke laughed to himself and responded, "Are you kidding? I can't even remember the last time I owned a tie, much less a suit. Why do you ask?"

"Never mind, I'll take care of all that at this end. Just get your butt up here Friday afternoon early. E-mail me your fitting sizes, and include your shoe size as well."

Robert logged off, leaving Luke in the dark, but Luke did what was requested in the forlorn hope that his friend knew what he was doing.

THAT FOLLOWING FRIDAY, AFTER FIGHTING the northbound weekend traffic, Luke arrived at the address indicated on the map. He was stunned to find a whopping great edifice that looked like it had been transported brick by brick from Versailles. The Palace, as Robert referred to it, was situated on six acres of land that included numerous fruit trees, vast raised rose beds, and even a half-acre fishpond that Luke passed on the way up the long drive from the automated gates. When he pulled up to the house there was a middle-aged Hispanic gentleman dressed in overalls waiting to take Luke's open Jeep to the garage. When Luke appeared confused, the man pointed to the graying sky that soon promised rain. Luke nodded, handed over the keys, and grabbed his bags.

The expression on Luke's face when Robert greeted him at the front door caused his host to break into a broad grin. "I've been waiting in gleeful anticipation of this moment. Just to see the look on your face is reward enough, but in fact this pile of vanity isn't mine. My father acquired it in lieu of a very substantial debt, and I live here more as a live-in caretaker than anything else. In fact, the only part of this place that's furnished is the north wing, but it has three bedrooms, two baths, a living room, dining room, and its own kitchen. There's even a marble-trimmed swimming pool out back. Come on in, put up your feet and stay awhile."

Luke saw at once that what Robert said was true. The foyer and the south wing were naked, but Robert's apartments in the north wing were handsomely furnished with expensive copies of fine antiques, which Robert said came with the house. And knowing his son's busy schedule, Robert's father had also employed a housekeeper named Mrs. Martinez, two gardeners, and a Chinese cook who made the best green chili con carne and shoestring fries Luke had ever tasted.

After supper the rain started to come down in buckets. Robert and Luke retired to the living room, where Mrs. Martinez had set a comforting blaze in the ornate-mantled fireplace. When he was sure they were alone, Robert began to discuss the purpose of their meeting.

"I hate to say this, Luke, but I've come up with nothing at all useful. And the sad fact is that I know why. Despite my family name, I just don't have the rank or chops to get anyone to cooperate with me. It's going to take the efforts of someone far more powerful than myself to loosen sealed tongues."

Luke nodded. "I haven't made any progress either. Every

thread I follow leads nowhere." Luke changed the subject. "But that's enough bad news; I must assume you wouldn't have invited me all the way up here if you didn't have something more interesting in mind."

"Well, I don't know how viable this suggestion will sound, but I'm serious all the same. I just couldn't make a move without consulting you first." Robert paused to gather his thoughts. "I think we need to bring in a third party. Someone who just might have as strong an interest in this affair as we do. And since the search, if it goes on much longer, is going to start costing us some serious bucks, we're also going to need someone with deep pockets as well as deep interest."

Luke nodded. "I know you well enough to assume you have someone in mind."

"I do in fact. I think we should talk to my father. He's a man of legendary discretion with a passion for Chinese history. I've refrained from mentioning anything about this to him, per our agreement, but I believe he can help us if he has a mind to. In addition, my father has the ability to help us set up an appropriate corporation to secure our interests. But most important of all, no one in the Chinese communities or the existing tongs would dare refuse any request made in his name."

"That sounds most convenient."

Robert shrugged self-consciously. "I haven't mentioned this before, I suppose because I foolishly believed I could do this all on my own. I thought my old man would be really impressed if I could pull this off, but that proved little more than conceit on my part. Even so, this entails a subject very close to his heart. Let me tell you a little something about my father. His company is the largest Asian import-and-export concern in the United States. They handled three and a half billion dollars worth of trade last year alone, and even more than that the year before. He gives fortunes to domestic Chinese charities, and every Chinese of any importance refers to him as Grand Master Wu. They deny him nothing. If anyone can help us, he can. So what do you say? Do you feel okay about talking to him about all this?"

Luke sat back and thought for a few moments. He tried to flash through all the possible scenarios and pitfalls. He'd speculated about arriving at just such an instance, but he hadn't bothered to carry on the daydream because it seemed patently improbable. Finally, with no handy negatives on which to hang an objection, he gave in to the moment. "Well, we're just spinning our wheels right now. The whole thing seems to hang in expectation of acknowledgment from somebody. So okay, I'll go along for the ride if you think it's in our best interest, but only if you and I get the intellectual credits. Otherwise we'd just be doing all the legwork for somebody else's benefit, and I'm not up for that."

"I wouldn't worry about that if I were you. I know my father pretty well. You'd be surprised how many spectacular things he could have taken credit for if he'd wanted to, but that's just not in his nature. He's a quiet and modest fellow at heart, which is why so many people trust him with their fortunes."

"Okay, I'm in. But what's all this business about a suit?"

Robert smiled. "I've already taken care of that. You'll find everything you need in the closet of your room."

"Why do I need a suit?"

Robert blushed slightly. "Well, there's something about my father you've got to understand. He's a man of great formality. Do you know that in my whole life I've never seen him without a suit and tie? When I was a kid he once took me to the beach to watch a surfing competition. It was eighty-five degrees in the shade, and he wore a three-piece blue pin-striped suit and a black fedora. My father believes that one doesn't dress well from a standpoint of self-respect, but out of respect for others. He also taught me that if you're looking for money or influence, dress like you're in need of neither. People with money and power rarely invest time or effort in those who look like they're in desperate need of it."

"I suppose that makes sense, but then I've never had either, so I wouldn't know."

"Well, tomorrow you're going to look like you've got both. Now, did you bring all the paperwork?"

"Yes, of course I did."

"Good. And if my father wishes to see the originals, how long would it take for you to get your hands on them?"

"One day at the most. The material is relatively close by. But what have you got planned?"

Robert got up and went to warm himself by the fire. "I took the liberty of inviting my father to come down here for lunch tomorrow. After lunch we'll make our pitch. I bought a display easel today. We'll set it up in the south wing with a couple of chairs and no distractions from household interruptions. We can show him what you've discovered and tell him what we believe is needed to further the search. Now, I warn you, my father is a cunning and circumspect fellow, and he chooses his words very carefully, so you probably won't see any appreciable reaction at first. He'll mull things over in his head for a while, and then get back to us when he's made a decision."

"Does he speak English well?"

Robert laughed. "Are you kidding? He's an honors graduate of Harvard Law and pulled second billing in a class of ninety-three. And like that lovely friend of yours at the aquarium, he speaks better English than I do. And you know something odd, in my whole life I've never seen him lose his temper or swear. Not once. Not even in Chinese."

"And your point is?"

"My point is, think before you speak. My father believes that lazy or haphazard use of language indicates lazy and disordered thinking. He once fired one of his top men because he over-heard him swearing on the phone to a supplier."

"Well, perhaps you should do all the talking."

"Not at all. He'll want to ask you questions. Just answer him as simply and succinctly as you can, and never embroider your sentiments for his consumption. He hates flattery and glib responses, and can spot a hustle while it's still over the horizon. Would you believe it, I never got away with a single thing as a kid. It was like he had eyes in the back of his head, and he was always five steps ahead of me in everything. But no matter what I did, he never once raised his hand or his voice to me. He didn't have to. I lived in terror of his lectures. All he had to do was say that I had disappointed him, and dishonored my ances-tors, and I would break down in tears and confess to everything. Hell, I'd even confess to things I didn't do, just in the hope he'd let up on the lecture."

Luke sniggered. "Well, I do hope you've learned a few new moves since then. I didn't drive all this way just to witness your long-suffering father administer corporal punishment for the first time."

Robert let the comment pass with a nod and suggested that they make an early night of it. He said that they would have to be on their toes in the morning to make plans for the presenta-tion, something best done with a clear head and sharp percep-tion. Luke agreed and said that he could really use the sleep.

The day had been long and the weekend traffic like a slow parade of escaped mental patients.

The bedroom reserved for Luke was large and beautifully appointed. It had an attached bathroom that was bigger than his kitchen at home. Robert said that Mrs. Martinez had taken the liberty of unpacking his bag and that he would find everything neatly hanging in the closet. Luke would also find a suit, shirt, tie, and shoes to wear at the meeting. He then bid his friend good night and retired to his own room across the hall.

Luke found all his things had been laid out neatly. His shaving kit had been placed in the bathroom, and when he checked the closet he found all his clothes had been placed on hangers. But he was even more surprised to find a beautiful pearl-gray Armani suit hung up there as well. On the floor of the closet he discovered a handsome pair of expensive oxblood dress shoes. Out of curiosity Luke tried them on, and they fit as though they had been custom-made for him.

The next morning at eight thirty, Mrs. Martinez awakened Luke with a tray of coffee and the morning paper. She said that breakfast would be served in thirty minutes.

Over generous portions of bacon and eggs, Robert told Luke how he believed the meeting should be conducted. He would make the introductory remarks, and then Luke would take over. He should explain how and when the discovery of the papers had taken place, and how he had come to seek out Robert at Stanford for help. He cautioned his friend to answer all questions honestly, but to volunteer nothing beyond what was asked, and to voice no unfounded opinions, as it would sound like a sales pitch. Robert said his father was in the habit of making up his own mind without encouragement to believe things one way or the other.

Next, Robert would take over and contribute his own translation of the inscriptions, as his father would be unfamiliar with many of the more esoteric characters in the ancient text. Though he was fluent in Mandarin and Cantonese, Wu senior was not versed in ancient forms of either dialect. Finally they would show Dr. Gilbert's old photographs of the artifacts, which would stand as proof that the rubbings had come from the artifacts themselves. In closing, they would state what they believed was needed to further their search by way of information, tong cooperation, and financial assistance. Lastly, Robert said they should leave his father alone to read Dr. Gilbert's journal for himself, as he preferred privacy when reading. He was also in the habit of making his own notes, so a notebook would be supplied.

After all the material arrangements had been made, Luke and Robert retired to shower and get dressed for lunch. Robert expected his father to be diligently punctual. It was one of the things he demanded of himself, and of others.

Robert and Luke, warned by the gate buzzer, were waiting outside when Mr. Wu senior arrived at the door in a chauffeured town car. The driver was a large, muscular Chinese gentleman. Luke could only assume he also served as Mr. Wu's bodyguard.

Robert introduced his father as Lawrence H. Wu, and Luke was surprised to find such a close physical resemblance between father and son. Mr. Wu senior was a tall, dapper gentleman of erect posture, patrician bearing, and indeterminate age. His hair was jet black and impeccably trimmed, and his features were handsome and open, though one side of his mouth hinted at a face that preferred smiling. He was handsomely dressed in an expensively tailored but understated black silk suit.

During lunch the elder Wu politely queried Luke on his

background and education, and seemed moderately impressed with what he heard. Everyone meticulously avoided any mention of business while eating. Robert had warned Luke that his father never discussed matters of importance when at the table. He thought it uncouth, and believed that meals were to be enjoyed without mundane references tainting the experience.

After lunch they retired to the south wing, and Robert began the presentation. Then Luke took over as planned. However, Robert was quite unprepared for the response his father exhibited. Routinely polite but unresponsive to most things, his father surprisingly became quite animated by what he was hearing and seeing. It appeared that the subject of Zhou Man's discovery of California had touched a nerve that, for the moment, completely engrossed all of Mr. Wu's attention and enthusiasm.

Robert was so amazed that when Luke looked at his partner for an insight, all Robert could do was raise his eyebrows and shrug his shoulders in confusion. He'd never seen his father so engrossed in anything before. And then, quite unexpectedly, Wu senior politely requested that Mr. Lucas stay while he read Dr. Gilbert's journal, just in the event that he had any questions about the professor's entries. Again, Robert could do nothing but shake his head and shrug as he left the room to arrange for tea to be served.

When Robert's father left the house, promptly at 3:30 p.m., Robert and Luke were standing in the driveway to see him off. Under his breath, Robert told Luke to bow, but only slightly, as his father's car drove off. "It's more respectful than waving," he whispered.

When Robert knew they could no longer be seen from the car, he abruptly turned to Luke and, with the expression of a wife who has just been embarrassed by her drunken husband, said, "Just what the hell did you say to my old man while I was out of the room! I've never seen my father like that in my whole life."

Luke shrugged innocently. "I don't know. I just did what you told me to do, and worded everything as speculative supposition. You told me he loved history, so I played to that. But I also hinted that whoever claimed patronage for the discovery of Zhou Man's stone marker on this continent would obviously garner international prestige and respect, especially in China."

Robert quoted an old saying in Spanish: "For honor will bloom like the jacaranda, and where the petals fall, influence will increase."

"Yeah! Something along those lines, I suppose, but not quite so bucolic. Anyway, listen, I've got to get home before seven. I've got a fair bit of work to do before class on Monday. Thanks for the loan of the Armani."

"It wasn't a loan. You can keep it. Hopefully you'll have a chance to wear it again soon."

"Well, I do have a date tomorrow. Thanks."

THE FOLLOWING SATURDAY FOUND LUKE anxious to be off for a day of surfing down the coast. In the last week he'd spent a good amount of his not-so-spare time doing his own research. With the help of two old "freaks" from the Stanford computer lab, Luke began his own line of inquiries into Mr. Lawrence H. Wu. However, that particular morning he'd received a green "surf alert" on his e-mail. Seven-to-nine-foot swells were generating some interesting sets offshore on the north-facing points and beaches. The accompanying map attachment picked out some favorable spots just south of Point Sur.

Luke had been anxious to try out his new surfboard. It was actually an old board that he had modified with a little help from a friend at the surf shop. Luke had been influenced by filmed experiments of scuba divers rigged fore and aft with a couple of battery powered discs that emitted just enough of a charge to create an electric field around the swimmer. Even with the diver suspended in the midst of a darting frenzy of feeding tiger sharks, not one shark could tolerate the electric field for more than a half second. They all immediately closed their second eyelids in distress and rolled away like wounded aircraft. Thinking of the kid who had been killed by a great white off Lover's Point, Luke wondered if he couldn't rig out a surfboard the same way.

To that end Luke had made all the necessary wiring modifications, including cutting out a small, watertight compartment into the center of the board that held two small rechargeable twelve-volt batteries. Luke's tank tests in seawater showed a dependable battery life was somewhere around eight hours. More than enough electrical discharge to discourage shark attacks for a six-hour day in the surf, if in fact one were all that enthusiastic or crazy.

Luke had just finished loading up his Jeep with his wet suit, beach gear, and cooler. He was strapping his board to the padded roll cage when his BlackBerry began to chirp at him like an enraged sparrow. He swore and reached into his backpack, withdrew the source of unwanted distraction, and checked to see who was calling. It was Robert Wu, and Luke, suspecting the worst, thought of ignoring the call, but he answered it anyway.

"Hello, Robert, what can I do for you? And I hope to God you say 'nothing.'"

"I need you to grab your best togs and meet me at Monterey Airport at three o'clock this afternoon. Your suit is cleaned and pressed, I hope."

Luke tried to sound disgruntled, but his curiosity was piqued. "Yeah, it's cleaned and pressed and still in the bag, but you're going to have to explain this airport business. I'm just on my way down the coast to do some important research off Point Sur. Can't you take a cab to town? I'll meet you when I get back later this afternoon."

Robert chuckled. "You don't understand, Luke. I'm not coming in to stay, you're going out at three fifteen, but I'll be there to escort you."

"Would you mind explaining to me just why I should drop everything I'd planned for today?"

"It has nothing to do with me, it's my father. He earnestly desires that we join him for dinner at seven o'clock this evening. Knowing him as I do, I have ample reason to expect something unusual. He's as keen as a diamond, mind you, but he isn't normally this animated. He's more the contemplative tortoise type."

"I'm sure that's nice for you, but I said I was doing research!"

"Yeah, yeah, whatever you say . . . Well, are you coming or not? I really believe this is important for both of us."

Luke sighed like one belabored by the world's cares, but only to mask the fact that he was secretly intrigued by the receipt of such a brisk response to their presentation. "I'll be there on time, Dr. Wu." Luke ended the call with a push of a button and began to unload the Jeep, beginning with his experimental surfboard.

Luke changed clothes, packed quickly, and called for a cab to the airport without knowing quite what to expect, but ripe with expectation all the same. He stood in the airport lobby looking around hopefully for almost five minutes. Then he felt a tap on his shoulder and looked around to find Robert smiling at him. Robert looked pretty much the same except that he now wore his long hair slicked back and joined in a braided queue at the back. He motioned to Luke. "We've got to step on it, the pilots don't want the engines to cool down. You'll enjoy this."

The twin-engine Learjet was a plush affair in soft black leather, set off with bird's-eye maple veneer everywhere, including the head. No sooner had Luke buckled himself into his leather recliner than the Lear began to quickly roll out toward its takeoff position.

Robert looked over at Luke with a serious glint in his eye. "Tell me again, Luke, how difficult would it be for you to retrieve Dr. Gilbert's original documents?"

"Not too difficult. They're relatively close by. Why do you ask?"

"Well, if my father wanted to see the originals tonight, could that be arranged? I know it's really short notice, but I was told to ask. Of course, no one will press the point if the inconvenience makes it impossible."

Luke nodded toward the flight deck. "If you can get your boys to set this flying limo down at the Watsonville Municipal Airport, and stake me forty bucks, I could have the papers back at the airport in thirty minutes or less, but I'd have to make a call first to announce my coming." Luke smiled to himself. "The documents are being held under very tight security, you understand. Even I have to make an appointment to pass security."

Robert picked up the pilot's intercom, spoke to the pilot, and nodded at Luke. "Please make the call, I really think this is important. I will personally see that my father guarantees the safety of the goods. I'll call him after takeoff."

Before Robert could finish the sentence, the Lear throttled up its engines and began racing down the runway at remarkable speed. A moment later they were ascending altitude in a steep climb. Both Luke and Robert were pinned to their overstuffed recliners.

Robert looked over at Luke with a big grin on his face. Over the roar of the engines, he shouted, "I just love this kind of stuff. They pop this takeoff just for me. Wait till they bank out of the pattern. That's a real toe-kisser."

In Watsonville, Luke took forty bucks off Robert and sped away from the airport in a cab. He told Robert that twenty was for the cab, and twenty was to grease security into speeding up the withdrawal process. Which secretly meant flowers for his grandmother.

Thirty minutes later Luke returned to the airport with the paper-wrapped portfolio, which he kept tightly clutched under his arm. Robert was waiting on the tarmac and looked notice-ably relieved when Luke returned. Eight minutes later they were in the air again.

A TALL, BLACK-HAIRED, WELL-DRESSED GENTLEMAN with Indian features met their Learjet with a limo in San Fran-cisco. Luke's unspoken question was almost instantly answered when Robert introduced his father's personal secretary, Mr. Shu-RI Ram Sing. This gentleman smiled with humility and invited Luke to call him Mr. RI. With a self-deprecating grin, he said it was far easier to remember.

Mr. RI escorted his charges to a small but very elegant hotel between the Embarcadero and Chinatown. It was so under-stated that the management didn't display a name of any kind, and the lobby looked like a fashionably appointed Victorian living room. The new guests were invited to make themselves comfortable on a plush red leather sofa in front of the marble fireplace, while a pleasant young man brought snifters of what-ever was requested. They then filled out their check-in cards, and by the time they were shown to their suites, the bags had preceded them. Nonetheless, despite all courtesies offered, Luke never let the folio out of his sight.

Luke's suite was opulent in the extreme, and he was quite pleased with himself and the arrangements. He had just hung up his clothes when a knock came at the door, and a very polite Chinese gentleman in a white coat said he had come to pick up a suit and shirt to be pressed, and a pair of shoes to be shined. He promised to have everything back in twenty-five minutes or less. Luke shrugged, but he happily complied and handed the little man his whole hanging bag to save time. Then he went off to check out the six-headed shower installation.

Luke had almost made it to the bathroom when another knock sounded at the door. This time it was a house waiter pushing a folding table piled high with fruits, cheeses, breads, pitchers of exotic juices, bottled waters, and God knows what else. Robert followed the waiter into the room. He appeared rather pleased with himself as well.

"This is all pretty slick, don't you think? If it was just me, my old man would be happy putting me up at a motel, but you pop along and suddenly we're camped out at the most exclusive members-only hotel on the West Coast. And if that weren't enough, Mr. RI tells me we're to have dinner at the Great Kahn. Mind you, my father is a generous fellow when it comes to my education, and my room and board, but he believes the rest is up to me."

Luke looked up from the mountain of food on the table. On top of this abundance rested a card that indicated that everything came with the warm compliments of the house. Luke shook his head. "Why go out? There's enough fruit here to loosen the bowels of an elephant, and enough bread and cheese to stop him up again . . . So what's so great about this Great Kahn place?"

Robert looked somewhat deflated. "Well, to tell you the truth, I've never been invited there before. The Great Kahn is the most exclusive and prestigious eating emporium in the western United States. In fact, it's not a public restaurant at all. It's more like a millionaire's private food club. They only allow a membership of one hundred and six. Don't ask me why, this is all hearsay, but I've heard it costs one hundred and fifty grand to be admitted, and a yearly fee of twenty thousand, and you still haven't paid for the food."

Luke was suddenly curious. "How do you go about getting to be a member?"

Robert shook his head as he picked at the cheese. "That's the dark part. Someone has to die and leave it to the prospective member in his or her public will. Of course, some places come up because the expense proves too great, or the member no longer cares to participate, but that's rare, and those seats change hands for serious money."

A perplexed expression shadowed Luke's features. He was slightly anxious about all the secrecy and blatant exclusivity. "So why are we to be so honored just now? What's your father's real interest in all this? He doesn't strike me as the hard-boiled academic type, despite his background."

Robert smiled and shrugged. "Beats me. Your guess is as good as mine at this point. I swear, Luke, he hasn't told me a thing, but then he never really does. My father infers, he doesn't tell. Come to think of it, I've never even heard him give an order. Things he wants done just get done."

Mr. RI picked up his charges in a chauffeured town car promptly at seven that evening. Luke carried the sealed folio under his arm. The car drove down the Embarcadero toward the Bay Bridge in the last orange-purple rays of twilight. Near the bridge, the car pulled up to the garage ramp of a nondescript three-story commercial building. The only front entrance appeared to be a green metal door with a camera dome mounted above. After a moment, the large metal garage door began to roll up, and Luke noticed a camera dome above it as well.

Once inside, the car coasted down a steep ramp and then leveled out in front of a pair of red elevator doors. The overhead lights came on just as the car doors opened. When he got out, Luke noticed that the car wasn't in a garage. Some basic instinct, probably inspired by watching too many spy movies, forced him to clutch the folio more tightly under his arm. The ramp continued up on the other side to meet another garage door leading out to another street. There was room for only two vehicles in front of the elevators at one time.

Robert exited the car looking just as confused as Luke. For a moment they stood blinking at each other like toads, then Mr. RI motioned them toward the elevator. There were no buttons, simply a key plate. Mr. RI withdrew a key from his vest pocket, inserted it with a quick twist, and the large elevator doors opened to reveal a plush Victorian, leather-paneled room, with generous green leather benches on both sides and cut-glass lighting sconces on the walls. Luke surmised that the space had once been a large freight elevator. This was confirmed when they arrived at the second floor and the opposite wall slid back to reveal a Moorish-looking foyer with a pair of ornately carved wooden doors on the far side.

Luke looked at Robert and shook his head, and again he tightened his grip on the folio. Mr. RI politely motioned them to approach the doors, but remained behind himself. Slowly the doors opened inward to display a scene that Luke could only later describe as a cross between a tented Mongol palace and a film set from *The Last Emperor*. A tall, dapper blond gentleman dressed in a white silk suit, tie, and gloves was waiting to greet them.

Luke judged the room to be about eighty feet square, but he couldn't really be sure with all the fabric hangings. They had entered on the balcony floor that ran around three sides of the room. Below lay a single large space broken only by the place-ment of elaborately carved screens. To Luke's surprise, there was only one table visible in the whole space, and it was set alone in a rounded V pattern at the center of the floor and il-luminated with three Tiffany table lamps. The rest of the room was kept in relative darkness. Two of the high-backed chairs were set on either side of the V, and the third was set imperi-ously at the head—the result being that no one person faced another directly, and one had to turn slightly to address the other guests.

Robert's father was not present when they entered, but the gentleman in the white silk suit and gloves escorted the young men to their seats, whereupon two similarly clad waiters ap-peared out of nowhere to stand behind their chairs. Luke care-fully placed the folio next to his leg where he could feel it.

They hadn't been seated fifteen seconds when Mr. Wu senior also appeared as if out of the dark void. Both Robert and Luke stood up for their host. Robert greeted his father in Chinese and bowed slightly from the waist. His father caught sight of the queue, smiled, and mistimed his response, which seemed to amuse Robert. He winked at Luke.

Mr. Wu then turned to Luke and bowed slightly. "I'm so happy you were able to make this journey, Mr. Lucas. I will attempt to make your time with us as profitable as I can."

Luke smiled and looked around. "With all due respect, I'd say you've already outdone anything I was expecting. You've been most generous, sir."

Robert's father smiled and nodded. "I think it's always best to let history make those judgments, Mr. Lucas. Please, take your seats."

The three table waiters helped with the chairs in one motion and immediately turned and came around to the front of the table to deliver small silver platters, centered with steaming silver finger bowls scented with jasmine and roses. Soft napkins were uniformly rolled at one side, and a small green sea turtle, deftly carved from lime peel, floated on the water.

Luke looked across at Robert and copied whatever he did. Mr. Wu turned to Luke again. "Mr. Lucas, I really do appreciate your feelings about security, which, by the way, is the principal reason we are meeting here tonight, but I'd be a poor host to allow you to sit there all evening with that package chafing up against your leg . . . If you'll look to your right, you'll find that a low table has been placed there for your convenience. You can safely rest your burden there within reach. I assure you no one will touch it without your permission."

Luke did as suggested. "Thank you, sir. But this portfolio is more of an emotional burden than anything else. Thankfully, by Monday it shall be back under tight security once more."

Mr. Wu interjected. "That was one of the things I wished to discuss with you, Mr. Lucas, but that can all wait until after we've enjoyed our dinner. I hope you don't mind, gentlemen, but I've taken the liberty of choosing the menu and wine in advance. Do you like French food, Mr. Lucas? I know my son does."

Luke smiled. "Yes, sir, I do indeed. My dear mother tried her best to raise me well, and she was a genuine 'Four F': frenzied French-food fanatic. However, she always claimed I had an un-tutored palate, by which she meant I ate too much garbage in the student union, I suppose."

The elder Wu laughed with insight and turned to Robert. "I had the same problem with my esteemed son, but I unknow-ingly nurtured a future addict. He even wangled a stint at the Sorbonne in Paris to study ancient Chinese texts collected by French Jesuits on the island of Ceylon. However, his credit card bills indicate that he spent six hours of every eight eating a wide swath all over Paris, and all of southern France, I might add." Mr. Wu bowed his head toward his son. "It's in my son's honor that I have chosen our menu."

Robert looked pleased. "That's most kind of you, Father."

The meal was excellent and consisted of numerous small dishes, each calculated to make the portion that followed taste even better. Robert said it was like a French dim sum, and he inhaled every morsel.

When the last course was cleared away and coffee served, the waitstaff disappeared completely. Mr. RI and Mr. Wu's chauffeur appeared out of the shadows. The secretary super-vised the placement of a covered table nearby, and two more lamps were brought in to illuminate the surface. Mr. RI then produced a wrapped package, approximately two feet square, and carefully placed it at the center of the table, and then he and the chauffeur disappeared back into the gloom, but Luke was quite sure they had not left the room. He imagined that they were in the dark somewhere close by watching their master's every move for a hint of distress.

When he'd finished his coffee, Mr. Wu turned to his guest. "With your indulgence, Mr. Lucas, perhaps you will allow that it's about time we discussed the purpose of our gathering."

"As you wish, sir. As long as it's within reason, and within the bounds of propriety, I'm at your service."

Robert's father nodded. "As you say, within the bounds of propriety, to be sure. Now it occurs to me, Mr. Lucas, that I know a great deal about you, whereas you know very little about me, aside from what my son has most likely told you."

Luke politely interrupted. "I hope you'll forgive me, sir, but Robert has told me nothing that an observant person could not deduce for himself." Luke turned to his friend. "In fact, I might add without fear of contradiction that at present he's probably more mystified about what's happening here than I am. And in that light, perhaps our business would advance somewhat if I were to tell you what I do know, and you can correct me if I'm wrong in my details."

The elder Wu's eyes almost twinkled with an air of confidence that spoke of amused defiance. .

Luke smiled confidently. His "freaks" had hit pay dirt. He looked at Robert and smiled again. Having no knowledge of what his friend was up to, Robert appeared somewhat pensive. Luke carefully folded his napkin, set it to one side, and turned to face his host. "To begin with, your son has told me little or nothing of importance beyond your exceptional scholastic credentials, and those are public knowledge. However, this is what I've discovered on my own. Your real name is not Lawrence H. Wu, it is in fact Dr. Lao-Hong Wu, and your grandfather was Dr. Lao-Hong. From my calculations he was a contemporary of Dr. Gilbert's. Next, your family's association with a company now calling itself APITC, or the Asian Pacific International Trading Company, goes back almost eight generations. It was then called the Three Celestial Corporations. I can only assume that modesty later inspired the elders to shorten the name to the Three Corporations. In effect you are CEO and president of the oldest credentialed Asian trading house in the United States. Your company's reported net profits for last year alone amounted to $3,900,758,000. On a personal note, you were born on the second of August, 1944, in Nanjing, China, and came to this country under the sponsorship of American relatives when you were five years old. Your academic career was exemplary, if somewhat narrow in focus, and you have been employed by APITC since your graduation from Harvard Law School. You have only one son, the eminent linguist Dr. Robert Wu." Luke grinned at Robert. "And I can only assume, from what I know of Chinese practices, that you have tried on numerous occasions to bring him into the family business, so far unsuccessfully."

The elder Wu and his son suddenly appeared almost dumbstruck. They looked at each other with raised brows, and then looked back to Luke.

Mr. Wu forced a smile. "Please continue, Mr. Lucas, you seem to be doing quite well for the present."

Luke nodded. "Thank you, Mr. Wu, I will. Your corporation owns a controlling interest in six overseas banks, as well as extensive holdings in commercial real estate, both domestically and in Asia. It is also reported that you sit on the board of two of the largest West Coast shipping companies, and you control a cargo airline that operates twenty-six heavy-lifting 747 aircraft. I could have found more information, but this was all I needed to fit the parts of the puzzle together."

Robert's father leaned forward. "And what puzzle would that be, Mr. Lucas?"

Luke smiled with an air of self-satisfaction. "Well, sir, first I asked myself why you would go to such expense to have us here, and just why you would be so intensely interested in what we've discovered. But I think I know the answer to that question. In fact, I'm certain of it."

Now both father and son looked at each other with expressions of concern. The elder Wu nodded again without the polite smile. "Please go on, Mr. Lucas."

Luke obliged. "Well, from my research I've deduced that the Three Corporations at the time of the discovery of Zhou Man's artifacts were more powerful than any of the California tongs, and I'm quite sure they have always kept far better records. When we said at our last meeting that we needed access to better information, you knew exactly where to look for it: in your own files. In fact, I'm fairly persuaded you already knew all about Zhou Man's testament. It's also my belief that the Three Corporations have known about this matter since 1906. But then something unforeseen happened, and all trace of the artifacts was lost." Luke nodded toward the table with the wrapped package. "It's also my belief that tonight you have brought records that indicate your proprietary interest in those artifacts."

Mr. Wu nodded. "It seems I've underestimated you, Mr. Lucas. But do you mind telling me where you came by all your information?"

Luke clasped his hands together, looked down, and chuckled with slight embarrassment. "Please forgive me, but in truth, my last two roommates in college were the most outrageous computer geeks you'd ever want to meet. They're first-class, full-blown savants, if such a thing exists." Luke smiled and blushed slightly. "Well, to make a long story short, they owed me big-time for getting them through their humanities courses, so I called in a few chits. Frankly, Mr. Wu, if I'd been so inclined, I could have had your social security number, your FICO score, your passport records, and any driving violations you might have collected over the years. But those particulars were none of my business . . . How am I doing so far?"

The look of surprise on the faces of both son and father was palpable. After a moment Wu senior spoke again. "So far, Mr. Lucas, you have exceeded all expectations, and you are correct in almost every particular. And the fact is that we do have a proprietary interest in Zhou Man's artifacts. Indeed, though we're somewhat embarrassed to admit it, you might say that the artifacts were technically in our possession when they were lost. You will need my son to do the translations, of course, but in that package on the table you will find all the original records of a transaction my company initiated with the Bao tong in Monterey. They concern two treasures discovered near the shores of Monterey Bay. They are referred to in those documents as Zheng He's Warrants. But that's a polite way of saying that Admiral Zhou Man, who left the artifacts in Monterey, was sailing under the orders and authority of Admiral Zheng He, who in turn received his warrants from the Ming emperor Zhu Di."

Mr. Wu paused, looked at his son, nodded, and then continued to address Luke. "But I think, Mr. Lucas, that in the end you must be the judge of what I say, as I must be the judge in light of other interests." Mr. Wu's expression brightened. "So now, to leach a punch line from an old joke, I'll show you mine if you'll show me yours."

Luke was amused that this austere Chinese gentleman would even know the joke, but he nodded, arose from his seat, and invited father and son to join him at the table. Luke pulled out a penknife and carefully opened his package. He laid out the original rubbings, the photographs, and Dr. Gilbert's hand-penned journal. Then Mr. Wu raised a finger, and Mr. RI appeared from out of the shadows and opened the other parcel. He laid out a series of Chinese documents as well as ink-and-brush illustrations that appeared similar to the artifacts described.

Luke called upon Robert to look at his father's papers, while he sorted out material for his father's examination.

After a couple of minutes Robert stood up. "These look like the real thing to me, Luke. They even contain some rather arcane characters that haven't been used since the turn of the century, and the paper looks about right for the period, but I'd have to check the watermarks to be sure."

Robert's father pondered his son's remark and grinned to himself. "I can assure you those records are the originals." Then he nodded and bent over the table to examine Luke's photographs and rubbings. Without looking up, he motioned to Mr. RI, and almost telepathically, Mr. RI handed his master a folding magnifying lens. Noting every minute detail, he continued to examine the photographs.

A bizarre but interesting possibility slowly breached the surface like a whale, and Luke instantly felt stupid for not recognizing the prospect before. He addressed his host in a serious tone. "I respectfully suggest that I feel we're going through some kind of charade, Mr. Wu. In fact, I believe you may already know where Zhou Man's artifacts are. That is to say, even if you can't lay your hands on them at the moment, you know approximately where to look. You profess to have paperwork indicating a legal and proprietary interest in the artifacts, so why don't you just go get them? One way or the other, you don't need us. You already know more than we do. So why all the window dressing and mystery?"

Mr. Wu straightened up and riveted Luke with a stern expression punctuated with a sardonic grin of logical superiority. "You seem to have a very good mind, Mr. Lucas, and it appears you know how to use it with some dexterity. Yes, in fact, we do know what happened to the artifacts, but we don't know how, or where, to find them after all these years. You'll obtain this information in those ledgers, but I'll give you a shorthand picture. The Three Corporations paid out a great deal of money in gold to take protective possession of the artifacts. The Monterey tong, being small and poor, could not secure the treasures properly, so we made them a generous proposition, which they eventually agreed to. My grandfather Dr. Lao-Hong was a young man at the time. His uncles sent him on behalf of the Three Corporations to Monterey to negotiate the exchange, which he did successfully. When the time came to bring the treasure north, a small steamer was chartered, and one of our most trusted secretaries was sent south to escort the artifacts via the chartered steamer to Santa Cruz, and from there by mail packet to San Francisco."

Luke interrupted. "I don't understand. Why would you transport such valuable material by water, and in a small steamer at that? Why didn't you take it north by railroad?"

Mr. Wu smiled. "The San Francisco earthquake of April

1906 did more than just destroy one city, it shattered numerous outlying communities, and with that, many railroad lines were made unserviceable. It took many weeks for some lines to restore a regular, albeit limited, schedule. At the time, ships were filling in for the railroads in every capacity. Aside from putting the artifacts in a cart and walking them north, ocean transport was deemed the safest way to go."

Luke suddenly caught the drift. "And your ship sank on the way to San Francisco."

"Not the ship, Mr. Lucas, the chartered excursion steamer taking the artifacts to Santa Cruz to meet the ship. According to the survivors, deep swells and whitecaps made for a rough passage. Suddenly there was a boiler explosion and fire. The people escaped to a small boat relatively unscathed, and were ultimately rescued by a passing fishing boat, but the steamer drifted away from land engulfed in flames; it then presumably sank. There was no one around to witness her last moments, but she took Zhou Man's treasure down with her."

An incredulous expression crossed Luke's face like a blush. He felt as though he'd lost the thread. "I hope you'll forgive me for asking, but what's the problem? Your company has more than enough money to mount a search of its own. All you need is a dependable research vessel and crew, a couple of side-scan radars—computer-linked to a broadband sonar, of course—throw in a couple of RUV units and a half dozen deep-water divers, and off you go. It shouldn't take you more than eight months to plot every piece of debris off the coast of Santa Cruz for a hundred-mile radius. If you run a thorough plot with the best equipment and the best people, the search shouldn't cost much over three hundred thousand a week. But of course, that's not counting little things like food, a qualified medical officer and supplies, diesel fuel, maritime insurance, and a bunch of stuff like that."

Luke carefully watched Mr. Wu's expression for a hint of what was on his mind, but drew a blank and continued. "Assuming that the steam launch was made of wood, which is par for the course in that era, and that she did in fact burn to the waterline, the chances of finding any trace of the hull itself are negligible at best. Being a screw-driven, steam-powered vessel means the only metal you're likely to find would be a simple two- or three-cylinder engine and a boiler and firebox. But if there was an explosion as reported, you may not find the boiler or firebox in the same location. Then there's the matter of a hundred years of silting. If the artifacts weren't already effectively shattered by cold seawater coming into contact with red-hot stones, they'd probably now be buried under several meters of silt, depending on where the burning hulk ultimately went down, of course."

Luke could see that Mr. Wu was getting the point, but the man was still curious. "Tell me, Mr. Lucas, why do you presume the stone objects were destroyed by the fire?"

"I didn't say they were destroyed by the fire itself. The stone artifacts were most likely wrapped and sealed in some kind of waxed cloth, linen most likely, and packed tightly around with straw inside an appropriately sized wooden shipping crate, because that's what people did in those days. Agreed?"

Mr. Wu nodded. "I will take your word for such details, but finish the equation if you please."

"Of course, sir. So now we have a stout wooden crate packed tightly with flammables like dry straw and waxed cloth, and a fire breaks out all around. The box then becomes a self-consuming furnace; the waxed cloth and tightly packed straw make stupendous fuel. One must assume, therefore, that the temperature of those stones during the fire must have been very considerable. And if they didn't shatter to pieces from the heat, then certainly immersion into cold seawater from that state would have done the job quite nicely. So it's very possible that what you'd be looking for now might be little more than unrecognizable chips and chunks of stone."

Mr. Wu was silent for a moment. "So you don't hold out much hope of finding either the wreck or the cargo intact?"

"I didn't say that. Anything is possible. Perhaps the boat sank before the fire reached her cargo. There were no witnesses to the final moments, so no one knows. But these days they seem to be finding every important ship that ever went to the bottom. I just don't believe that in this particular case a full-blown research expedition is appropriate, at least not right now. For one thing, it's far too expensive, and second, if you don't know what you're looking for or where to begin looking for it, you're just wasting money. It's far better to spend that money on preliminary research first. There is a mountain of information out there to be gleaned and cross-referenced. Things like old tidal charts, known wrecks and obstructions, historical data, even local newspapers of the period can prove helpful. Perhaps some passerby onshore saw the smoke from a fire at sea and pointed out some landmark to draw a heading upon. Who knows? But you won't find anything without looking."

The elder Wu nodded. "I understand. So you're not altogether discounting the possibility that the stones could still be found intact."

Luke chuckled. "I'm not in a position to doubt anything at all, Mr. Wu. It's all up for grabs to my way of thinking. Perhaps the explosion blew the cargo overboard, I don't know. But I am saying that it really doesn't matter to me one way or the other."

Mr. Wu looked surprised. "What do you mean, Mr. Lucas?"

"Well, I can't speak for my colleague, of course, for I'm sure he has his own ideas on the subject, but personally I have enough evidence here to publish one whopping great paper without finding the stones at all. Your son and I have even discussed coauthoring a paper together. Our combined fields of study draw on some very powerful arguments for credibility. And now that we know the other half of the story, I really don't believe we would be faulted for not finding the solid evidence. But perhaps someone else might, and then you can show them your ledgers. That's going to make for a very interesting court case."

The elder Wu appeared to be seriously digesting everything Luke had to say. After a few seconds he motioned Luke back to the dinner tables, where, magically, three snifters of fine brandy and small pots of coffee had been deposited by unseen hands. Robert stayed bent over the ledgers, making notes.

Luke resumed his seat, tasted his brandy, and smiled. "If you're at liberty, might I ask you a question, Mr. Wu?"

"By all means, Mr. Lucas. I'll answer if I can."

"Since your company has known about the loss of the steam launch since 1906, how many attempts have been made to find and salvage the contents before now?"

"It's odd that you should ask, because I only recently discovered that two attempts had been made. In 1921 a group of Japanese abalone divers were employed to make a search in a promising location. Unfortunately, the information used was erroneous and after one man died, and nothing of interest was located, the project was abandoned with bad feelings on both sides. The second attempt took place in 1938 using salvage divers from San Francisco. Both attempts proved fruitless, deadly, and rather expensive."

"So why, may I ask, would you want to jump through that hoop again? Admittedly the equipment is better today, but the launch has had more time to bury its secrets even deeper under the silt and sands. Even if someone were successful in narrowing down the search area, there could be no guarantees of success. The launch could have drifted for hundreds of miles before she sank or, if the explosion holed her, she could have gone down very near land. Without the use of the proper equipment and the appropriate computer programs, the odds of finding the target aren't even worth mentioning. Even with all the bells and whistles, the possibilities are slim to none. Do you have any idea how many fishing boats have gone to the bottom in the last hundred years in Monterey Bay alone? The last historical estimates indicate over one hundred and eighty reported sinkings in that span, and about half that many again that went to the bottom unreported for one reason or another. So you see, Mr. Wu, by the time your people had checked out every reasonable or promising target between Monterey and Santa Cruz, you'd be old and broke—well, perhaps not broke, but certainly poorer."

Mr. Wu pressed his fingertips together over his mouth and contemplated Luke's words. Robert now joined them at the table. He was still making notations on the screen of his iPhone as he sat down. He stopped once he spotted the brandy, raised his glass in salute, and took a large sip. "This is marvelous brandy, Father, thank you. But if I may, I'd like to throw a penny in the cup. From your ledgers, and they do appear most precise and thorough, including the price paid to the tong for the artifacts, which was later covered by insurance, and taking in the costs incurred during the two failed attempts to recover the cargo, I calculate . . ." Robert consulted his iPhone again. "Yes, I calculate that at present dollar value, since 1906 the company has invested at least twenty-five thousand dollars in Zhou Man's artifacts. Which is certainly not a great deal of money by present research standards. In fact, according to Luke's numbers, that wouldn't begin to pay for a six-hour cruise on any properly equipped NOA research vessel."

Robert's father continued to contemplate his pressed fingertips. He appeared to be far away, and neither Luke nor Robert chose to interrupt his reverie. Instead, they sat back to enjoy their brandy and coffee.

After a couple of long minutes Mr. Wu sat forward and spoke. "I'm most grateful to you both for such honest appraisals of the situation, and I have listened very closely to all you have said, Mr. Lucas. Now, please feel free to correct me if I've misunderstood anything. You say that with enough scientific research, documentation, and the appropriate computer programs, one might narrow down the search considerably." Mr. Wu paused. "But isn't there an existing body of information concerning what rests on the bottom of Monterey Bay? I mean, hasn't it all been mapped before?"

Luke nodded. "To be sure, and they're still mapping the Monterey trench with a small atomic submarine. But if the steam launch went down over the trench, the cost of retrieval, if it were found, could be astronomical. Still you are correct, it has all been mapped before, but if someone used that existing information and programmed the right computers with all the reliable information available concerning the tides and currents for that period of time in history, and if they also created computer models of the launch, with information scanned from period photographs or even plans, it might be possible to create a pretty accurate model of probabilities. With the right programs one could reproduce the explosion and fire on board with relative accuracy, and possibly even create a plausible timetable for the sinking based on known data."

The elder Wu nodded. "And all things being equal, Mr. Lucas, how long would you suppose all that should take?"

"To tell you the truth, sir, I'm not sure, but with the best equipment, and a couple of hotshot data programmers to do the legwork, perhaps six months of steady effort, or perhaps a year, it's hard to say."

Robert's father sipped his brandy and smiled. "And what do you think, on a professional scale, of course, the budget for this category of research might be?"

Luke shook his head. "Well, now, I couldn't tell you that for sure. I've never budgeted an experiment on this scale. But I know of some serious mapping projects, using GPS-guided sonar, side-scan radar, and cross-linked computers coordinating all the information, and a half million is not an exorbitant sum. However, all that wonderful scientific information is for sale to credentialed clients, and there's probably no reason to repeat the surveys. If the launch is there, you can be fairly sure it hasn't moved since it went down in 1906. So, to answer your question as best I can, I don't know.

"But let me build you a hypothetical model. First, you'll need two qualified people with unquestionable discretion to oversee the project and keep the object of the search down to a minimum, need-to-know basis. And then you're going to require the services of at least two, and possibly three, platinum-plated programmers. However, no one need be aware of the true significance of the search. They simply lay out and piece together the complex mapping of programmed plots with corresponding computer graphic overlays to complete the visual features on the bottom of the bay . . . So, for six to eight months, the job should cost approximately two hundred and eighty thousand in salaries, about twenty-five thousand for equipment and customized computers, fifteen to twenty-five thousand for prepublished maritime data, access to top-drawer nautical research, and, of course, a roof to put it all under. I won't bore you with the rest, but in all I think it might pan out at three hundred and eighty thousand dollars, give or take twenty grand, but that's only a ballpark figure, you understand. It would require about a month to compile a proper budget. But you've got all the time in the world. If your boat is down there at all, it's a sure bet it's not going to wander off any time soon. And if nobody else is looking for it, you have all the time you want."

Mr. Wu appeared lost in thought once more. A few moments later he rose from his seat and made a slight bow to his guests. "I am most grateful to you both for the time you have taken to counsel me on this matter. You have given me a great deal to contemplate, but now I see it is getting late, and I for one have an early schedule tomorrow. The car will take you back to your hotel whenever you are ready. But do please stay and finish the brandy at your leisure."

Luke and Robert rose from their seats to thank Robert's father, but he said it was nothing compared to the value of what he'd just learned. He passed his son a small silver box with a mother-of-pearl button set in the center. "If you wish more brandy or coffee, press the button once. When you're ready to leave, press it twice. My driver will come up to escort you down and take you back to your hotel. Again, thank you both. You will hear from me before you leave tomorrow." Mr. Wu gave another slight bow, which was returned by his son. Then he turned and silently walked off into the dark at the back of the hall. Not another sound was heard.

It sort of gave him a shiver, but for all Luke knew, his host was still in the room somewhere, patiently waiting to hear what would be said when he was supposedly out of earshot. Luke was determined to say nothing colorful until they were back at the hotel, and maybe not even then. Still standing, Luke finished his brandy and then went to the table to gather up the folio. He was not surprised to find that Mr. Wu's ledgers had mysteriously disappeared, but Luke's papers had not been touched. He began to pack them away.

THE NEXT MORNING LUKE AND Robert were waiting in the hotel's foyer for the car to take them back to the airport. Luke would fly back to Monterey on the Lear, and the car would return Robert to Atherton. Luke was therefore a little surprised to see a full limousine pull up in front of the hotel. And then Mr. RI stepped out and announced that Mr. Wu was waiting in the car to escort them to the airport. This was a wonder, as Luke hadn't expected to see their host again this trip, if ever. Luke looked at Robert for insight, but his friend just shrugged again with implied ignorance. They entered the car and sat across from Mr. Wu.

Robert's father was all smiles as he welcomed his guests into the limo. He asked after their comfort the previous night and offered them coffee. They hadn't gone far before Mr. Wu, in something of a roundabout manner, began to explain his presence. "Mr. Lucas, I was impressed by what you said last night at dinner. And you are perfectly right, blind searches, like blind pigs, generally find little of value. But you have also reminded me that pure research is always profitable in a world that craves answers. As my son would say, we Chinese practically invented the vice of insatiable curiosity. I would be remiss if I didn't take at least one opportunity to find the objects at the heart of the mystery."

Mr. Wu pulled two thick brown envelopes from a thin leather briefcase at his side and handed one to Luke and the other to his son. "Those are contracts of employment for the next eight months, with salaries totaling seventy-six thousand euros each."

The elder Wu sipped his coffee and continued. "Should you agree, Mr. Lucas, there is also a letter of credit giving you both a commercial account to draw against. I believe it's a two-hundred-and-fifty-thousand-dollar line, but if something promising should appear, more funding could be made available."

Luke was stupefied. He looked at the envelope like it was a loaded pistol. "And just what do you want me to do with it, sir?"

Mr. Wu smiled. "Just what you said last night. Bring together all the available existing information, feed it to a few custom computers, and see what they come up with. You are free to hire whomever you please, and my company will lend you every credential to see that you get the very finest equipment available, and at the best prices."

Luke looked to Robert for support, but his friend appeared just as confused. "And just where are we to set up this operation?"

"Well, you can choose any place you please, of course, but I suggest that the house in Atherton would make an ideal location. There's room for everything and everybody in that pretentious pile of rocks, and it has the added appeal of becoming a tax write-off if used for business purposes. It's also quite close to the Stanford campus and, most especially, a university-trained labor pool who are presently, if my informants are correct, sweeping floors, waiting tables, and flipping hamburgers to pay off their student loans. I really don't think qualified assistance will be difficult to employ."

Luke balked for a moment. "But I have a life in Monterey. I can't spend all my time in Atherton."

Mr. Wu nodded. "I've already thought of that. There's no reason to give up your apartment; my company will subsidize half your rent, so you can keep the place and come and go as you like, which, I've no doubt, will prove advantageous in the long run. As for your work at the aquarium, I've also included a personal letter to Julie Packard. It requests the loan of your services, without penalties, for eight months, on a special marine research project. Since we've contributed substantial funds to that organization over the years, I think we can settle on an arrangement suitable for all parties. And besides, you're going to need that affiliation to accomplish your ultimate goals. Which is, as I see it, to maintain scholastic credibility should the time come that we actually find what we're looking for. You see, Mr. Lucas, I totally agree with your estimation of events. This is no undertaking for commercial treasure hunters. The mantle of science always disarms speculations about profit, so I see no reason to sever any professional relationships whatsoever. And as far as your studies are concerned, I believe I can be of some help there as well." Mr. Wu nodded toward Robert and smiled. "Thanks to my son's academic gluttony, I have channeled a great deal of money into the Stanford coffers. I believe I can induce the powers that be to allow you an extended sabbatical, especially since you will be ostensibly working and studying in your chosen field."

Luke shook his head and looked at the envelope again. "You have the advantage on me, Mr. Wu. I really don't know what to say just yet, but you certainly know how to get a man's attention." Luke looked over to Robert, who appeared to be following every detail like a cat watching a bird. "But I hope you'll forgive me when I suggest that we've skipped rather gingerly over the fine print. I can be something of a pessimist at times, and I swear I smell a caveat or two in my Christmas stocking."

Mr. Wu laughed. "You are a very perceptive young man, Mr. Lucas. But I think you'll find this stipulation a rather tame creature. All I ask is that you both delay the publication of your papers until we have some reliable scientific information on which to base a yes or a no. After that, you may do as you please with my blessings and support."

Luke turned to Robert and nodded toward his envelope. "You've been uncharacteristically quiet through all of this, Robert. What's your considered opinion about the offer in hand?"

Robert sat back and tapped the big envelope on his knee and smiled to himself. "Since you ask, old son, I think it's a truly amazing offer. Just think of all the toys we'll get to play with." He gradually grew more animated. "Throw in a top-notch, broad-spectrum laser scanner to read the rubbings, and your photographs, and we could virtually re-create the artifacts down to the slightest detail, warts and all. We could feed all the stats into a computerized milling machine and make exact copies of the artifacts in resin; that way we'll be able to show our divers just what to look for on the bottom. And I can also harness up a calligraphy program to clean up any distortions in the various texts on the stone and seal. We could reproduce them to look just the way they did the day they were buried under that cypress centuries ago."

Robert grinned like a boy with a new bat. "I don't know

about you, Luke, but I see a way here to use the esoteric skills my father so dearly paid for on something really remarkable and historically pertinent. Expensive toys aside, I don't believe this is a waste of time no matter what happens. With better technologies comes a far greater chance of success."

Robert's father interjected a serious note. "If you'll forgive me, Mr. Lucas, I would like to have your response before we arrive at the airport. A great deal depends on your answer, especially if matters are to be put in place without delay."

Luke sat back, looked down, and wiped his face with his hands. When he opened his eyes he focused on the wrapped folio at his feet. Luke thought to himself, *Well, my board's already in the water, so I might as well ride this "boomer" all the way.* Then he looked up as if just coming awake. "My answer is yes, sir. Yes indeed. I think I'd like to follow this as far as it can lead us. Whatever we find, it's sure to prove a remarkable piece of science, engineering, and history all rolled into one. It will also help authenticate existing documentation. I'm extremely grateful you've asked us to participate, Mr. Wu. We'll do the very best we can, but we'll keep our fingers crossed all the same."

Mr. Wu gave a broad smile. "In that case, would you both please sign the two copies of the contracts you'll find in those envelopes? The checks are in the amount of fifteen thousand dollars each. Ten of that is an advance on your salaries, and the remaining five is to cover individual business expenses until the line of credit clears whatever bank you choose. Keep strict records of every transaction, no matter how small. Others will be looking over our shoulders eventually, and it's best not to feed their envy with questionable expenses." Mr. Wu sipped his coffee and watched his new young dragons sign their contracts. He continued speaking upon receipt of his copies.

"Now, I want Robert to accompany you back to Monterey. He can help you get your business affairs in order, and also help you pack whatever you choose to bring to Atherton. If you'll give me your landlord's address, I will arrange for a check to be sent every month; you will be responsible for the other half, of course."

"That's very handsome of you, Mr. Wu, but I wonder if you'd think it out of place if I made a couple of suggestions of my own."

"Not at all, Mr. Lucas. I'm most interested in what you have to say."

"Well, first I think that the less mentioned about the stones the better. For our purposes, all anyone need know is that we're doing research in multidisciplined submarine topography, which is, in fact, exactly what we'll be doing most of the time. And second, that we choose a name for the corporation that reveals nothing of our goals, and even less about our methods."

Robert piped in with a suggestion. "Let's go with an old Chinese standby. We'll call it the IAS Project."

Luke did a double take. "What does IAS stand for?"

Robert giggled. "It's A Secret. IAS, pronounced like 'ice.'"

Luke turned to Mr. Wu. "What do you think, sir?"

Mr. Wu barely stifled a chuckle. "I have no objections to bad puns; you can call it anything you like. You can call it Porky Pig for all I care, but let us hope the ghost of Zhou Man is not sitting in opposition to our best intentions. Otherwise, I leave the IAS Project in your capable hands, but keep me informed at all times. I will send down my purchasing agent to see you next Thursday. Give him a list of the equipment you will need. Whatever it is, I can arrange for the best possible prices, no matter where it's made. And what we can't buy, we will lease."

As soon as possible after takeoff, Luke got the thumbs-up from the Lear's captain and began texting his old roommates in Virginia. He asked for the names of the best programmers in northern California. Luke got an immediate response and was told to search out the website for the Flying Rodriguez Brothers of San Jose. He was informed that they were verifiable computer geniuses.

When Luke texted back inquiring about their lateral computer qualifications, his friends informed him that the preeminent Flying Rodriguez Brothers could reprogram a duck to give six pints of milk every day, and if that wasn't lateral enough, then Luke would have to look elsewhere. Luke contacted and made an appointment to meet with the Rodriguez brothers even before they landed in Monterey.

Mr. Wu was as good as his word, and within three weeks Luke and Robert had the IAS Project up and running. They had rewired the north wing of the Atherton house to handle the increased power needs of their computers and other equipment. They installed a phone bank and rented all the office furnishings that seemed necessary. Soon they were masters of a very impressive array of powerful new computers and large-format scanners.

Luke began petitioning every possible source for topographical submarine maps of Monterey Bay and the coast of California a hundred miles north, west, and south of a line plotted between Monterey and Santa Cruz. In that regard, Luke's association with Hopkins, Stanford, and the Monterey Bay Aquarium were extremely helpful. As soon as any material came in, it was coded and put into a custom program designed by the

Rodriguez brothers. It created a kind of multidimensional effect.

Maps from the turn of the century indicating sunken ships and other submarine hazards were layered with recent radar and sonar scans, which were then again layered with satellite radar images, and Navy and NOA topographical scans. The Rodriguez brothers even scanned a number of early Spanish and English maps of the bay. Then they layered in the tidal and current tables for the past one hundred years, which was an easier job than Luke might have surmised. He happily discovered that maritime records were the most assiduously preserved of all documents.

AFTER EIGHT WEEKS, PACO RODRIGUEZ informed Luke that they now possessed the most comprehensive data field on Monterey Bay in existence anywhere, and more information was becoming available every day. His brother, Estéban, suggested that it was about time to bring in a top CAG specialist to meld the whole data bank into a complete and comprehensive virtual 3-D map. Paco wrote out a list of talented candidates and Luke hired the most promising: a young Vietnamese woman named Françoise "Skipper" Nuygen. She ultimately proved to be the hardest-working and most creative member of the team.

But it was at night, after everyone had left, that Luke and Robert did their own work on the computers. Luke focused on current and tidal charts for the period, while Robert dealt with the artifacts as agreed.

From the very first Luke was amazed by how much garbage

littered the bottom of Monterey Bay. If he was going to get his computers to do a comprehensive search, he would need to know a great deal more about the missing steam launch. He found all kinds of links that gave him designs and dimensions, but they were mostly Edwardian lake or river steamers. What Luke needed was a picture of the boat itself, and through the clever auspices of a talented Monterey historian, Kent Seavey, a photograph was soon found in the Hotel del Monte historical archives. Luke hit the keyboard and traced backward to find that the Billings and Joyce Boat Works had built several passenger steam launches in their Oakland yards. In 1885 they specifically took an order from the Hotel del Monte. Luke thought the name sounded familiar. It was called the *Del Monte Princess*. Unfortunately, the famous hotel burned to the ground in April of 1887, and the vessel was sold as a local mail and passenger packet to service Big Sur.

Luke's search eventually coughed up the exact designs for the launch, its dimensions, its displacement, the weight of the engine and boiler, and every other pertinent fact he could conceivably wish to have, including the costs charged to the owners of the Hotel del Monte. Because the clients demanded that only the best materials be employed to impress their guests, the elegant fifty-nine-foot steam-screw launch came down the shipway at a whopping fourteen thousand dollars. And it proved a great success for the hotel before the fire.

Thanks to the generosity of the Rodriguez brothers and Skipper, Luke found he was discovering more about complex computer programs than he ever thought possible. Under their guidance he practiced maneuvering through the numerous programs, and soon found he could navigate around the submarine topography with considerable dexterity. He learned to code in specific GPS coordinates and watch the program instantly take him to that location on the virtual 3-D map. The layout also included all known sunken vessels and other foreign debris, so Luke could cruise in a leisurely fashion, like a sounding whale, loitering at points of interest and then moving on. It was like flying underwater, and Luke began to enjoy the process for its own sake.

And that wasn't all Luke enjoyed. As much as he loved Monterey, Luke found life at the mansion in Atherton quite to his liking. He had the use of a new Lexus, his salary was more than generous, his commute to work was all of eighty-five feet, and the food was always exceptional. Plus the location had the advantage of being closer to Rosie, though he had to admit that she was now so heavily preoccupied with leaving for Duke that their time together became more infrequent, and somewhat strained.

Working on his own programs, Robert had accomplished his reconstruction of the stone artifacts, complete with all three texts and ancillary decorations. The next step was to have three-dimensional models carved on a computerized milling machine, but there was one problem: they needed more computer enhancements to make the engraved texts stand out on the model.

The Rodriguez brothers had pretty much finished their work after three months, and only came in now and then to tweak a program here and there, or to layer on a new update. Skipper was now of far more use to the project than anyone else, and Luke and Robert debated whether to bring her into their confidence full-time, or just conditionally, telling Ms. Nuygen the least critical part of the story. They decided to clue Skipper into the fact that they were designing a broad and comprehensive submarine search program that required the best graphics available in the industry. To prove the program viable, they had decided to try to target a small wooden steam launch that had gone down between Monterey and Santa Cruz in 1906. So far no one had been able to find the target, so it had naturally been chosen as a perfect test subject. If, using only their multiprogram-generated maps, they could find the missing steam launch, they would have adequately proven the efficacy of their approach.

Skipper seemed content with this revelation, and since she already harbored an abiding crush on Robert, any excuse to stick around the office was just fine with her. And believing, as she did, that the enigmatic stones were a separate project controlled by Robert's interests alone, Skipper happily volunteered to help him streamline and clean up his computer models for eventual physical reproduction.

Thirteen weeks into the project, Luke and Robert decided it was time to show their results to their backer. Subsequently an appointment was made with Mr. Wu for the following Monday evening. Luke leased a big-screen monitor to show off their new program to the best effect, and he also arranged that no one else would be present when they made their demonstration.

Up until now Luke had been so busy tweaking the finer details of the current and tidal charts that he had put off doing a general search for the launch. Robert teased him about getting his feet wet, but suggested that they wait and run the complete search program with his father present so he might appreciate the complexity of what had been accomplished. He also put forward the idea that even if they didn't find the target they were looking for, the program itself might be of great commercial value in other fields, such as deep-ocean mining, marine salvage, and oil exploration. The possibilities were wide-ranging.

Even if their original goals went unfulfilled, at least all parties could realize some reasonable profit from the work they had already completed. Luke admitted that he had not been looking that far ahead.

MR. WU WAS MOST IMPRESSED with what Luke and Robert had accomplished. First, Robert showed his father the jade seal and the stone tablet as reconstructed by the computer. He mentioned in passing that it would be possible to have more copies of the artifacts made through a computer milling process, but said that hopefully that wouldn't be necessary if they found the originals. Then he showed his father the complete translations of the various texts on the stone and the inscription and chop on the jade seal. He said there was no doubt whatsoever that the seal was once the property of Zhou Man. His name and imperial titles were clearly indicated on both the stone tablet and the seal.

Then Luke took over. He showed Mr. Wu the computer reconstruction of the steam launch, and the probable location of the boxed artifacts in the passenger cabin with the company courier. Using computer animation, Luke demonstrated the probable cause of the explosion and the subsequent fire. When the rate of the conflagration was estimated on the computer model, the steam launch was shown to burn to the waterline in less than twenty-five minutes, after which the remnants would sink. However, Luke pointed out that if the explosion had blown a hole in the hull, the launch might have gone to the bottom before being completely destroyed by fire. Either scenario was possible. Only discovery would answer the question.

Luke began to demonstrate how the various marine topographical maps and sonar surveys were overlaid with more recent side-scan radar and even satellite images. He went on to illustrate how the various maps, when overlaid on a detailed Coast Guard survey, pinpointed the various shipwrecks of known or unknown origins, as well as smaller debris fields from other maritime accidents. The computer program illuminated everything from the 1935 wreck of the Macon airship off Point Sur to the recent sinking of the trawler *Bella Stella* off the coast of Half Moon Bay. Luke then had the computer eliminate every known shipwreck, leaving only eighteen unidentified targets. He set the launch in its approximate position when the boiler exploded. Using the tidal and current charts, Luke showed that at the approximate time of the accident, the tides were slack, verging on the outgoing tide. The program illustrated just how far the burning launch would have drifted before sinking. This eliminated another ten targets. Then Luke eliminated any wreck that showed no magnetic anomalies, meaning it had no engine or substantial metal parts. This reduced the targets to four. Two were of the wrong length, and a third was broken up so badly that nothing could be determined of its original size. But the fourth was a strange anomaly that showed up as a cross-shaped image on the sonar and radar scans.

At first Luke thought that perhaps it resembled a sidewheeler, but there was no indication that such a vessel had ever sunk in that location. Then he suggested that perhaps, against all reasonable odds, a longer ship had gone down perpendicularly over another sunken vessel. The upper image was approximately seventy feet long, and showed a strong magnetic response amidships, but the cross-shaped member beneath corresponded in length and width to the fifty-five-foot steam launch.

To make sure that nothing had escaped their notice, Luke ran the program again, and again they got the same responses. Just in case he'd calculated the tidal chart wrong by a few hours, he expanded the search another twenty miles north, west, and south, but still there were no viable matches that could possibly correspond with their target parameters. When he had finished, Luke turned to Mr. Wu and nodded. "That's it, I'm afraid. Despite the best efforts of all concerned, I really don't believe there could possibly be any targets that we've missed. We've included the best sources available anywhere, including the United States Navy and a half dozen government surveys, not to mention all the historical maps we could find. If your launch is down there, it has to be in that last location. Even the magnetic indications seem to be telling us that there are two vessels in that one spot."

Robert's father looked thoughtful for a moment, and then smiled and spoke with finality. "I'm most impressed with what you've accomplished in so short a time. Now all we have to do is go down and see if you've hit the mark."

Luke smiled and shook his head. "Well now, I can't speak for your son, of course, but I'm a research biologist, not a salvage diver. I'm afraid you'll have to find some professional types to take care of that part of the search. Still, I think you should know that even with all this information, the odds of finding what you're looking for are still not very promising. And given all the legal and technical hurdles that still stand in your way, it might be quite some time before you'll be able to exploit this information."

Mr. Wu nodded. "I understand, but I do hope you will stick to our bargain not to publish your findings until we've had an opportunity to search for the wreck."

Luke nodded. "Of course, Mr. Wu, but that agreement was

predicated on the understanding that you would not take an overly long time to come up with an answer one way or another. In the meantime, if I might suggest, it would be a good idea to get ahold of the Rodriguez brothers and have them streamline this program for commercial use. It could easily offset the costs you've incurred so far, and possibly bring in more than you expect. And, if you offered the Rodriguez brothers twenty per-cent of the copyright, their dedicated enthusiasm would be ce-mented for sure. You could have this program out on the market in less than three months."

"And what about you, Mr. Lucas? What about the IAS Proj-ect? Don't you feel you're entitled to part of the profits?"

"Not really, Mr. Wu. I mean, if you should choose to toss me a bone, I certainly wouldn't object, but you've paid me very handsomely for my efforts, and I have no expectations for fur-ther profit from a program I didn't really design anyway. It's the Rodriguez brothers you want as partners, not me. I wouldn't have thought of the whole thing except for this project, which you paid for . . ." Luke paused and smiled. "But there is one thing I'd like to have."

"Name it, Mr. Lucas."

"Perhaps, when you're ready to go public with all this, you might let me have a copy of the program for my own private use. Aside from that, I can't think of anything more I need or want. However, I would appreciate being kept in the loop about any discoveries you do make."

Robert looked at Luke as though he was crazy, but he said nothing. Mr. Wu nodded. "Very well, Mr. Lucas, you shall have what you wish."

TWO WEEKS LATER LUKE WAS back home in Monterey, and very happy to be there. It had taken about ten days to draw all the materials together in an easily workable format, which the Rodriguez brothers accomplished with remarkable proficiency and speed. Then Luke and Robert supervised the removal of the equipment to a commercial location in Palo Alto provided by Mr. Wu. The Rodriguez brothers were put on retainer, as was François Nuygen, and Robert supervised their work for his father. For the first few weeks Luke and Robert consulted almost daily, but for the most part Luke returned to his scholastic routine with little interruption.

Now that he had more than enough cash to invest, Luke went back to work on his shark-repelling surfboard. With the help of another enthusiastic surfing friend, Eddie Andrews, who made fine customized boards in his garage, Luke produced three viable prototypes. However, the problem of testing these under real conditions required that they find someplace where they could locate enough large sharks of the most dangerous species to use as test subjects.

After a little research Luke found a location off the west coast of Baja California that seemed to fit all their projected needs. They planned to take several regular boards, as well as the electrified models, rig them with wet-suited dummies well stuffed with chum, and tow them slowly behind a boat in shark-infested waters. Luke had seen films of this procedure being used by researchers wishing to study the method of shark attacks on surface-swimming sea lions, and the results had been spectacular. Some of the larger great whites had made steep ascending attacks with such speed and ferocity that they literally lifted themselves and their prey ten feet into the air. But when a shark realized that its intended victim wasn't food, it usually ignored the target and moved off.

Luke and Eddie had planned to make the trip in three months' time. If the tests proved successful, Luke and his friend intended to go into limited production. Luke even thought he knew where he could find a wealthy investor, but he never mentioned Mr. Lawrence H. Wu by name.

In the meanwhile, as time allowed, Luke went back to work on his paper concerning Dr. Gilbert's discoveries. Robert did his part by supplying all the text translations, as well as his own analysis of the authenticity of the inscriptions, which he stated were unequivocally correct in every detail, and impossible to forge without a thorough knowledge of the ancient forms of the languages included in the stone inscriptions. In every other detail, the stone plaque was similar to markers found at other locations known to have been visited by Zheng He's fleets. Robert also stated that Zhou Man's seal would have been impossible to forge, in part because the size of the piece of pink-white jade used to make the seal would have carried a prohibitive price tag, and the skill to carve a piece of jade that size would require the talents of the finest Chinese craftsmen. Additionally, any forger would have needed access to information concerning Zhou Man's chop and his imperial titles, which no longer existed in the official records anywhere.

About two days before Luke was to leave for Mexico with Eddie, he received a call from Robert. His friend said that his father had made all the necessary arrangements to have a salvage crew dive down and inspect the target wreck. He asked if Luke wanted to go along and see what they discovered. Believing that little or nothing would come of the search, Luke begged off and said he was on his way to Baja to do some important research, but that if anything turned up, Robert could text him. Otherwise he would be back in two or three weeks and they could talk then. He wished Robert and his father the very best of luck, but some intangible instinct told Luke that they would somehow be disappointed.

There was a quality of impenetrability in every detail of the mystery that Luke couldn't quite put his finger on. There had obviously been strong motives for deception behind every element in the sequence of events that had led them this far, as though blind passages had been specifically designed to thwart all those looking for a clear exit. He didn't know how he foresaw this, but he felt that no westerner would ever unravel the whole story, and perhaps that was as it should be.

LUKE AND EDDIE RETURNED TO Monterey wreathed in glory. Their experiments had been rewarded with total success. All three unelectrified boards, with their chum-packed dummies, had been victims of furious shark attacks, while Luke's rigged boards remained totally unmolested despite the numerous sharks that had been drawn to the location by the odor of fish blood. Luke wished he could have watched the action from a submerged location, but that would have been impossible with anything other than a shark cage, which would have been impractical from a moving boat. Next time he would make arrangements to have some small video cameras mounted to the bottom of his boards so he could get a better picture of what was happening below the surface.

Luke was somewhat concerned that he hadn't heard a word from Robert in the three weeks he'd been away, but he just assumed that Mr. Wu's salvage divers had found nothing of interest. He was therefore surprised when he found a note from Robert pinned to his apartment door, dated the previous day. It said, "Your landlady says you should be back tomorrow afternoon. I'm staying at the Spindrift Inn down on Cannery Row. It's important that I see you whenever you get back. I would have called, but I didn't want to speak about the toys on the phone. Come find me as soon as you can, as I must return home tomorrow. All my best, RW."

Luke knew the only thing that might be the cause of such secrecy was the long-odds possibility that Mr. Wu's divers had indeed found Zhou Man's treasures.

As soon as he had taken a shower to wash off the road, Luke changed his clothes and headed down to the Spindrift Inn. He asked for Dr. Wu and was directed to a large bay-view suite on the third floor. Robert was waiting for him, but he seemed to be in a strange mood. He led Luke out to the small balcony and offered him a beer.

"No thanks, Robert, I've been driving since early this morning, and a beer would just put me to sleep. I still have a bunch of unpacking to do. So what's this all about?"

Robert gave a strange smile. "Well, first of all, you'll be pleased to know that the program worked. We found the launch just where you said it might be, under the wreck of an old trawler."

"That's fantastic! So did you find the stones?"

Robert shrugged. "That's the rub, Luke. The answer is yes and no."

"What are you talking about? You either found them or you didn't. Which is it?"

"Well, the divers found the rotting remnants of the box the treasure was shipped in, and it was approximately where you said it might be. But the contents weren't quite what we expected."

"What are you talking about, Robert?"

"Well, this'll slay you. It seems that the Point Alones tong completely snookered the Three Corporations."

"What?"

"You heard me. The divers found a stone all right, but it was an old flagstone roughly the same size and weight as Zhou Man's plaque. And instead of the jade seal, they came up with a crude clay figurine of something that looked more like a long-necked duck than a giraffe. Both items still showed trace remnants of the waxed silk that they were originally wrapped in."

Luke was more than surprised. "But how did the tong think they could get away with the switch like that? The fakes were bound to be discovered when the crate was unpacked at its destination, and then there would have been hell to pay all around."

Robert chuckled. "But don't you see? Those cagey old fishermen knew that, so they arranged to destroy the launch before the switch could be discovered. They never believed that anyone would recover the wreck, and so they were home free."

Luke was perplexed and shook his head. "But why would they do that? It doesn't make sense. What did they have to gain?"

Robert smiled. "They must have had their reasons, because the whole scam took some sharp planning to be sure. The tong obviously didn't want to give up the artifacts, but they knew that if they refused the Three Corporations' offer, the treasure would most likely be taken by force or outright theft. But whatever their motives were, they got away with the deception very handily. And if we hadn't found what was left of the burned launch, everyone would still believe the treasures were lost at sea."

"So where are the stones now?"

Robert laughed. "Your guess is as good as mine, but after all this time I don't believe there's anybody left alive who could tell us. I'm afraid the whole thing will have to remain a mystery until someone accidentally stumbles across them again."

"How does your father feel about all this?"

"Well, he's disappointed to be sure, but like everything else, he seems to be taking the whole thing in stride." Robert grinned. "Though in fact, I think he's secretly rather impressed with those canny old fishermen. After all, they not only got their money, but they kept the treasure as well."

Luke just shook his head. "I think I'll have that beer after all, if you don't mind."

Robert retrieved an imported beer from the minibar, and when he returned he handed Luke the beer and an envelope. Luke took the beer, but looked confused about the envelope. "What's this for?"

"It's that bone you were talking about. My father was so impressed with the search program that he decided that you deserved it now. It's a check for ten thousand dollars. He said you could expect more later if everything works out with the Rodriguez brothers."

"That was very generous of him."

Robert laughed. "Not really. You probably saved him many times that amount, and besides, he's already convinced several important salvage companies to buy into the marine search program for big bucks. It's the Rodriguez brothers and Skipper who will probably see the lion's share, but that's only as it should be."

"So what do we do now, Dr. Wu?"

"I suppose we go ahead and publish what we have. I'll let you know next week when you can expect my end of the work. In the meantime, I guess we go back to what we were doing before all this happened. Though I'm somewhat persuaded that after we publish our papers, we're going to be busy enough covering our butts. The pros and cons are going to jump off the dog like hungry fleas, and come after us instead."

LONG BEFORE HE'D FINISHED HIS paper on Zhou Man's artifacts, Luke went back to the Hopkins storeroom to make sure that Dr. Gilbert's small trunk was where he had hidden it. He was very pleased to discover that the lab's housecleaning chores hadn't progressed any further than they had some months before. The trunk was still there behind the file boxes where he had hidden it. At the first safe opportunity, Luke returned Dr. Gilbert's papers to the bottom of the trunk. Then he moved the trunk to a place where it easily could be found by anybody looking for it. Luke had no intention of having his work tainted with the charge that he had purloined university property to accomplish his ends. On the other hand, there were no rules against research secrecy. That kind of thing was commonplace in the academic world. If the Stanford dons didn't know what was in their own possession all along, it was not his problem. As a credentialed postgraduate student in good standing, Luke had every right to use university files for his own research. He and Robert knew only too well that before publication would be allowed, the first question asked by their faculty advisers would be where and how they came by their source material. Once that was answered, the university would rush to secure Dr. Gilbert's papers for its own library, which was exactly what Luke and Robert wanted. Once the papers had been properly examined, and their authenticity verified by the university archivists, Luke's work would be defended by competent authority. And that is precisely what happened.

When Luke and Robert at last published their work, it caused an international tremor that would ripple through academic circles for years. And, of course, they got more than their fifteen minutes of fame. They were hounded for interviews by every conceivable news organization and invited to lecture about their discoveries everywhere. The Chinese press, both mainland and otherwise, camped out at their doors, and they were even invited to go to China to deliver lectures to university scholars, which they did, if only to avoid the domestic breed of hyenas.

Then, as might be expected under the circumstances, all kinds of people came out of the woodwork with claims of knowing where the treasures were hidden. But they were proved wrong in every instance. The whereabouts of Zhou Man's stone testament and his beautiful jade seal were never discovered, but Dr. Gilbert's papers became world famous. Luke hoped that somehow this turn of events would have pleased the old scholar.

Luke went on to create another sensation with his shark-repelling surfboards, and he profited far beyond his expectations. But his greatest reward came in knowing that perhaps he'd saved the lives of many of his fellow surfing enthusiasts around the world.

Robert Wu garnered two more doctorates before he became totally bored with academic achievements. He at last bowed to his father's desire to have him join the firm. He went on to be voted his father's successor, and thus found he'd become immensely wealthy and powerful, which bored him even more. But in the end, Robert's father didn't get everything his own way. To everyone's surprise, and especially Luke's, Mr. Lawrence

H. Wu's only son fell for, courted, and eventually married the lovely Françoise Nuygen, and they soon produced twin boys. This turn of events made his father relatively happy, though he had really wanted his only son to marry a nice Chinese girl.

And every May 10, which they counted as the anniversary of their first meeting, Luke and Robert met for dinner at the Great Kahn. They ate handsomely, drank expensive brandy, and reminisced about their adventures and accomplishments. They always ended the evening with a toast to that illustrious explorer Admiral Zhou Man, the venerable patron of their greatest success.

Luke never married Rosie. She eventually dumped him for a successful orthopedic surgeon she had met at a medical conference. Luke was not particularly disturbed by her decision, for he intrinsically knew that their differing interests and ambitions would eventually lead to an emotional breach of some kind. Instead, Luke fell for, and married, a beautiful blond champion surfer from Santa Cruz named Gail Lightfoot. They had met over the Internet when she had written to ask about the validity of rumors she had heard concerning his shark-repelling surfboard. She then traveled to Monterey to meet the inventor personally. Once convinced that Luke's credentials and scientific principles were sound, she had courageously offered to test his electronically rigged surfboard in the shark-infested waters off South Africa, where she was soon scheduled to participate in an international competition.

Luke was immediately attracted to this courageous and willful beauty with eyes the color of light green jade, and so naturally he agreed to rig her competition board with his device. With Eddie's help they worked together on the setup so she would completely understand every detail of the apparatus, and the methods necessary to facilitate repairs if that should prove necessary.

A well-tanned Miss Lightfoot returned three weeks later with a second-place silver medal, and potential orders for sixty-five shark-rigged boards. A month later, while the couple surfed the poststorm waves off Lover's Point, Luke plucked up the courage to propose marriage. Gail said she was truly flattered, but coyly strung him out for two months just to see how he would react. When she eventually discovered that Luke was just as tenacious and patient as she was, Gail agreed to a formal engagement. Luke marked the blissful occasion by presenting her with a platinum ring set with sea green diamonds to match her eyes. They were married in Pacific Grove three months later.

Luke often said that marrying Gail was the most propitious and enlightened thing he had ever done. And as passion's destiny would have it, they ultimately produced two lovely, tow-headed girls name Olivia and Sophie.

Luke eventually became a full professor at Stanford, a position he could easily afford because Gail took over the business and eventually made them both very wealthy. After several shark attacks on surfers who had fallen off their boards, Luke finally decided that the Australian diver/inventor who had first designed the shark-repellent device was correct in attaching the current generator to the surfer and not the board. However, this didn't faze Luke one bit. He just moved one step sideways and conceived of a method of attaching an enhanced version of his watertight devices to the undersides of inflatable life rafts. He even adapted a model to be easily retrofitted to the existing survival rafts used by military pilots and commercial airlines. After that, the money just seemed to roll in all by itself. Luke and Gail even received several prestigious commendations from the United States Navy and the Marine Corps. Not to mention a whole wall of impressive plaques from the airline pilots associations of twelve countries, and the naval and air services of six more. They also received testimonials from whole fishing fleets, and enough smoked salmon, smoked whitefish, and frozen crabmeat to open a Broadway deli.

Robert and Luke always acknowledged that they had been blessed by a heretofore unknown historical event of great consequence, one that would ultimately force a revision in all the history textbooks, but they were not the only ones who found blessings entwined in the mystery of Zhou Man's treasures.

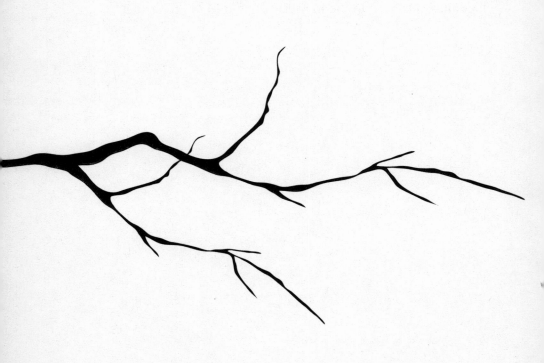

BENEDICTIONS

"Only fools and the faithless rail at
Heaven."

—CHINESE PROVERB

EVERY FEBRUARY 6, ON THE eve of the lunar New Year, a small group of Chinese elders secretly gather in Monterey. They are all direct descendants of men who had met upon the same mission and in the same place for a hundred and two years. In the dead of night, at precisely eleven o'clock, they secretly make their way to a young cypress tree overlooking the bay. The tree itself is but a little older than the quiet ceremony they then perform. Incense sticks are lit and placed in an ancient copper urn filled with sand from China Point. A libation of gold-infused rice wine is gently poured at the base of the tree, and small strips of gold-edged, red rice paper, upon which many prayers of benediction have been inscribed, are burned in another ancient bronze bowl. The smoke carries these prayers to Heaven. The ashes are then reverentially sprinkled around the tree with the ceremonial clapping of hands, three times.

At the conclusion of this simple ceremony a special prayer is said for the illustrious spirit of their benefactor, Dr. Lao-Hong, whose intrinsic sense of integrity and justice, undeterred even in the face of conflicting clan loyalty, had been instrumental in making this auspicious and honored observance possible. The elders then quietly depart in the firm knowledge that they have kept faith with the spirit of their ancestors, and honored the long-departed hero of their race, Admiral Zhou Man. In this way they confidently appreciate that his blessings have been secured for another year of hopeful prosperity. These faithful gentlemen, or their assigned heirs, will gather at this very spot, on the same date and time, for as long as the memory of the esteemed admiral and his intrepid sailors lives in the hearts of their wide-ranging countrymen. And as far as these venerable elders are concerned, that will be for as long as subsequent generations and reverential commemoration allow, or as long as Admiral Zhou Man's treasure rests undisturbed beneath the bent and weathered cypress overlooking his Bay of Whales.

"To souls seeking wisdom devotion is prologue."

—CHINESE PROVERB

EPILOGUE

IT WAS MY FATHER, A fine historical scholar in his own right, who long ago first suggested to me that the Chinese had visited and explored the west coasts of the Americas long before Columbus discovered which side of the planet he was on. I well remember that my father was the only person I had ever known to point out that the Aztec deity Quetzalcoatl (god of knowledge, creation, priesthood, and the winds) was depicted, in the remarkably un-Aztec stone carvings at the Ciudadela complex in Teotihuacán, as a feathered serpent, a creature totally unknown in the Western Hemisphere, but well-known in China as a dragon. If viewed head-on, the Aztec depictions of Quetzalcoatl, with his feathered collar, resembled almost exactly the polished bronze plaques carried on the flat bows of the largest capital ships in Admiral Zheng He's great treasure fleet. Subsequently, I became an enthusiastic student of maritime history in general, and Chinese maritime engineering and history in particular. When I later learned that Chinese anchor stones, quarried in China, had been discovered in Monterey Bay, I came to realize that my father must have been instinctually correct. From that moment of childhood enlightenment, nothing has absorbed my interest more than the study of maritime contacts between ancient cultures. I now also believe, after long study, that the same might also be true for maritime connections between Africa and South America's Olmec civilization via the Yucatán peninsula of Mexico. It is only a personal opinion, to be sure, but anyone viewing the great stone helmeted Olmec heads found in that part of Mexico must admit that the depictions of their facial features appear far more African than they do the indigenous native population of that period. But that's another book altogether.